Broken Earth: Devastation

By Barbara J Barker

Dedication: To Tom and Jarod, who were both

invaluable on this journey.

Contents

Chapter One: The First Day..5

Thingvellir National Park, South Iceland: 8 a.m. local, 2 a.m. CST................................5

Keflavik Airport, Southwest Iceland: 8:30 a.m. local, 2:30 a.m. CST 7

Chapter Two 11

Holden, NE: 3 a.m. CST 11

Atlanta, GA: 6 a.m. local, 5 a.m. CST 14

Tasmin Sea: 200 miles southwest Sydney, Australia, 10 p.m. local, 5 a.m. CST 16

Chapter Three 19

Mid-Atlantic Ridge, North Atlantic Ocean: 11:30 a.m. local, 5:30 a.m. CST...........................19

San Miguel Island, Azores: 12:30 p.m. local, 6:30 a.m. CST.......................................20

Atlanta, GA: 7:45 a.m. local, 6:45 a.m. CST 22

Chapter Four 25

The western coast of Portugal: 1 p.m. local, 7 a.m. CST..25

Port St. John, Florida: 8:30 a.m. local, 7:30 a.m. CST 27

Southwest Argentina: 10:30 a.m. local, 7:30 a.m. CST..29

Mid-Atlantic Ridge, North Atlantic Ocean: 12:15 p.m. local, 8 a.m. CST............................29

Chapter Five...32

Merritt Island, FL: 9:30 a.m. local, 8:30 a.m. CST..32

Boothbay Harbor, Maine: 9:30 a.m. local, 8:30 a.m. CST 34

New York City, NY: 9:30 a.m. local, 8:30 a.m. CST 36

Nags Head, North Carolina: 9:30 a.m. local, 8:30 a.m. CST 37

Washington, D.C.: 9:30 a.m. local, 8:30 a.m. CST..38

Chapter Six 42

Emerson, GA: 9:30 a.m. local, 8:30 a.m. CST...42

Southwest Argentina: 11:30 a.m. local, 8:30 a.m. CST..43

Sydney, Australia: 1:30 a.m. local, 8:30 a.m. CST 45

Holden, NE: 8:30 a.m. CST 48

Sacramento, CA, USGS Office: 7 a.m. local, 9 a.m. CST 53

Chapter Seven 55

Holden, NE: 9:15 a.m. CST 55

New York City: 10:30 a.m. local, 9:30 a.m. CST 58

Scottsbluff Regional Airport, Nebraska: 10 a.m. MST, 11 a.m. CST 61

Tennessee: 11 a.m. CST 63

Chapter Eight 66

Cullman, AL: 3 p.m. CST 66

Cheyenne Mountain Complex, Colorado: 2 p.m. MST, 3 p.m. CST 69

Chapter Nine 73

Holden, NE: 4 p.m. CST 73

Northwest Nebraska, Highway 29 North: 3 p.m. MST, 4 p.m. CST 76

Hendron, KY: 4 p.m. CST 77

Chapter Ten..80

Holden, NE: 6 p.m. CST 80

Cheyenne Mountain Complex: 7 p.m. MST, 8 p.m. CST..83

Chapter Eleven..90

Southwest Argentina: 11:45 p.m. local, 8:45 p.m. CST 90

Beijing, China: 2 p.m. BST, 12 a.m. CST..95

Southwest Argentina: 4 a.m. local, 1 a.m. CST 98

Chapter Twelve – Day Two..102

Holden, NE: 5 a.m. CST 102

Hendron, KY: 6 a.m. CST..102

Cheyenne Mountain Complex: 5 a.m. MST, 6 a.m. CST 106

Chicago, IL: 7 a.m. CST 109

Chapter Thirteen 111

Southwest Argentina: 10 a.m. local, 7 a.m. CST 111

Titan Three, Pacific Ocean, off coastal Chile: 10 a.m. local, 8 a.m. CST 113

Cheyenne Mountain Complex: 8 a.m. MST, 9 a.m. CST 115

Southwest Argentina: 12 p.m. local, 9 a.m. CST 116

St. Louis, IL: 10 a.m. CST 117

Chapter Fourteen...121

Moca, Dominican Republic: 10 a.m. local, 12 p.m. CST 121

Cheyenne Mountain Complex: 12 p.m. MST, 1 p.m. CST...123

Holden, NE: 2 p.m. CST 125

Yucatan, Mexico: 2 p.m. local, 2 p.m. CST..126

Chapter Fifteen 128

Moca, Dominican Republic: 12 p.m. local, 2 p.m. CST 128

Cheyenne Mountain Complex: 2 p.m. local, 3 p.m. CST 129

Holden: 3 p.m. CST 133

Cheyenne Mountain Complex: 3 p.m. local, 4 p.m. CST 135

Chapter Sixteen...138

Southwest Argentina: 7:30 p.m. local, 4:30 p.m. CST 138

St. Louis, MO: 8 p.m. CST 141

Chicago: 8 p.m. CST..144

Southern Pacific Ocean: 10 p.m. local, 10 p.m. CST..145

Chapter Seventeen 148

Cheyenne Mountain Complex: 12 a.m. local, 1 a.m. CST...148

Southern Pacific: 12 a.m. local, 12 a.m. CST 152

Epilogue 164

Chapter One: The First Day

Thingvellir National Park, South Iceland: 8 a.m. local, 2 a.m. CST

The ground trembled ever so slightly. Birds of various sizes and colors suddenly launched skyward, spinning in the cold air. Flying overhead, wings straining with effort, the birds soared north, their cries of alarm largely unnoticed by the tourists below. This was no orderly migration of a flock; these birds flew chaotically, crashing into each other, lost feathers catching gusts of wind. Something unseen had terrified them, yet the people visiting Thingvellir National Park were oblivious to their fear.

Dr. Helgi Briem, a professor at the California Institute of Technology, watched as one of her geology students, Sandy Lupo, raised her phone for another shot of the Mid-Atlantic Ridge, the most famous site in the park. Helgi, born and bred not far from here, always enjoyed sharing the heart of Iceland with others. These annual excursions kept her connected to her home and her family. So far, this year's trip had been amazing. She loved this park, and sharing it with her students was like giving them the most beautiful gift in the world.

Most of this ridge stretched thousands of miles under the Atlantic Ocean, reaching from the icy top of the planet almost to its frigid bottom. Shaped like a writhing snake, the fissure was part of the planet's mechanics, creating a new ocean floor as the Earth's tectonic plates spread apart. The tiny bit that surfaced across Iceland was the only part of the massive fault sitting above salt water. Seeing it here today was a geology student's dream come true.

Helgi's Caltech undergraduates worked hard to earn a spot on this field trip to Iceland. It was open to a select few second-year geology students, and grades were definitely part of the criteria. Once they made the cut, Sandy and her friends moved Heaven and Earth to arrange the funds and get their parents on board.

"The rest of our class is going to flip when they see these pictures," said Kyle Austin beside Sandy.

"This is great! Makes all those shifts worth it." Sandy clapped him on the shoulder and then turned around, drinking in all the sights. She and Kyle had worked at the same restaurant for a time, both saving for the trip. "Everyone in our class wanted to come. I can't believe we are the ones standing here. It's so beautiful," she concluded with a sigh.

Helgi walked on down the path, enjoying the view. Gray and brown walls of rock rose on either side, cracked and broken, chunks of geology caught in sprouts of green grass at their feet. Ahead, the walls leveled out, the ground dropped, and twenty feet further, a pool of bright blue water collected in the faults. It was so clear she could see the broken pattern, the rise and fall of the crevices, and the water at the bottom turning darker the deeper it flowed. Behind her, the kids continued their conversation, comparing photographs on their phones with excitement.

"Look at this one," Sandy waved the device so hard the picture was a blur.

Kyle laughed and tried to catch her hand.

"Tomorrow, we go to Almannagja." Becky Pruitt, another of Sandy's classmates, scanned the pamphlet she had picked up at the tourist center. Her blond hair whipped in the wind. Her blue eyes and pale skin resembled those of the majority of the Icelandic population, and she could have passed for Helgi's younger sister. Becky was fascinated to read the brochure's description of how Scandinavian settlers initially populated the island, bringing their genetic heritage with them. There were not many Icelanders with black hair and dark eyes like Sandy.

"It's a good thing it's July and not January," Kyle commented. He rubbed his scruffy haircut in a mock shiver and pulled his nylon jacket tighter. "I wouldn't want to make that hike in the snow."

Helgi agreed silently, a smile curving her small mouth. Almannagja Gorge, Iceland's principal dry land rift, presented a challenging trail. Over eight kilometers of ridge coated in lava rocks, you could stand among massive heaps of broken tectonic plate crust with your toes touching the planet's geology. After all, it was literally the point where Iceland was rising from the ocean.

Last year, she taught the class about these very cliffs and how these rock faces marked the meeting point of the North American and

Eurasian continents. The gradual pull of the tectonic plates allowed for new features up and down the gorge as the process continued. Thingvellir truly was a natural wonder, and it was her favorite place in the world. She glanced back over at her group, keeping an eye on them.

Sandy was grinning; tomorrow's itinerary was at the top of her thoughts. The day included snorkeling in the Silfra Fissure, with its crystal-clear spring water, some of the purest in the world. The visibility was touted as being absolutely amazing.

California natives Sandy, Kyle, and Becky all loved to snorkel, but none of them had ever had a chance to swim in a fissure. Sifra was believed to be the only spot on the planet where you could snorkel between two tectonic plates. The day would end at the spectacular Oxararfoss Waterfall. The professor had told them that the pictures they had found on the internet hardly did such a natural wonder justice. All of the students were quivering with excitement—despite Kyle's reservations about the temperature.

At least, Sandy *thought* it was excitement that was causing the trembling. But, looking down, she suddenly realized that the pebbles at her feet were moving in little jumps, and she could feel tiny movements under the soles of her boots. Frowning, she began to speak when a solid vibration rumbled up beneath the path and through their legs.

Deep unease filled her, and a glance at her friends confirmed their fear, too. Becky's smile had disappeared, and Kyle's forehead was wrinkled in concern. Up the trail, she saw Dr. Briem hurrying back in their direction, concern stamped on her face, and other people pointing ahead and behind her, talking frantically. She didn't know which way to look and spun around, trying to see everything at once. A grumbling noise started low, and then shouts filled the air. She whipped around as the other tourists on the trail began to run back towards the tourist center, stumbling as the ground moved beneath them. Kyle grabbed her arm, steadying himself.

"Earthquake?" he exclaimed in astonishment. Even though they were all aware of Iceland's geological record of thousands of tremors a year, most were small shakes that could not even be felt. The professor had told them they probably would not feel any vibrations their whole visit, let alone experience a real shaker.

"I think it is," Sandy stammered.

Helgi slid beside Becky, pushing the girl towards the Visitor Center. "Go!" she yelled. She didn't know how bad this tremor would be, but she wasn't taking any chances with her students.

The rumbling noise behind Sandy drowned out the words, but she could read her professor's lips. Shock snapped up through her stomach, making it hard to breathe. Dr. Briem's fear became her own, and she turned to start running. The noise grew louder, becoming a sustained bass roar in seconds. The ground jolted, and Sandy gasped as she realized this earthquake would be a monster. Kyle screamed just then, a high-pitched shriek of fear.

Sandy turned back to him, unwilling to abandon her friend. The sight that met her eyes froze her brain. The pretty pool resting at the end of the path was gone. In its place was a hole in the ground, dark sides violently tumbling into a growing maw. She grabbed Kyle and pulled him down the pathway after her friends, now more than one hundred yards ahead.

A massive section of the path split before Helgi and Becky as they tripped and skidded across the ground, frantically working to stay upright. The professor threw up her arms in a futile gesture to save them both. The piece elevated sharply and slammed into the cliff wall, disintegrating and burying the two women in rubble. Sandy screamed, stopping, clutching a moaning Kyle. More slabs of the ground were torn free, forced into the air, blocking their way.

The roaring increased to a level that hurt her eardrums, and to her horror, she watched as the Visitor Center toppled and fell, crushing those around it. Car alarms burst into a wail, the mournful cry echoing a warning. Then, even more horrifying, the whole area sank: Visitor Center, buses, cars, people, the walls of the cliffs, and spires of rock all came crashing down before they disappeared into a new hole, one that was eating the earth like a Pac-Man. The ground between them fell away at an astonishing rate as it was devoured. Sick with fear, she could not see the bottom. And suddenly, Sandy knew there was nowhere to run. In just a few minutes, as the ground shook and roared, the two holes met, everything fell into the darkness, and not a trace remained of Thingvellir National Park.

Alvar Haarde pressed the radio transmit button. "Ground Control, this is Cessna two-six-niner-foxtrot-uniform requesting clearance. The itinerary to Reykjavik Domestic Airport has been filed. The intended altitude is ten thousand feet. The weather is fair, and the winds are to the north. Over."

As he waited for a reply, he checked the fuel gauge on his Cessna 172 again. It indicated that the tank was full. Alvar knew—he had personally just finished filling it—but he always paid strict attention to such details. He liked to say that good judgment resulted from meticulous, punctilious, and scrupulous behavior with a healthy dose of double- and triple-checking. That formula hadn't let him down yet.

Opening the throttle and turning on the master switch and fuel pump, he eased the gauge to establish a stable fuel mixture. Snapping the beacon lights on, he started the ignition switch and listened to the rumble as the engines caught and fired. Oil pressure was good, and avionics set; he was ready when ground control called back.

"Cessna two-six-niner-foxtrot-uniform, cleared for runway five. Caution: Wind turbulence, with winds picking up speed north by northeast. Over."

"Ah, Cessna two-six-niner-foxtrot-uniform, cleared for runway five. Thanks for the update on the winds. Heading for runway five, over."

He started to move the plane forward, a smile on his cheerful face. This was the best part of his day. The short hops back and forth between KEF and RKV might have been annoying for some, but Alvar loved to fly every chance he had.

Today, he was picking up a couple of engineers in Reykjavik. They wanted to see the Mid-Atlantic Ridge from the air. This wasn't the first time he had flown engineers, but these fellows sure seemed to be in a hurry. They called last night and offered twice his usual fare for the experience. Alvar briefly wondered why and then shrugged. It was none of his business, and he did not care.

9

He moved up in line on the runway and called to the tower requesting departure information. While he waited, he saw out of the corner of his eye something dark hurtle overhead, and he craned his neck around to peer out the window and above the wing. With a start, he realized a massive flock of birds was driving through the sky to the north. There were so many their shadows cast a gloomy cloud over the tarmac.

"What the. . .?" he whispered to himself in surprise.

As he watched the birds, the chatter on the radio took on a new urgency. Voices overlapped, exclaiming about the birds as the other pilots caught sight of the phenomenon.

Then, in shock, he listened to the panicked cry from the tower as the controller cut into the babble. "Mayday! Mayday! Mayday!" The controller's voice shook as he tried to speak quickly. "Declaring an emergency. This is not a test; repeat, this is not a test. A massive earthquake in south Iceland! Get off the ground as fast as you can! *Go! Go! Go!*" The controller said more, but the plane in front of Alvar jumped forward, seizing his attention. As it gained speed and turned the curve to the runway, Alvar sped up, following the sleek aircraft onto the tarmac, noting a big 747 just lifting off ahead. Behind him, another plane roared forward, moving too fast.

Terrified of running into the plane in front and equally terrified of being run into from behind, Alvar tried to look across both runways and drive simultaneously. He didn't feel the Earth shake or see the ground kilometers behind him split and collapse. He hoped the birds would be long gone by the time he lifted, but in panic, he didn't stop to check the sky. He started down Runway 5 and watched breathlessly as the plane in front of him gained speed taking off from the blacktop with a much shorter takeoff than usual.

Before its wheels left the ground, his Cessna 172 was moving. Suddenly, he could feel the jolts; the tires lifted and slammed back to the concrete, skidding as they grabbed the asphalt. *The earthquake was here!* Faster and faster, trying to attain flight speed, he swallowed hard and jerked up on the elevators, pushing the stick forward as far as it would go. Jagged fissures ate up the ground behind him as the Cessna hurtled down the runway. Cracks on the tarmac raced past him, widening as he watched helplessly, and he knew he was out of time.

The ground bucked hard, throwing his plane at least fifty feet into the air, and suddenly, he was airborne. Frantically, fearing a mid-air collision, he searched for other aircraft, lifting as fast as the little Cessna would go. He saw no birds or other planes in his flight path. His chest straining, he tried to slow his breathing. Blinking at the blue sky, he fought off the panic that threatened to choke him and struggled to get his bearings. Looking down at the ground, he started a turn back towards the airport. The radio had fallen silent, and the cab was now filled with static.

He gripped the stick, trying to steady the Cessna as the sight below him took his breath away. The airport was gone. Everything was gone or in the process of going. As he watched mesmerized, the land to the north and west crumpled, broke, and sank. Everything to the south and east was already gone, and the ocean had poured into the cavities left behind.

The last of the land beneath him broke away as he stared, and the Atlantic Ocean rolled over the scraps, meeting itself in a collision of waves. The surface was wild, swells striking from all directions, and the froth filled the air. Debris and flotsam littered the ocean surface, and pieces of wreckage were tossed together and agitated in the roiling foam. A plane wing forced its way up through the mess, then was slammed back down by a vast gray sheet of something else riding the next surge. He could not see any bodies but knew they were there, under the dark green water.

Barely able to believe what he was seeing, he wondered if the earthquake's results had pressed into the mainland, or if only this peninsula were now submerged. Then he remembered the Mid-Atlantic Ridge. He imagined it carved through the country. Iceland has been built over the ridge through millions of years of massive magma eruptions. It wasn't possible to take it all back in just one day—was it?

He suddenly remembered the engineers he was supposed to be picking up. Shaking, with sweat dripping across his eyes, he tried to pull himself together.

Muddled with anxiety, fearing the worst but unable to think of any other course of action, Alvar turned the nose of the Cessna to the west and headed for Reykjavik. The sky was free of birds now and still a bright summer blue. No other planes were in the air, not even the 747 that took off just before he did. Fatalistically, he wondered if they made it and, if so, where they went. It seemed impossible for the sun to shine and the sky to be so blue while the land below had just sunk and disappeared.

More than two hundred thousand people lived and worked between here and Reykjavik. Alvar despaired at the thought as he gazed down. He usually followed the coast on his routine flights, but there was no coast to follow today. Jagged stone teeth split the waves here and there, remnants of the land where little villages and farms had once stood. The beauty was gone; devastation and salt water were all that remained. Even the fishing boats that typically dotted the waters were gone, lost to the giant waves created by the massive earthquake.

Alvar saw no sign of life, regardless of where he looked. Tears poured down his face, blurring his vision. Suddenly, he remembered the radio. With a yell, he grabbed the device, mashing the transmission button and calling for help. No words came back on the primary air frequency; it was just static and more static. Frantically, he switched channels, trying to rouse anyone, anywhere. The noise rose and faded and rose again. No one answered.

Finally, though his wet eyes could not believe it, the GPS receiver told him he was over Reykjavik. The city was gone; the ocean stretched as far north, west, and south as he could see. Giant icebergs calved from glaciers sailed over the tumultuous waters of the sea, and flotsam littered the waves. He kept flying west, praying for a radio response. He strained his eyes for even a strip of earth on which to land his plane while weeping for his homeland and all the people who had lost their lives today.

For the first time, he started to wonder what had happened. How could an earthquake of such magnitude stretch across such a distance? How could the land be sundered to such an extent that the ocean drowned everything? Why did no one know an event like this was possible? And who would help him if he could not find a place to land?

Fagurholsmyri Airport on the opposite coast of Iceland was several hours from his position. Darkness now covered the sky in that direction, but he could not tell from here if it was clouds, smoke, debris, or something else. He decided to fly in that direction and hope for the best. In the meantime, he watched the sun glint off the giant waves below and cried.

Chapter Two

Holden, NE: 3 a.m. CST

"MAC, turn on the jammers and call Max."

MAC swiftly initiated the call, with a speed only artificial intelligence could accomplish. Ben Stone's cell phone rang, signaling that his end of the call had connected. He picked it up and listened to the squeaks and tweets as the call reached Max's cell on an encrypted line. The young cyber engineer picked up on the first ring, even though it was the middle of the night.

"Hello," he answered, his high-pitched voice wide awake.

"It's started," Ben told him, clenching his fists. He stood, pacing a short circle, then sat with a frustrated thump. His tired eyes scanned the multiple monitors, trying to take in all the information simultaneously. "Most of Iceland is gone, subsided beneath the ocean."

Max was silent for a beat. "MAC, did you find evidence of linking activity?"

The artificial intelligence had already hacked into its computer counterparts in NASA, DARPA, and other black sites with acronyms for names. It gathered the relevant information, depositing it in the quantum mainframe built into the corner of the room next to Ben's desk. Running every calculation simultaneously, MAC answered in less than three seconds.

"Yes, Max. Coordinates: -64.984182, 161.894099 (64° 59' 3.1" S, 161° 53'38.8" E at 8 am Greenwich Mean Time, 2 a.m. CST, and 7 p.m. AEDT. That point is 269 miles north of Antarctica, south of Tasmania in the Indian Ocean. Those coordinates are the antipodes of the Icelandic coordinates, as you predicted. Based on the pulses, the strength of the Mantle Cannon was set at 25%. This was likely a field test. Original specs from five years ago indicate the destruction of Iceland was not the expected outcome."

"The idiots probably thought they'd pop a few of Iceland's volcanoes and were surprised. I bet somebody got a medal when over a hundred went off." A fatigued bitterness tinged his voice—incongruous in one so youthful.

Ben refocused on the monitors, the phone tight to his ear. He practically buzzed with anxiety. "So, maybe they will pull back? Rerun the equations and recalculate. Maybe they'll finally see the truth of what we've tried to warn everyone about?"

Max snorted. "Not a chance. Field test two will commence in hours. You can bet on it."

The AI helpfully displayed a map of the North Atlantic, indicating the initially planned site for the second test. With a ship anchored two hundred miles southwest of Sydney, Australia, its antipode was centered in the North Atlantic Ocean near the Azores. Potential weak spots on the Mid-Atlantic Ridge and other likely mantle flaws identified by MAC were colored with alerts.

Ben studied it, unsettled again by the amount of red. "I warned Newsom and Hart multiple times. Iceland is bad enough—all the lives lost. But messing with the Mid-Atlantic Ridge..." Max's voice trailed off, then rose again. "That dumb-ass Newsom said it was a few fish and the bottom of an ocean. He never understood the science, even when I dumbed it down to kindergarten level. You saw the projections, and so did they. They said I was an alarmist, worried too much, all exaggeration. We'll see."

Ben had stopped listening to Max's rant. He had heard it hundreds of times. He agreed with Max, but it was pointless to rehash history.

Hunching over the desk reminded his complaining muscles that he had not left this seat in the last several hours. It was a lot harder to pull these all-nighters in his fifties than it had been in his thirties, that was for sure. He attempted to sit straighter as his stomach rumbled, commiserating over its missed dinner. His sweaty shirt read, "*SCHIST HAPPENS metamorphically speaking.*" If he hadn't been so anxious, he would have gotten a chuckle out of the phrase again.

"I'm calling my brothers and sounding the alarm. Max, you need to get out of there too."

"Packed, strapped, and ready to roll," Max snapped back.

"Will you come here?"

"Maybe. I have a few things to do. Take care of yourself, Benny." The call cut out before he could say anything else. Swearing,

Ben dropped his phone on the desk. He knew better than most that Max could not be controlled. The kid had called all the shots since they teamed up.

Not that he was complaining. Max really was a certified genius. The proof was in the quantum computer the self-taught engineer had built and bequeathed to him. The value it provided Ben was worth any aggravation from the young prodigy. Okay, not so young anymore, he reminded himself. They had been collaborating for four years, so he had to be in his thirties now. His poor social skills and his vendetta against Dror Hart and Victor Newsom-, CEO and CFO of Titan International, made him seem younger than he was.

He picked up his cell and checked the encryption status, though MAC never let him down. Still paranoid, he knew the last thing he needed was for Titan International to find his location. He tried to dial, and watched as the information scrolled across multiple computer screens simultaneously.

The phone continued to ring unanswered, and he grumbled under his breath. Pulling his eyes away from the computer, he texted a hasty *"Call me"* to his brother Arthur in Atlanta. Art, two years his junior, was probably prepping for the early a.m. news—he worked as an anchor for FOX 7, a prominent network. Art would call back when he saw Ben's message; he was good that way.

He dialed again, trying to reach either of his two other younger brothers. The middle of the night was not the ideal time to make calls, but he wanted to warn them.

There was no answer at Augie's, so he left a message. "Augie, wake up, man. Iceland's gone. It was a mega eruption, and it looks like most of the volcanoes on the island vented. It tore the land mass apart. Now, MAC is projecting more movement in the Atlantic, something major. It doesn't look good for the coastal countries in the Northern Hemisphere. The East Coast is going to get walloped. MAC isn't decisive on how long before the faults let go, but if they are related to the testing of the Mantle Cannon as we extrapolated, we're talking hours, not days. Call me!"

He tried Will last, even though he knew his youngest brother was likely off the grid: he was currently reconnoitering another angle of this problem in Argentina. Will was a retired military ranger. If anyone could find Titan International's compound, it would be him.

There was no answer again, so he left another frustrated message: "Will, SOS. The world is about to take a major hit. Call me."

No point in saying more, even on encrypted lines. Will knew what was at stake. He swore at the phone in his hand and dropped it on the table.

Just as it landed, it rang with a soft chime. He snatched it back up, trusting MAC to encrypt it. Despite his paranoia, he did not even look at the caller ID. "Art!" he barked out.

"It's Frank, Ben."

Stunned to hear Frank Robbin's voice, Ben took a deep breath, not answering for a moment. He had not spoken to his old boss at the USGS in three years—not since he had left under a cloud of his own making.

Ben had been a geologist with the government's geological branch for thirty years. He loved his job. The saying could have been coined specifically for him: 'Do a job you love, and you'll never have to work a day in your life.' That was Ben's experience. Up until the end, anyway.

When he tried to convince his bosses at the USGS of the potential threat Titan International represented, no one believed him. A machine that could produce a combination of mutated pressure and heat pulses, strong enough to blast missile-like energy through the Earth, with the intended purpose of superheating and cracking the mantle on the other side of the planet? Yeah, his peers laughed at him.

Otto Brecken, a German geologist from The Technical University of Munich, discovered the frequencies that made the farfetched process work and promptly sold his research to Hart at Titan International. Ben's superiors said Brecken's "concept" was science fiction. The idea of positioning on the antipode of known magma lakes and repeatedly firing at the target was a joke. They pointed out that most volcanic material in such huge chambers is solid. The idea of producing the amount of heating required to melt the rock was inconceivable. But, say you could get it to work?

You'd be talking about creating pyroclastic flows and rivers of lava that could eradicate miles of land, if not hundreds of miles. Pick the right area to aim at— the chain of currently dormant volcanoes in Beijing, China, for example—and you could eliminate one of the world's most significant political problems in one day. Victor Newsom thought the collateral damage was worth it, and apparently, so did DARPA since they funded the build of the Mantle Cannon. And who would get the blame?

Mother Nature.

Like all political arms of the government, the USGS listened not very politely and did nothing. They only reacted to intel from the top. He knew that better than most, since that was how his career ended. The day he was forced out was the second worst day of his life. It demonstrated to him, beyond any doubt, that no independent thinking would be permitted. His bosses deemed the idea ridiculous, and it and his career died that afternoon.

He scratched at the stubble on his usually clean-cut face. "No point in dwelling on the past," he told himself as he pushed away that stab of memory for the millionth time. Easy to say, hard to do. He sighed.

But hearing from Frank Robbins in the middle of the night, especially tonight, was a surprise. He glanced at the clock on the wall. It was 1 a.m. in Sacramento.

"Ben, answer me. I know you can hear me." Frank sounded winded; his tone tinged with hysteria.

"I hear you," Ben replied gruffly. "What do you want?"

"This is it, isn't it? Iceland? This is what you tried to warn them about? Is it finally happening?"

Ben relented. Frank had not been responsible for his job loss and reputation. Frank had tried to help, even to the point of nearly being cast out along with Ben. Besides, he wanted to warn someone, even though he knew it was too late to do anything.

"Yes." He closed his eyes and opened them again, and the monitors filled his view. "Are you watching the satellite feeds?"

One of Ben's monitors displayed Geosys, a real-time cloud-based imagery service. Another displayed a NASA version of the same data

18

type but with better resolution, thanks to the networking connections of his brother, August, a research meteorologist at NASA. The two technologies were linked to different satellites, but Ben had both pointed at Iceland. Or at least where most of Iceland used to be. Numbers scrolled across a third monitor as MAC crunched the new data gathered in the last few hours while trying to correlate potential outcomes.

"Yes. I can't believe it. Ben, we're losing it here. No one saw this coming. For God's sake, Albert is on with the president and his people." Albert Longfield, the USGS director, had publicly embarrassed Ben at that doomed meeting with all the department heads.

Frank got right to the point. "Do you think Titan built the weapon?"

"Iceland meets the criteria for the potential outcome."

Frank's tone rose. "What do you think will happen next?"

Ben hesitated.

Frank knew what was wrong. "I'm not sharing this. They didn't ask me to call you. But I always was afraid you were right, Ben. I kept your phone number within reach."

Ben gripped the device; confident MAC had encrypted the call.

"Somethings happening with the Mid-Atlantic Ridge. And it's going to be soon."

Atlanta, GA: 6 a.m. local, 5 a.m. CST

Max Ungle gripped the steering wheel and pressed harder on the Subaru's gas pedal. He needed to be in and out of Atlanta fast. When he set up the first of his safe deposits, he hadn't anticipated the risk to Atlanta. He should have moved the data once MAC uncovered Titan's test plan and the potential repercussions for the Atlantic coast. The work of a whistleblower was never done, he thought mockingly.

As he drove the last hour into Atlanta, he brooded over the choices that had led him to this point. It had been rad when he first got the job at Titan International six years ago. The money was sweet, too. His reputation for software development and manipulation was legendary among his peers; he was the go-to guy to get anything impossible done. He took one look at the blueprint Brecken dropped in front of him, and he was hooked. Never one to turn down the unachievable, even if it was just for bragging rights, he dove right in. He had an unlimited budget and resources at his beck and call. Never having worked for a corporation before, he assumed that this was how all great projects worked. It didn't occur to him that he was building a weapon of mass destruction until he built the simulations.

A flash of anger crossed his narrow face as he thought about the simulations. Not one of them had helped humanity. He couldn't dream up a single benefit. The only thing the device was suitable for was destruction. And Max, for all his shortcomings—he would be the first to admit he had quite a few—was not into world destruction.

That jackass Newsom tried to give him more money to get on board. But Max wasn't fooled by some greedy corporate stooge. He realized the score once he dug around and discovered DARPA was paying for everything. His peers had been saying it for years: government and corporations were toxic.

Drawing on what he considered to be incomparable tech skills to go along with his immodest self-regard, the self-proclaimed punk nerd hacked around the company's weak-ass firewalls to download and smuggle out the specs of their Mantle Cannon. Every time he thought about it, he sneered at the stupid name.

It didn't take a hacker of his stripe to get the job done. It was easy to take the data. Since then, however, staying one step ahead of Titan's goon squad had been much harder than he anticipated. Those guys never gave up.

Meeting up with Ben Stone four years ago was a game changer, and it was lucky for Max. They had both frequented an off-brand source for cutting-edge computer modification hardware. A hole-in-the-wall dump in the Lincoln corridor in Pasadena, the owner was mainly a crook. The whole front end was piled with vintage and obsolete equipment, dirty and haphazardly displayed. The back was where the real business occurred, somewhat illegally, as one could never be sure where the parts had come from. The resulting lower prices attracted economy buyers like Max.

Max was there most days during those hot summer weeks he spent building the quantum computer. He kept running into this old guy, who was also trying to make a computer and asked some decent questions. Only a few people impressed Max and even fewer when they opened their mouths—but Old Guy had some excellent ideas and never tried to converse with Max. His equipment purchases were surprisingly intelligent, too.

When Titan's enforcement agents showed up on a random Thursday evening asking questions, Old Guy and Max were trolling in the back part of the store, ignoring each other, hidden by stacks of ancient equipment piled in the middle of the room. The men in black tried to bully the desk clerk, scaring the kid with questions about Max in loud, mean voices.

Old Guy looked at Max's white face and motioned him to follow. They slipped out a back door he didn't even know was there and into a small car parked behind the store. They were gone in less than two minutes.

Old Guy, of course, was Ben Stone. It turned out that Ben Stone had been a geologist for the USGS. Ben was the first person to take Max seriously. Not that Max told him right away about Titan International and the jerk twins, Dror Hart and Victor Newsom. He was justifiably paranoid by then. One thing Max did very well was keep secrets.

The two geeks stuck to computers for a while and hit it off immediately. They worked on building hardware and programming the software for months. Max was a genius-level developer, and Ben was in awe of his engineering capabilities. The geologist assumed that the shake-down and questions about Max in the computer store that day were related to unlawfully hacking or appropriating computer equipment. Max knew Ben didn't care about minor stuff like that.

However, over the weeks of working with a guy whose day job was geology, Max couldn't help himself, and started bringing up potential geological doomsday scenarios. Ben really was smart, and he understood people better than Max. He figured out something more was happening and leaned into Max until he earned enough confidence to get the hacker to spill.

Max finally showed him the stolen specs. He had hacked back into Titan and found project plans confirming the company had moved forward with the project after he walked. They found themselves another brilliant programmer (though not as clever as Max) with less strict morals, and that guy had made progress. There was a lot of progress, as it turned out. Ben knew enough about geology and technology to understand this weapon's risks.

Once Ben was convinced by Max's story, being a straight-up guy, he tried to warn his bosses. But he hit the same ignorant wall Max had every time he tried to alert anyone who could shut Titan down, to the point that they fired Ben. No one believed the weapon could be built, or would work if it were built.

So, making digital and print copies of everything he raided from Titan, Max started leaving safe deposits in the big cities. Atlanta was the last one he had created, and with the most recent data, so he particularly wanted to collect what he had left there. He wouldn't take a chance on Atlanta being flooded by Titan's immoral activities.

He pulled into the Eastview Cemetery parking lot ten minutes later. The Mausoleum was five minutes down the gravel path. The beautiful marble foyer was empty—it was too early for visitors—as was the hall with Max's crypt. He pulled out the gold key the administrator had given him when he bought the vault and slipped it into the keyhole. The door opened easily, and his urn, filled with paper and digital devices, sat right where he had left it. He grabbed the vase, slipped it into his knapsack, and beat a hasty retreat.

Pulling out, he headed for ATL, the Hartsfield-Jackson Atlanta International Airport. He had booked the next flight out to Bahia Blanca, Argentina. Will Stone, Ben's brother, would meet him there. It was time to go on the offensive.

Tasmin Sea: 200 miles southwest Sydney, Australia, 10 p.m. local, 5 a.m. CST

Titan One surged in the rough waters of the Indian Ocean. The ship heaved like a staggering drunk as the captain tried to stay anchored on this spot. Victor Newsom was oblivious.

The first test, launched on *Titan Two*, 1500 miles south, had been a complete success. The Mantle Cannon had outperformed all expectations. He scanned the specs, noting the amount of energy released and how broad an area was affected. It was a bigger than their estimates, but clearly, the weapon met all test parameters.

Dror Hart, CEO of Titan International, strode into the cabin, his well-trained personal assistant Cynthia at his heels. He grabbed the wall as they bobbed right again. Cynthia sprawled across the desk. Both men ignored her clumsiness, and she hastily pulled herself back up.

"Well?" Hart asked.

"It's good—no, it's great, Dror." Newsom could not contain his glee. A big grin split his brown face. "Three-quarters of Iceland is gone. Activating the volcanoes caused a major subsidence, and what's left is hardly worth the conversation. We have met our end of the contract."

"Contact General Wolfe," Hart ordered Cynthia. "Let's ensure he knows the first test was a complete success."

"Yes, sir," Cynthia hurried to comply. They could hear the phone ringing.

"Wolfe," the general barked. Cynthia handed the device to Hart.

"General, I believe you are aware of the results of the first test?"

Wolfe laughed. "I'm aware Iceland had some volcanic and earthquake activity this morning. How do I know you aren't just taking credit?"

Hart's face turned crimson, but his tone remained modulated. "Well, let's ensure that's not an issue for the second test. In one hour, we will implement Test #2. Watch the Northern Atlantic. I think you will be happy with the results."

"I'll be watching." The general hung up.

"Pretentious ass."

He tossed the phone back to Cynthia and gave Victor a dead-eye stare.

"One hour. Make it happen."

"It will be my pleasure." He glanced at his cell and saw a text from Dr. Brecken, the lead scientist on this project. "Brecken needs to talk. I'll update you if needed. I'll be in the control room."

Hart barely looked up from the device as Newsom walked away, scrolling to Brecken's name. Once he was far enough down the corridor, he pushed the connect button.

"What do you need, Brecken?"

"Sir, we're getting some concerning numbers from the first test."

Newsom frowned. "I read the results; the device worked perfectly."

"Yes, sir. Sorry, I should have been clearer. We have readings that we took after the test. Ground readings, sir, measure impacts on the core as the waves pass through. That's what I am concerned about—the core. It seems to be reacting to the waves we sent through the planet."

"That's impossible. You told me that was impossible. You said there would be no impact."

"I may have been wrong," the scientist admitted quietly.

"We are doing the next test in less than an hour. We'll discuss it after that." Newsom hung up on Brecken's protestations, thinking furiously.

The Mantle Cannon was the company's only viable product, and DARPA was their only paying customer. Titan had been incorporated to produce the cannon after Hart obtained Brecken's designs. The bulk of the money to get started came from DARPA once Hart sold Wolfe on the idea. Hart brought in Newsom to ensure a successful delivery. No cannon, no payout. If this failed, not only would they be bankrupt, but he would be out of a job that paid extremely well. So, whatever it took, this product was not going to fail.

He scrolled again, reaching the head of security on *Titan Two*. "Dr. Brecken seems to be feeling poorly," he told the man who answered. "Please arrange for him to sleep for the next twenty-four hours until you hear from me."

"Yes, sir," came the crisp response.

Newsom smiled as he put the phone away and continued to the control room. He liked running the show. He had no plans to stop doing so.

Chapter Three

Mid-Atlantic Ridge, North Atlantic Ocean: 11:30 a.m. local, 5:30 a.m. CST

The MCS Madrid was one of the largest container ships in the world. Carrying over twenty thousand containers and weighing in at more than two hundred and seventy thousand tons, she moved goods from Europe to the United States and back. With the hull painted a bright red, a white boat deck, and thousands of multi-colored containers, she stood out against the waves as she crashed through the big swells. As big as she was, the men and women on the bridge could still feel the hull rock as the ship road up and down the sea.

"Pilot, let's slow, drop to six knots." Captain Harald Larsen rechecked the display. His shiny dome forehead wrinkled with worry. The waves may have been high because of that business in Iceland earlier today, but the ocean floor here bothered him. There was enough sea-based resistance on his screen to make him sweat. He studied the monitor, disturbed as the sonar image jumped, broke up, and cleared. He could not get a straightforward reading of the ocean's depth in this area. The colors that marked the depth kept changing, bleeding into each other, and the brighter yellows that indicated a strong sonar echo spread across the window, overtaking the blues swiftly. In other words, the ocean seemed to be getting shallower—but that was inconceivable.

He should be picking up the Mid-Atlantic Ridge here—a long, snaking rift nestled between two mountain ranges. It should plunge a thousand meters or more below them in this area. The equipment would not verify, and to his frustration, he could not get any reading that made sense. A tech was on the floor at his feet, squeezed under the counter, trying to determine what was interfering with the signal. He heard the pilot talking to the engine room but did not look up. He studied the information on the various boards, navigation charts, sonar readings, radar, rudder, and thruster controls with increasing annoyance.

With a catch in his voice, the third mate suddenly called out. "Captain, look here!"

Captain Larsen turned. Irritated by the interruption, he strode over to the big bridge windows to see the trouble. The waves had increased in just a few minutes, and Larsen was shocked to see them crashing over the main deck. But that was not why the third mate had called him. The young sailor pushed the binoculars into the captain's hand, pointing over the bow.

Raising the glasses, he braced himself as the sea heaved more furiously beneath his feet. The air shimmered, like during a heat wave. It took a moment to focus the glass and sweep the waves. They looked peculiar close up, almost like enormous bubbles in a giant pot of boiling water. Then he forgot the waves, and his mouth fell open.

"All stop!" he screamed, knowing they could not stop in time. Even without the waves pounding on her, the ship needed ten to fifteen minutes to come to a complete stop.

Modern cargo ships were constructed with a complex arrangement of steel plates and strengthening beams. Iron blended ribs held the 14-gauge steel plates welded with millions of steel and wrought iron rivets. All that strength would not help them now. With a mighty crash that broke every window and threw everyone and everything to the floor, the MCS Madrid collided with the top of a vast black mountaintop just visible above the waves and came to a dead stop. Unforgiving rock tore the bottom of the ship wide open, and they rested at an awkward forty-five-degree angle.

Larsen lay on his side, dazed, bleeding from multiple cuts from the glass, and hearing the screech of hot wind as the waves scraped the ship against the rock. Seemingly from a distance, he could hear his crew screaming, but he could not move. He realized his exposed flesh was burning. The red skin started to bubble, and the air, on which could be smelt a whiff of sulfur, scorched his lungs. He could hardly draw a breath.

He felt his strength leaking away, and his eyes milked over, blurring his vision. In his last minutes, the shrieks of the steel hull pulling apart loosened his bowels with terror. As his consciousness faded, he envisaged the hell that must be roiling under the ocean's surface, and shuddered as he expired.

"This is Jade Perez, reporting from CNN Portugal, here in the beautiful Azores Islands. For the last twelve days, San Miguel Island and all of the islands in the Azores have been suffering minor earthquakes, some magnitude two point six and worse. Caught in the clutches of multiple offshore undersea earthquakes, the locals ask how long this disturbing activity will go on."

Jade gestured with her entire arm to the area around her. "Known for its great catches and safe coves, this once tiny village has grown into a leading port and the economic capital of the Azores Archipelago. Located on the southwest coast of San Miguel Island, the city of sixty thousand has learned to live with volcanic activity. But the recent earthquakes are causing concern among the local population."

Tossing back her glossy, dark hair, the young news reporter tilted her pretty face, ebony eyes set above prominent cheekbones. Standing with her was the owner of one of the local marinas, a reasonably handsome, wind-worn type who seemed ready to flirt with her if she gave him the opportunity. This, however, would have to wait for the news. She pushed the microphone over to him with a secret wink.

"I'm here with Sr. Luis Carvalho, the owner of the largest fishing fleet on San Miguel Island. Can you share with us what you have been experiencing these last few weeks, Sr. Carvalho?"

"Call me Luis, Senhorita." His eyes were so dark in his tanned face that Jade thought she could see herself. She moved closer. "Most shakes have been minor, a nuisance to the good people of San Miguel trying to go about their business. For others, the endless tremors and the odd marine behavior are causing worry. The outside world has noticed the activity as well. This happens every few years, so it is not unprecedented. Living over the Mid-Atlantic Ridge comes with its risks. But when the Earth shakes, the fish, they flee, and our fishermen struggle to bring in a catch."

"What are you hearing from the coasts?" she inquired, anxious to keep him talking.

"Geologists, marine biologists, and even volcanologists have flown in to examine the sea mounts that litter the ocean floor in this area.

A geologist explained to me that these knolls are left over from hotspots under the tectonic plates. These underwater hills and mountains have increased hydrothermal activity to the point that the waters around the islands have warmed significantly in just a short time, chasing away our usually abundant sea life. Ponta Delgada fishermen are frustrated, and we need help understanding how long this will continue."

His earnestness played well for the camera. Jade knew her producers would appreciate this segment—time for a bod to tourism concerns.

"I understand that on the other side of this island, you have a small town named Furnas, literally built deep in the crater of an active volcano."

He laughed. "Yes, that is true. A thousand people live there. There is no lava, of course. But hot springs bubble up through the black rock. Tourists flock to stay in the hotels and swim in the mineral pools. It is a beautiful place. Maybe while you are here, I could show it to you?"

Jade leaned forward, the answer in her eyes, but she didn't have a chance to share a breathy affirmative. As she opened her mouth, with a deafening explosion, all six volcanoes and hotspots on the island erupted at once, even those thought to be long dormant.

Dull, booming bellows startled the fishermen working on the docks, the tourists at lunch, the homemakers, shopkeepers, and the farmers. The island groaned and jerked, the quake making it impossible to stand. Jade and Luis grabbed each other as they fell, and her cameraman swung around, trying to balance himself and record everything simultaneously.

Doors and windows rattled violently, spewing their glass shards into unprepared people, buildings, and streets. Roof joists snapped, crushing those too slow to get away. Dirty water sprayed from broken pipes. Dogs started baying their fear, and birds launched themselves from their perches in a frenzy.

The ground shook again, much harder jolts than what the islanders had been experiencing in the last few weeks. Smoke suddenly poured from old calderas as new splits in the earth formed, vomiting up even more darkness to quickly blanket the sky. In minutes, ash started to fall from the clouds in thick veils. Pumice pounded the earth. Dozens of electric bolts jumped between cumulous black clouds, and in their brief light, the terrified populace could see the gigantic columns of smoke and ash now rising into the sky.

For those close enough, the glow of lava pouring from the calderas on either side of the island threw a ghastly orange smear that reflected the heat. In Furnas, the entire township, including tourists, animals, and infrastructure, sank into an abrupt upwelling of magma as the caldera awakened, instantly burning to ash. Great gouts of lava exploded skyward, splattering the plateaus in streams of red like huge Jackson Pollock paintings.

The other islands in the archipelago were experiencing the same violent shaking. The buildings groaned and shivered. The ground bucked and rippled in a series of waves to the shore. Fuel lines ruptured, spewing gasoline over the towns and the docks. Sparks ignited, sending deep orange fire streams in all directions as the burning liquid splashed in wide sweeping arcs. Detonations destroyed whole blocks as convulsions kicked up from deep in the Earth. The debris burned fiercely and started more fires.

In the towns, people flocked to the streets. Some were injured, to hurt to move far. Many tried to hide from the burning air in the buildings that still stood and were not on fire. Others ran through the ash for the docks, frantically hoping to get away on a boat, only to be stopped by walls of hungry flames springing up in front of them. For those who made it around the fire, there was still no respite on land or in the sea today.

The Earth itself rocked with intense side-shifting motions. The water surged in giant whirlpools and immense crashing waves. Huge mats of pumice expelled from far beneath the Earth's surface pelted any boats still lucky to be floating. Boulders and lava bombs holed sails, decks, and men, casting everything into the furious waves where drowning replaced the fiery deaths their families suffered on the land.

The misery would have lasted longer, but deep beneath the archipelago, high pressure was building up between the two underlying tectonic plates. Blasts of heat and pressure slammed into the mantle from below. Ocean water forced itself into the resulting cracks, mixing swiftly with the magma. The Azores Islands rode high over huge magma chambers on both sides of the plates. The heated steam on either flank expanded rapidly and explosively, resulting in intense pressure. With a final mega eruption, an area over eighty kilometers in circumference, islands, and seafloor shattered and blew itself out of existence.

Atlanta, GA: 7:45 a.m. local, 6:45 a.m. CST

"I'm Art Sone with your morning Atlanta News on 7. I'm hoping you have a great day, Atlanta!" He signed off with his customary confident smile, but as soon as the cameraman signaled off, Art frowned. The world news was bad, but he had done this long enough to know they weren't getting the whole story.

He waved, catching the director's attention. "I'm going to my office; yell if you need me."

"Sure, sure, good job today." Farley had run the morning news long enough to feel comfortable dismissing his anchor without a recap. He turned back to the cameraman, ready to discuss stills.

Art rushed through the hall, dodging others in a hurry. He was anxious to get to his cell phone. Sure enough, he had a missed call from his brother, Ben. Neither the government nor USGS had much to say about what happened to Iceland this morning and literally nothing to say about the ongoing situation in the Azores. Ben had warned him. Test #1 was planned for Iceland. Now, the island had been wiped out. Aware of Titan International's potential volcanic and earthquake weapon, Art knew more than was good for him. He knew enough to fear that things were going to get worse.

He dialed and waited impatiently as MAC encrypted the line, then connected.

"Art. It's happening." Ben's voice was tight. "It's going to be worse than I thought."

"What do you mean?" Art sat up straight in his chair.

"You saw Iceland? That's Test #1. After crunching the data from the Iceland event, MAC's model predicts that the results will be catastrophic if Titan International commences Test #2 anywhere in the Northern Atlantic. MAC alerted me that they started the test and upped the strength of the pulses in the last fifteen minutes."

"My God, they really are going through with it? After Iceland?"

"It's worse than that. The Mid-Atlantic Ridge is already in a period of heightened activity, which is why the Azores have experienced all those minor earthquakes recently. Blasting that area with the Mantle Cannon will add pressure exponentially and could cause a fault of epic proportions. We're talking about massive tsunamis, earthquakes, and the East Coast flooding. It is not just floods; most of the water could remain on the land. The East Coast might subside, and we'll be redrawing all the maps. After this is over, the United States will possibly have a new coastline. You need to get Marta and get out of there."

"It's too late for her to be at the apartment. She's at the hospital seeing patients; she does office visits on Tuesday."

Dr. Marta Jenson, General Surgeon, was one of the most dedicated in Atlanta. Art worried she wouldn't leave Atlanta willingly, even though they'd had this "be prepared" conversation a few times over the last two years.

He asked what he knew Marta would ask. "You think Atlanta is going to be hit? We're three hundred miles from the coast. That's impossible, right?"

"I told you. The crust isn't the only thing that's affected. The oceans are going to shift, too. And anyway, Atlanta is only one thousand feet above sea level. The incline between Atlanta and the ocean is shallow, and the waves will easily run up to the city if the impact is big enough." Art could hear Ben moving around. "Iceland and the Azores are just the first act. But it will be soon. And the oceans will move, too. The model predicts the Appalachians will be the new coast. You need to leave *now*."

Art ran a hand through his wavy hair. "We have to warn people."

"I tried that three years ago." Ben's bitterness echoed Max's earlier feelings. "The only people who believed me were my family."

Art exhaled forcefully. "That wasn't hard. You and Max were pretty convincing."

Art had been shocked—hell, they all had been shocked when Ben lost his job at the USGS. But that was nothing compared to when Ben pulled the brothers together and walked them through Max's synopsis. MAC's simulations had convinced Art and Augie. Will seemed more skeptical, but he was the most pragmatic of the brothers. They all knew better than to push him.

But the Army Ranger believed now. Over the last few years, Will had used his contacts in the military to investigate Max's claims. Officially, the Mantle Cannon didn't exist, but Will had uncovered enough information to substantiate key facts about DARPA's project, as wild as those facts seemed in the beginning.

At first, Art and Augie insisted the USGS didn't understand what Ben was trying to explain. But when he heard the scope of Titan International's goals, Art knew the problem was more significant. Men and women lived in denial. They did not want to believe science would take risks that could doom everyone. Knowledge was a tool to improve the world, and most people trusted what their leaders told them. Art saw it every day in the newsroom. MAC's predictions were terrifying, which made them difficult to accept.

MAC was beyond cutting edge; it was built with AI intelligence that did not exist just a few years ago. Constructing an artificial brain was way past anything Art could comprehend, but there was no denying Max's genius; even he could see that. The whistleblowing of Titan International was a different story. Until Max came along with his accusations, Art's opinion of Titan had been positive. He'd reported on the company a few times, and it seemed genuine.

Ben's cyber hacker added further complexity. Max could be hard to talk to; he was angry and paranoid about almost everything. But in this instance, he rang sincere with Art, and Art considered himself a good judge of people.

In the last several months, he had researched the mega-company that had burst onto the technological scene out of nowhere three years ago. They were almost too well-funded, and were working with some top names in their fields, whom they recruited almost instantly. It was a suspicious setup. Augie's wife Kay was a detective on the police force in Merrit Island, and she had looked into the CEO Dror Hart and the CFO Victor Newsom. She didn't find anything that could be substantiated, but they both felt those two were shady. He had been watching the company ever since, and while he'd only noticed little things, everything he found just increased his misgivings.

Ben interrupted his thoughts. "It's going to hit both sides of the Atlantic. Europe is closer, so you'll hear from them first. You need to get out of there."

"Any chance this will be less severe than MAC predicted?"

"No, I told you. It's going to be worse. Get out of there and get on the road. It's not going to be the same world tomorrow. We need to face it together." Ben paused. "I'll call Augie again. Move!"

Chapter Four

The western coast of Portugal: 1 p.m. local, 7 a.m. CST

Along the western coast of Portugal, it seemed just like any other day. Serving the deadbeats in a ratty old bar on the beach, Consula Reyes pushed another cerveja across the scratched bar to an older figure perched on a rough, crooked stool. In his late fifties to early sixties, his faded shirt's top two buttons were open, exposing a tuft of gray chest hair. His face was heavily wrinkled and deeply tanned. He gave her a two-fingered salute, barely touching the washed-out cap shading his leathery face.

"Nice day today, Consula."

She rolled her eyes. Alonso was one of her regulars. She didn't know if Alonso was his first name or last, but it worked for her either way.

"The sun shines, the breezes move the trees and the grasses, and the waves roll in, Alonso. It is the same day as yesterday, and the same day it will be tomorrow." She shook her head, her springy ginger hair framing a lined face.

Alonso seemed to consider her words. "The ocean seems rougher than usual, but only the fishermen and the tourist's care. Maybe it is a result of Iceland's destruction?"

Consula waved him off. She didn't want to talk about it.

Thanks to smartphones and tablets, even the baristas in bars on the remotest beaches had already heard about the catastrophic land destabilization and the loss of much of Iceland. Still, it was thousands of kilometers away, making it just one more story in the news. If one was interested in that sort of thing, there was news much closer to home on the television hanging on the wall, even if it only had three channels.

Consula shuffled off to serve another patron at the bar, leaving Alonso to mull over the loss of Iceland. Over the last several days, continuous tremors had been recorded way out in the deep waters of the Atlantic. He knew the other fishermen were watching; it had been the topic of conversation all day yesterday. He took a sip of his drink, contemplating the risks. He didn't know it, but it was already too late for him to act.

With the Azores over sixteen hundred kilometers west, no one on the mainland could feel the continual shaking. But, with a terrifying sudden flash, everyone from Norway to Liberia to Greece suffered the destructive blasts radiating from the ocean floor, ripping the Azores to shreds at that moment. They grew successively more powerful, louder and more violent, as if the air itself were being ripped in terrible cracking detonations.

It was bad all over, but along the coast, it sounded like the end of the world. Men and women flinched where they stood; children screamed in fear, their voices drowned in the roar. The assault by such a concussive wave of sound shattered any composure. Many fell to the ground, covering their ears in pain. Endless thunderous booms followed the last mighty explosion until it finally faded into a crackling noise and stopped.

Precious minutes were lost while people picked themselves up, recovered, and regrouped. Alonso helped Consula up onto her feet, trying to brush her off while she pushed him away. "I'm fine, let me alone," she growled at him.

He backed up, hands raised, and then picked up the bottles that had shuddered off the shelves. His ears felt as if they were stuffed with cotton wool, and he wondered if the muffled edge to the conversation around him was a sign of permanent hearing damage.

He didn't think to look out at the ocean, but if he had, he would have recognized what was happening as the surf rolled out and did not return. When the thirty-meter tsunami roared in half an hour later, no one in the bar, and very few on the beach, had grasped the situation and moved to high ground.

Alonso and Consula drowned in the first wave, along with thousands of coastal Portuguese citizens. Though a bit smaller, the next several waves added enough water to obliterate the flat southern half of Portugal well into the Spanish plateaus. Towns, farms, and entire families were wiped from existence.

The mountain chains protecting the land in the north meant that the tsunamis driving up and over the Spanish coast found fewer victims.

35

Those same mountains had resisted considerable waves in the past and, once again, protected the millions of people who lived in the high country.

France, England, Ireland, and other northern countries were also targets in the line of seismic sea waves. By the time they struck, tsunami warnings had gone out where they were available, but casualties were still in the millions. The coastal areas were submerged under twenty meters of ocean or more. Belgium, the Netherlands, and Denmark suffered a steep surge as the water poured through the English Channel, and even the famous dikes protecting low-lying Holland were destroyed, unable to hold back waves of this magnitude. Salt water poured over the cities, towns, and fields, creating new shorelines.

Morocco and the Sahara caught the final west-traveling waves along the African coast. The water crashed over beaches and sand dunes and roared across the flat land. Parts of Casablanca and Rabat became lakes in the desert, and most of their populations perished beneath the waves. When the news of the giant tsunamis finally reached the United States and Canada, there was little time left for the Americans to evacuate.

Atlanta, GA: 8:30 a.m. local, 7:30 a.m. CST

Art couldn't just walk away. He had worked with his team for years. He owed them more than that. A few inches shorter than Ben's six foot two, his slim figure and casual suit were rumpled today. It matched the state of his mind. He called everyone in his office and waited impatiently to start until the last person showed up.

"Look," he said, trying to be as calm as possible. "I know this is hard to believe. But a highly credible source warned me that something catastrophic would happen to Atlanta, maybe today. I'm leaving, and I wanted to give you the opportunity to go as well."

Five seconds of silence, and then everyone started talking at once.

"What kind of catastrophic?"

"Is this a joke?"

"I have kids; I hope you are kidding!"

"Wait, wait!" He held up his hands, trying to head off the babble. "You all heard the reports about the earthquakes in the Azores. Earthquakes can cause tsunamis. I know how crazy this sounds. How about this? I am giving you all the rest of the day off. I suggest you all get your families and leave Atlanta. Go to high ground. Think potential flood and get away."

Suddenly, everyone's phones started to go off. News alerts chimed frantically. Reports out of Europe described massive blasts out of the Azores, tsunamis, and floods hitting the coastal areas and sweeping inland. The causality estimates were unbelievable. Not since the Philippines in 2004, when an earthquake measuring a solid nine struck off the west coast of Sumatra, had something like this happened. His team was intelligent. After a little more discussion, they were gone.

Five minutes later, he was out the door and on his way to Mercy Hospital, where Marta tended patients. He hoped she would be easier to talk to than the group he had just left because he didn't know if they had time to argue. If he had to, he'd pull her into the car and argue all the way to Nebraska. While driving, he tuned in to the news and listened to the emergency broadcast. The Azores were gone, and the coastal cities of Europe were flooding at catastrophic rates. MAC had been right again.

Art called ahead, hoping to catch Marta alone. For once, he was in luck. She argued and questioned and threw doubt over every word he said. But by the time he pulled into the parking lot, she was waiting, bags slung over her slim shoulder and a dark look on her thin face. Her blond hair was disheveled, a clear sign of her agitation.

"It's on the television, and still no one believed me. They think we're too far inland to worry," she growled as she pulled on her seatbelt. "I tried. I talked to the chief of staff, but he said they would have been notified if there was a problem. He's heard nothing. And my patients, I can't get them moved out of the city fast enough." Her voice broke. "I did what I could; I had them moved to the higher floors. Thank God the neonatal is on the top floor. I couldn't live with myself."

"I know," Art said softly. He looked straight ahead with his Oxford heavy on the Honda's accelerator, concentrating on getting out of Atlanta. Luckily, the morning rush hour was lighter than usual today. The bug-out bags he had packed last year were in the trunk. He didn't have the heart to tell her he didn't think the hospital's six floors would be high enough.

Port St. John, Florida: 8:30 a.m. local, 7:30 a.m. CST

August Stone answered the phone while carrying bags to the Tesla. "I heard about Iceland. I got your message, and we're leaving here in five minutes." He heard Kay on her cell, instructing Lily, their college daughter, to be ready in thirty minutes. It would be a twenty-minute drive to the Eastern Florida State College campus, where she was in her last year of a biology degree, and another ten minutes from there to Merritt Island Airport, where he had booked a last-minute private plane. He worried they were cutting it close.

Far from doubting Max now, especially after working with the young whistleblower, he had become so sure of the outcome that he had planned for all of this in advance. Augie suspected Florida would be a casualty if Titan International went forward with their idiotic plans to run tests of such magnitude on the Atlantic basin. Surrounded on three sides by a potentially shifting ocean, he knew the water would have to move. Florida's topography was mainly flat. Water followed the path of least resistance. He could do the projections.

Over the last year, he had paid a local pilot to be on call. Kind of an odd fellow, Dave Skinner had been as good as Augie's money and was meeting them on the runway. But now he worried he had been too confident about their ability to get out of Florida. Everything was happening fast, with the warning signs he had expected to play out over weeks, in fact, arriving just hours apart.

"Titan started the second test a few hours ago. It took out the Azores Islands. You heard about the European coast?" Ben's voice was tense.

"Just did. Has MAC updated the model?"

"It's worse than we thought. MAC's projections are suggesting Florida won't exist after today."

Augie straightened and stopped. His bald head glinted in the morning sun as he started to perspire. It was one thing to suspect, but to have it confirmed shook him. "Did you reach Art or Will? How about Max? Have you heard from him?"

"Art is on his way with Marta. Will is in Argentina, but he has Max's tech. He knows what's going on. Max is being Max. He knows, but I have no idea where he's headed or what he is up to. Hopefully, he is in touch with Will. If MAC is right—and he has been so far—all the signs point to catastrophic results from Titan's testing today. There's going to be a massive ocean shift. How bad is still up for interpretation, but you need to get out of there. Are the authorities evacuating the coast? The first wave off of the Azores earthquakes will be there anytime."

Augie reached the house, urged Kay out the door, and grabbed the last of the bags. Hustling her to the Jeep, he did not even stop to lock the back door. "Nothing public. Nothing on our cells, television or radio, or sirens."

The tornado sirens would not have been much help. No one would have understood what to do. But tsunami alerts sent over the internet or television stations could have given some a chance to run. Probably not many, if he was being honest. With a "very low" hazard rating for tsunami strikes, few of the East Coast population would have reacted even if it had not been so early in the morning.

"NASA sent an alert warning employees and contractors away from the East Coast fifteen minutes ago. They would have sent out alerts everywhere, but these haven't reached the public yet. I'll contact you as soon as we are on the plane."

Ben agreed, then signed off. Jumping to his feet, he paced, watched the video display now covering the East Coast of the United States, and began to pace faster. His equipment could not pick up the deadly surge moving towards the Atlantic Seaboard, but he feared it was there and clenched his fists.

Lily Stone grumbled as she pulled her long, straight hair into a ponytail. This was so not in her plans today. Grady, her on-again, off-again boyfriend, watched her from the bed. He rolled his eyes as she pulled out an overnight bag and started stuffing it.

"Your father is so weird. Why don't you tell him you're busy? You've got classes today, and I'm here."

"You know I can't do that. If my parents need me for something, then I am going to help. I can make up the classes. And as for you," she threw a pillow at him. He grabbed it and slid it between his back and the wall, slouching with a pout. 'We can get together later too."

"Fine. I get it. I am not the priority here."

She sighed. Their relationship had definitely been more off than on the last few months, and it was this kind of whining that put her off spending time with him. She knew he was hot, with his wavy, thick hair, dark eyes, and deep, tanned skin. Her friends told her she was crazy and needed to ease up on some of his less attractive qualities, like this clingy thing he had going on. She just could not see herself staying with him.

She swung the bag over her shoulder, grabbed her purse and cell, and dropped a quick kiss on his cheek.

"I gotta run. Let's talk about this more tomorrow. I am sure I will be back by then." She headed out the door.

"Sure, whatever." His petulant tone followed her out into the hall. Shaking her head, she headed down the stairs to meet her parents. Tomorrow, they were going to have to have a serious talk. This relationship was going nowhere.

Southwest Argentina: 10:30 a.m. local, 7:30 a.m. CST

Will Stone remained motionless, hidden behind a giant gum tree. He could hear the faint whisper of the motion detectors probing the forest, but he was sure the high-tech watchdogs hadn't spotted him.

The drone shots he had photographed earlier matched the reality before him. Primarily single-level to keep the rubber-tiled roofs under the old-growth jungle, with a prefab center popping up another tier like a windowless silo. Modular segments sprawled over two acres, flanked by a crude rear courtyard and parking lot. A few aluminum casements broke the monotony of the vinyl panel walls. The whole place had an air of utilitarian practicality. Opulence was obviously not a factor.

Colorful shrubs and grasses muted by the late hour bordered a short path along which paced unfriendly-looking mercenaries armed with snub-nosed machine guns.

No signs anywhere. Titan International wasn't advertising. He eased back into the woods, careful not to draw attention. He had spent over an hour probing the facility for weaknesses, and believed he'd found a way in. He'd hike back a mile or more before he tried the satellite phone Max had equipped him with. Hopefully, his men, Murph and Blake, were onsite by now. He needed to be updated and determine the next move.

Mid-Atlantic Ridge, North Atlantic Ocean: 12:15 p.m. local, 8 a.m. CST

Iceland was one of the world's most geologically monitored land masses due to its volcanic nature, but its destruction still surprised geologists worldwide. An eruption or two was the norm. None of the models or real-time Earth systems predicted anything close to the reality of what happened. And it was not a one-off event.

It was worse for the Azores. The Azores Islands were trembling chronically. Their location on the Mid-Atlantic Ridge guaranteed they'd always experience ground shakes. Geologists wrote papers and articles defining such activity. But no one would have predicted the chain would, one morning, disappear in an enormous blast. Yet, that's what happened.

At the USGS laboratory in Sacramento, California, Frank and his peers were still frantically trying to make some sense of the science when they started getting indications of more trouble in the Atlantic: multiple little tremors popping along the Mid-Atlantic Ridge.

The seismograph data had seemingly settled from that part of the world, allowing the analysts to start calculating the magnitudes and reviewing the seismogram recordings. It was hard to understand. The first pass of the data indicated an enormous ground area of impact. No previously recorded earthquake came anywhere near the size estimated from the seismograph data on their screens. So, deep in discussions and lost in the analytics, no one was ready for what happened next. Suddenly, with a massive, planet-sized jerk, thousands of kilometers of rift blew, the explosive force twisting the Mid-Atlantic Ridge from what was left of Iceland south almost to the equator in a never-before-seen mega quake.

Billions of tons of melted rock, metals, and earth per second were violently shoved through massive fissures torn open in the rift valley as the continental plates diverged. The boiling hot material piled higher and higher on either side, covering the remains of the plates and cooling on the outside but red hot at the core. Expanding, swelling up, new walls rose on either side of the rift with the speed of an express elevator. A screaming hiss of steam, flame, and gas poured out above the water as black rock and smoke broke the surface, cutting through the waves and rising three hundred miles an hour. Twisting columns of smoke reached the clouds, shoving their way through the vapor. Heat blasted from the ocean floor, spreading over hundreds of miles, vaporizing vessels and islands alike, reducing them to ash and melted fragments.

The mountain that had forced its way up a few weeks ago as a precursor to this bigger event cracked and broke, subsumed by the monster driving up beneath it. It took with it the remains of the stranded cargo ship. Everyone aboard was long dead from the heat and the poisonous gases. Automated SOS had been sent, but the Portuguese Coast Guard could not get close enough to attempt a rescue.

An hour before the helicopter and its ten-person crew could have reached the area, radar and atmospheric conditions stopped them short. It was too late anyway. Every trace of the cargo ship and its thousands of containers was slipping beneath the waves to become part of the mount.

Instead, the Portuguese Coast Guard became the only living witness to the largest earthquake in history. The crew gawked at the dark horizon across which green lightning flickered. The tremendous black clouds rolled towards them, and bus-sized pieces of pumice shot like underwater projectiles from the sea. The crew of the rescue copter fled back the way they had come, screaming SOS warnings to those back at a base that wasn't answering. As it was, they arrived just in time to see the new tsunamis washing inland.

The shaking increased and then increased again, freeing even more ejecta. Enormous plumes of ash and sea spray were thrust into the atmosphere in an ebony slash following the ridge, stretching thousands of kilometers north and south. Static electricity built up at the top, and massive emerald electrical pulses zipped from the spreading umbrella clouds in the stratosphere down to the ocean surface in wildly erratic super bolts. Mega thrusts split the Atlantic floor wide open in huge unzipping motions.

The pressure waves spread at the speed of sound, overtaking and passing the giant tsunamis heading toward the United States and Canada. Twins of the surges that had hit coastal Europe earlier they had to travel a much longer distance to reach a western shore, spending some of their energy, but they were still deadly enough when they made impact.

This second round of uplifted ocean floor at the rift sent new and much larger surges racing in both directions. Where the Azores sent seismic waves from an eighty-kilometer circumference, the Mid-Atlantic Ridge continued erupting along a six-thousand-kilometer stretch. The amount of energy expended and water displaced hadn't been seen in millions of years. Still buried underwater from the earlier waves, when the earthquakes hit, Portugal, Spain, and the entire eastern European and African coastline became giant washing machines, agitating their loads.

Every alert and alarm screamed to life on the USGS network. Wide-screen monitors covering half the walls flashed with real-time data from the Atlantic. The seismograph traces tore across white screens and went crazy. Frank, who had been comparing data on oversized sheets of computer paper, clutched his work into a bulky bouquet against his chest, praying as the room erupted in chaos again.

Chapter Five

When the Mid-Atlantic Ridge blew, NASA had a front-row seat thanks to the satellites. The scientists were still feverishly discussing Iceland and the Azores' events.

NASA oceanographers had named the vast underwater waves the "Azores Surge" during those first minutes of the Azores' islands being blasted out of existence. The warning came from Seasat, the first civilian oceanographic satellite to monitor the oceans from space. After the destruction of Iceland hours before, some of the younger analysts working overnight turned the satellites south to view the North Atlantic area, anxious to see any other activity.

The NASA satellite was not pointed directly at the Azores' catastrophic blowout when the Earth let go. Still, the early birds viewed satellite-recorded data quickly enough to recognize the bulges racing across the ocean in multiple directions. With no time to analyze the depth of the surges, they went with disaster reflexes. Frantically, they sent emergency notifications, and though the warning went out across the internet immediately, they knew they would be too late in far too many seashore communities.

The alert also warned NASA employees and contractors away from Kennedy Space Center, hopefully west across Florida. This was the alert Augie had received. Lockdown and emergency protocols were driven into place by those who stayed on the island.

Unfortunately, after the disasters of Iceland and the Azores, no one had any idea that the rift had been wounded, and was now ready to spring an even more enormous catastrophe on an unsuspecting planet.

After several hours of rumbling and venting gas, the Mid-Atlantic Ridge unzipped.

The satellite view was unbelievable. A sudden release of vast amounts of stored energy blasted the water back in a mighty groove from the ocean floor to the surface across the ocean for thousands of miles. Thunderous blows sank ships close enough to see the white flash. The heat from the eruption boiled billions of gallons of water and sea life in the first minutes.

The primary seismic waves from the mega earthquake tearing through the ridge shot across the Atlantic and slammed into Merritt Island. So much energy had been released from the Mid-Atlantic Ridge that the tremors raced past the slower Azores water surges just arriving on the Atlantic Seaboard.

When Florida started to feel the first quakes, New York, Washington, D.C., and North Carolina were already shaking. The shock waves spread across the states, slamming through the mountains, the plains, and the Pacific floor. The seismic waves met their counterparts traveling in the opposite direction, coming off the Eurasian coast. The Earth rang with the detonations as the blasts rolled up from the Mid-Atlantic Ridge.

Augie and his family were belted in a Piper Cherokee Six heading southeast on the runway at Merritt Island Airport, lifting just as the first quakes plowed into the state. He leaned into the window, trying to see what was happening. In front, the pilot let out a yell. Behind them, tall palm trees swayed in jerking motions, uprooted, and fell. Buildings below slumped, with walls and roofs vibrating across the sand. People spilled over, buried when they were too close to the buildings, and bounced hard against the ground in concussive hits when they were not. Giant sinkholes opened, greedily swallowing vast chunks of land.

On the other side of the plane, Kay and Lily held each other in shock as they watched Merritt Island crumble.

"Mom, the island, what's happening to it?" Lily gasped. Kay shook her head in silence, her arm tight around her daughter, staring out the window.

The aircraft gained altitude, and the pilot, swearing steadily, swung them over the barrier islands, Sykes Creek, Banana River, and Cocoa Beach, before turning up the shore. The rest of coastal Florida was faring no better.

As Dave pointed the plane on a northern trajectory up the beach coast, he stared in shock at the destruction below them. Cape Canaveral had failed, allowing the ocean to take another bite out of the peninsula's shoreline. Seismic shear waves had liquefied the sands and silt the city rested on. Block after block flowed away, a mixture of millions of tons of soil, trees, rocks, motor vehicles, uprooted bridges, and buildings funneled as if in a slew into Port Canaveral. And people, he reminded himself numbly.

Three docked cruise ships were unloading. They never stood a chance. A landslide of debris hit them hard from just the right angle, the velocity so strong the sides caved and crushed, flipping the enormous ships on their sides. The landslide continued around them, striking the Cruise Terminal and the parking lots past it, swallowing everything up whole.

Then they were past and onto new scenes of destruction. Even from this altitude, he was able to see the bodies splayed in the fractured streets, partially crushed by collapsing debris, facades of brick, stucco, and glass mixed with fallen palms and evergreens. Automobiles and trucks smashed in lines of twisted metal along rippling roads. Electric poles fell, the lines yanked free, long whips sparking and crackling anything they touched. Fires ignited, surface faults broke open, and the ground failed faster. Then, it got worse when they reached the part of the island home to the Kennedy Space Center.

Just below them, the Azores Surge had finally made it to Florida. Welling up like water overflowing a bathtub, the surge raced across the beaches, over the wildlife refuges, and right through all the areas of Kennedy Space Center. Churning water covered the land below them, so deep the trees and the buildings disappeared beneath it.

"Oh my gosh!" Lily yelled. "It's a tsunami!"

"It's okay, honey," Kay tried to reassure her. "We're safe up here."

"Okay? What about everyone else? What about my school? What about . . .?" she stopped dead and went white.

"Will it reach the college?" Kay asked Augie, over Lily's head.

He didn't answer, but the look on his face said enough. He turned back to the window, listening to Lily frantically punch at her phone, trying to dial out.

Augie was very familiar with the layout of the Space Center, having worked there for twenty years. Despite that, the only building he could identify jutting from the water below him was the Vehicle

Assembly Building. The eight-acre, 160-meter-tall building NASA used to assemble rockets was too tall for the surge and, so far, had resisted the shaking of the Earth. He could still see the American Flag and NASA symbol against the gray and white walls, vibrating high above the surface of the churning, speeding waters. Mostly everything else, buildings, roads, parking lots, vehicles, storage units, and garages, were lost as a second, more powerful surge slammed ashore. The mass of water roiled with untamed power.

As the plane soared back over Florida, the ocean continued to run ashore. With so much water and such a strong tide, nothing was floating on the surface yet. He wondered how far west these waves would push before they ran out of momentum.

Augie fell back into his seat. He fumbled with his pocket, finally freeing his phone. No signal. He typed in a text message, trusting that it would be sent when they flew over a working tower, letting Ben know they made it out.

"My phone doesn't work." Lily held the device limply. Her brown eyes were wide with shock. Her long, brown hair, pulled back in a tail, made her high cheekbones and forehead even more predominant. She looked younger than her twenty-two years. "How far inland will the wave go?"

"Will it reach our house?" Kay asked. Augie could see her hands were still shaking. For that matter, so were his.

"I don't know," he answered honestly. "But I don't think this is over. Ben's house in Holden is the safest place to retreat to right now."

"But what about all the people in Florida? All my friends. . ." Lily asked quietly. He could see she already knew the answer.

"Hey, Augie! Get up here and explain to me what is going on!"

Tears slid down Lily's face as he reached the seat next to Dave. He could hear Kay comforting her, offering hope about the fate of her friends and teachers. He wished he had hope, too.

As he started to tell Dave what he did know, he watched the roiling water below them and wondered if the ground underneath had stopped shaking.

"The herring are running well!" Captain Pete shouted to his first mate as he pumped a fist. His gold front tooth gleamed in the sunshine.

The last few days had seen a great haul, and now the seas were cooperating, staying calm long enough to make it easy to get their catch back to shore—barely a white cap in sight. At the helm was Captain Peter Welles, the grizzled owner of the *Hungry Gullet,* a seventy-five-foot past its-prime trawler. They were about three miles out, returning to Boothbay Harbor to sell their load and then take a few days off. He pushed up his sunglasses, hiding the crow's feet cutting through the tan around his pale, blue eyes.

Suddenly, the ocean surface grew agitated. Calm one minute, wild waves the next; Captain Pete didn't know what to make of it. It was like driving into a giant fan! He glanced over at Rim Island as he passed and was astonished to see the trees shaking madly and the ground heaving. Huge chunks of land broke free and tumbled into the water.

"An earthquake!" he yelled to his first mate, who looked startled.

"What! Are we safe out here?" Ridley Parker may have held the title of first mate, but this year was his first real opportunity to fish the deep seas. Young and strong, he had shown great potential with the nets, and Captain Pete had congratulated himself on giving the boy a chance. Neither had family back on shore, but they had friends and people they cared about.

"Do you think they can feel this in Boothbay Harbor?" Ridley yelled back.

Both men swayed hard as they fought to maintain balance. Captain Pete held tight to the helm, and Ridley grabbed the deck counter. Though he had fished these waters for years, this was a first for the captain. He wasn't sure whether to keep going or stop, but he had so little control over steering that he chose the latter. He hit the worn knob that freed the anchor, and over the wind and roaring seas, he heard it clank as it dropped. He hoped it would hold them, but he had no idea what the earthquake-torn bottom looked like. The surface looked worse than ever.

The only times he had seen water this turbulent was during the nor'easter of 1991 or 1993. No one went out in these types of storms. But the sky was blue. It was pretty windy, sure, but the crazy squally ocean was the real problem—a big problem at that. The giant waves flooding over the gunwales were coming close to swamping them. He pushed the bilge pump on, hoping it would make a difference, and tried to assess what to do next. Squinting through the windows and hanging on to the helm at the same time, Captain Pete rubbed his eyes. There was so much spray and wind that he wasn't sure he was seeing things correctly.

But no, the current *was* wrong. Not only was it going too fast, it was going the wrong way for this time of day! He didn't understand what was happening. Trying to get answers, he grabbed the radio mic.

"Mayday! This is the Hungry Gullet off of Rim Island. We are experiencing turbulent waters, and the island is shaking itself to pieces. Can anyone hear me?"

He heard only loud static in response. Suddenly, the boat shifted hard around in the water like a toy swirling in a pool. Both men were caught off guard, bracing themselves the wrong way. The jolt threw them to the floor, and Captain Pete lost hold of the mic.

The current had shifted and was now heading back to Boothbay Harbor!

Younger and able to regain his feet more quickly, Ridley pulled himself up. Trembling, Captain Pete took the hand Ridley offered him, and he managed to stand, too. Grimly holding on to anything battened down, they rode out the next twenty minutes as the wind and sea battered them violently, and the current pulled hard to the west. Wave after wave lifted them high in the air, only to drop them a minute later. They watched in shock as the rogue waves washed Rim Island away until only a tiny knob stuck up from the surf. Trees and bushes torn from the land eddied around them, thumping the boat's sides as they hurled by.

Thirty minutes later, when the seas had finally started to calm, Captain Pete rubbed his wrinkled head, noting that his cap was nowhere to be seen. He held the wheel tightly, not trusting the ocean to remain quiet. The trawler rocked gently as if nothing had happened. Hoping the earthquake was done—or whatever it had been— he carefully raised the anchor, and they headed west to port.

Neither of them was prepared for what they found when they got close. The harbor was gone. The land was gone, everything swallowed up by the water. There were no buildings, stores, or boats, just debris and bodies in the water as far as they could see. The destruction was so great that they could not get close to where they estimated the land should be. Captain Pete tried to raise anyone on the radio, spinning the dial until he finally managed to catch a recorded alert.

He looked at Ridley in shock and despair as they both listened. Earthquake and tsunami! And another tsunami was headed right for them!

"We have to get to the open ocean." He swung the boat around and headed back through the harbor, praying to beat the next big wave.

"Can we make it?" Ridley's eyes were wide; his skin stretched tight over his cheeks. He tried not to think about Boothbay Harbor, his friends, and his home.

"I don't know; it depends on where it is. Hang on!"

Ridley clung to the central interior pole wrapped in heavy white rope. The trawler rocked as they crashed into debris and fought the outgoing current. The engine was wide open and screaming. He knew what was at stake. "Go faster!" he yelled to a grim Pete.

"This is as fast as she goes! We're survivors, boy, and we'll survive this!" They shot towards the mouth of the harbor, both of them praying until they saw what was headed their way. Then, they prayed harder as their necks craned upwards to see the top of the wave.

New York City, NY: 9:30 a.m. local, 8:30 a.m. CST

"An earthquake? Madre Dios!" Jose shouted with the first tremor.

The ground shook harder in New York City. In Times Square, the pavement vibrated so hard that the concrete snapped like glass shattering from a mighty hammer blow. The motion jerked the busy streets until, one after another, the skyscrapers swayed like a conga line as the hits kept coming.

Cars, buses, and taxis slid into each other. People had nowhere to run as everything jolted off balance and collided. Mashed between buildings and vehicles, thousands of New Yorkers died of blunt force trauma in the first few minutes. Food trucks toppled off the curbs, catching fire as hot oil and propane ignited.

Leaning out to hand a businessman his order of carne asada tortas, Jose was thrown from the window of his food truck, Chilio's, in the first sideways jerk. Dazed, he lay splayed across the sidewalk at the corner of West 47th Street and 7th Avenue. Only chance and the Good Saint Cajetan, to whom he prayed every night for help and good fortune, kept him from being smashed by his truck when it flipped over. The ground pitched in hard knocks, one after another.

Each jolt slid the colorful food truck closer, but those same jolts kept striking down his feeble efforts to move away. Car alarms were screaming around him, or maybe it was people—he could not be sure. The skyscrapers shattered above, and bricks and pieces of facade rained down. The air grew thick with dust, making it hard to breathe. Further up 47th St, a white plume of water shot out of the ground, as thick around as a redwood, creating a column as high as the buildings around it. White spray threw a shroud of mist, and droplets rained down the street.

He had never seen anything like this in the fifty years he had served on this corner. Even 911 affected only one small part of the city. This felt like everything, everywhere, and still, the quaking continued.

"Earthquakes only last a few minutes." He grabbed at the thought and held on even as another chunk of brick and rebar bounced off his skinny leg, slicing through his pants and flesh. He howled, but it was lost in the cacophony. Suddenly, a vicious jolt ripped the roof off his truck, the windows on the sides burst, and generously filled tacos and enchiladas were thrown all over the concrete like food bombs.

The streets surfed the violent waves, the buildings not so much, as more and more pieces broke loose. Ducking and scrambling across the sidewalk, Jose managed to pull himself over to a tiny cove in the old building next to him, a dirty, smelly hole probably used by drug abusers. There was nowhere else to go. He prayed the building would not fall on him. His prayer was answered.

With his arms covering his head and his eyes tightly screwed shut as he waited for the quake to stop, he never saw the sixty-foot surge sweep down the vicinity of Times Square. He caught the scent of salt and heard crashing water, but he did not open his eyes.

Like his fellow New Yorkers who ran from the waves hurtling through the city's heart, Jose was caught up in the maelstrom and swept away long before the building he was cowering under fell.

Nags Head, North Carolina: 9:30 a.m. local, 8:30 a.m. CST

Corey Davis whistled to himself as he strolled along. He had patrolled as a lifeguard on the world-famous beaches at Nags Head for ten years. Tall and tanned, he still cut quite a figure in his long-sleeved white shirt and red shorts. The job paid all right, but the women he met on the beach, gorgeous and usually rich, more than made up for anything he may have lacked in terms of a big salary. The ladies liked his rugged good looks and hazel eyes. And Corey liked the ladies.

He crossed around a sand dune and dodged a big sea grape tree on his way back to the Ocean Rescue Lifeguard Stand. Swaying sea oats caught the summer breeze, and the pipers picked at the sand. The sun was bright today, reflecting off the water, and he was glad he had his sunglasses on. He looked up towards the ocean, and then, as his eyes and brain connected, the bizarre sight stopped him short. Puzzled, he cocked his head, trying to make sense of what he was seeing.

The incoming waves were gone. The ocean had pulled back, so far back that he could no longer even see the water from where he stood. The wet, golden sand was left baking in the morning sun. Here and there, aquatic life rolled and flipped where it had been stranded.

Tsunami screamed through his thoughts, and the beach started shaking just then. Powerful, deep tremors roiled across the sand, and before he could wrap his brain around *earthquake!* the sand around his feet started to lose its firmness. Trying to balance, he realized he was sinking, as if the fine sand had suddenly morphed into quicksand.

Grabbing the sea grape, he pulled himself from the hole, his arms strong from years of swimming saving him now. He staggered back up to the boardwalk, the word tsunami chasing him as if it were the real thing coming up his back. Only it was the real thing coming, he realized fearfully.

"Tsunami!" he yelled as he tried to herd back the few beachgoers hanging onto the guard rail, trying to stay on their feet. Carrying their ocean gear, most looked at him in surprise, but his fear obviously appeared genuine. Maybe the earthquake convinced them, because they dropped their stuffed bags and chairs at their feet and ran stumbling back to their cars in the parking lot.

Corey reached his own Kia and got the door open. One last look back, and he could see the ocean returning, a long glistening ribbon on the horizon. A few stragglers ran into the parking lot to their cars. As far as he could see, the beach was empty as everyone ran from what was coming. He jumped in and sped away only to run into traffic snarling as everyone else tried to run with the ground heaving, traffic lights down, and the remains of buildings falling into the streets, cutting off any way out.

Desperately, he tried to decide what to do. Ahead, the seven-story Comfort Inn loomed. It was the tallest structure within miles. The earthquake might bring it down, but the tsunami would surely drown him. Corey jumped from the car, not even turning the engine off, and ran as fast as his legs would carry him. It was hard going. The Earth juddered endlessly, and the roaring was louder. His fear caused him to lose balance and stumble uncontrollably. Other people ran with him, and he wondered if they were all headed to the same place.

He reached the hotel before the water reached him, but he could hear it coming up behind him like a freight train. Charging into the lobby through the broken glass doors, he saw no one in the vast space. Chairs were overturned, and chandeliers lay over the fractured pieces of floor tiling that hadn't survived the quaking. The front desk sat empty. Corey and a few others running with him headed for the stairs. As he gained the second floor, he heard the water crash into the lobby below him and tried to climb faster.

The surging water raced up the tiled treads behind him. He heard the glass break and flinched as the roaring ocean forced its way into the rooms on the first six floors. Doors exploded off their frames, and the building started shuddering. The smell of salt water replaced the sterile air conditioning. Gasping, his chest screaming for air as the humidity increased dramatically, Corey dragged himself up the last flight of stairs. The water chased him to the last step, but as he dove onto the carpeted hall, it finally fell back, lapping at the floor as the hotel continued to sway. Terrified, he realized he could see the sky from the unbroken plate glass window in the foyer.

He staggered over to the window, lightheaded and heaving. The waterline stopped beneath his feet on the other side of the flat glass. Doors along the hall opened as guests, in shock, fell into the hall, yelling questions at him and struggling to stay on their feet as the earthquake shook land and water. Corey slid to his knees, settling into despair as he watched the next big wave climb the beach, heading straight toward him. He barely noticed the earthquake finally subsiding before saltwater washed over the hotel and beyond.

Washington, D.C.: 9:30 a.m. local, 8:30 a.m. CST

"Move, sir! Move! Move!" The Secret Service agent shoved the president of the United States harder through the door and onto the South Portico. President Ronald Tanner was not an easy man to work for, but he could certainly be relied on to value his own skin. He increased speed, crossing the porch like a hyena outrunning a lion, abandoning his wife to the skills of the Secret Service men pushing her along.

The skyscrapers in Atlantic City, New Jersey, had already cracked and fallen over the still-shaking streets when the first giant wave roared ashore. Anyone who avoided being buried by the earthquake was drowned under the mass of water that rolled through. Ocean City, Delaware, still jolting, was swallowed up next. By the time Virginia Beach was gone, broken by the rocking Earth and lost under the surges, word of the dual disasters heading their way had reached Washington, D.C. The Secret Service moved quickly, hustling their high-value principals onto the White House grass. Before his Gucci lace-up shoes touched the turf, President Tanner heard Marine One landing on the South Lawn.

Then, the first quake hit. The ground heaved up with a growl, throwing everyone onto the thick grass. The noise increased all at once, the pressure on their eardrums overwhelming. Between the helicopter's whomping and the quake's booming, it was hard to hear anything.

The closest Secret Service agent screamed into the microphone attached to his sleeve, "I've got the president. Hold your position!" The agent rolled back to his feet, trying to balance against the shaking ground. Despite the chaos, their training held. The four agents pulled the president and his wife up, tugging them over the lurching terrain to the helicopter. Behind them, a few staff staggered through the pitching Earth, trying to keep up.

The Sikorsky VH-92A Patriot hovered four feet above the moving ground. It proved to be a good choice, given its robustness in rough conditions. It was the only steady object in sight. Everything else jerked and shuddered in response to the waves of energy moving beneath the ground. The pilot had dropped the staircase, and the agents practically threw the president and his wife up the stairs. Other agents were waiting to catch and pull them through the door before they could fall back. Bob Hendriks, the chief of staff, and two assistants scrambled up behind them.

The Secret Security Agents dropped back on the lawn, motioning frantically for the pilot to take off. As the tremors increased, he did just that.

"Take off, take off!" President Tanner shrieked as he was pushed down the aisle. The helicopter rocked as it started to turn.

Tanner fell into one of the plush armchairs and stared out the window in shock as he watched colossal cracks race up the outer sandstone walls of the White House. The tremors pulled at the crevasses, causing them to widen until, with a mighty crash, the wall failed in multiple places and disintegrated. He looked down and was horrified to see huge fissures had opened in the South Lawn—there was no sign of his Secret Security Team. And still, the ground shook itself like a mad dog throwing off massive sprays of earth and rock.

President Tanner, numb with shock, tried to focus.

"What in the hell is going on?" he screamed as he grabbed the chair's arms, and the helicopter dipped hard to the right. "Bob, what is this? Is this an earthquake?"

His chief of staff collapsed in a seat in front of him, shaking and swearing as he watched the White House walls crumble into an unrecognizable heap. Only the steel frame, part of the reconstruction in 1949, still stood, a naked skeleton shivering in cadence with the tremors.

"Bob, answer me, you moron! Is this hitting the whole Atlantic Seaboard? What about those tsunamis? Did the surges hit the whole coast? We need to declare a national emergency!"

Bob Fredericks tried to pull himself together. He didn't have much more information than the president. He had barely answered the call notifying him of the president's immediate evacuation when the Secret Service burst into the Oval Office. He had only gotten a partial update before they were rushed down the stairs to the South Lawn. He'd be part of the White House rubble right now if he hadn't dropped his phone and run after them. With that thought, another wave of shivering twisted his stomach. Trying to calm Tanner, he gave what he had.

"Sir, a mega volcanic blast out of the Azores ninety minutes ago created these first tsunamis we're seeing hit the Atlantic Seaboard now. It hit the whole East Coast, up to Nova Scotia. All the way down to Miami. The warning came from NASA." His voice cracked, but he forced himself to continue. Tanner's face was flushed scarlet, beyond livid, and Hendricks did not want to goad him further.

"The surge may reach the Potamic River. Evacuating you initially was a precaution. But just before the Secret Service pulled us out, a ShakeAlert came through with a Class One Warning. It wasn't just the Azores Island chain that erupted. Thirty minutes ago, several thousand miles of the Mid-Atlantic Ridge blew! That's the quake that just hit us. Massive volcanoes are blowing the ocean floor into the atmosphere! Out in the Atlantic, it is a mega earthquake-volcano combination like nothing anyone has ever seen before!"

"We are feeling an earthquake from thousands of miles across the Atlantic?" Tanner asked incredulously.

Hendricks took a deep breath, trying to gain a minute. Fifteen minutes ago, it was an average day. He and his two assistants were meeting with the president, setting the afternoon schedule. Now, except for those two assistants, everyone he worked with daily was likely dead, and the shock muddled his thoughts. Tanner's screaming wasn't helping.

His assistants were keeping their cool. Jen James, a poised young black woman from New York, was already on her phone, getting internet through spotty satellite connections. Mark Avery, a recent transplant from the Capitol, had his tablet out. Neither looked as winded or as terrified as he felt. He didn't know much more than he had already shared and hoped those two would quickly collect more information for the president.

"Yes, sir. I don't know how it started, but we are trying to get the data now."

"Well, hurry up!" Tanner yelled. He turned to his wife, trembling in the next seat.

"Are you ok," he asked more quietly.

She smiled gamely. "I think so. Just scared to death."

"Me too."

He caught the eye of the closest Secret Service agent. He knew him from previous flights. Roy Johnson, one of the best men on his regular detail, stepped forward. He moved like a panther, all grace and sinewy muscle under his dark skin. Suddenly, Tanner liked his chances of getting somewhere safe a lot better.

"Roy, where are we headed?" he demanded.

"The Cheyenne Mountain Complex, sir."

Tanner scowled. "Not Raven Rock?" The Raven Rock Mountain Complex was an underground nuclear bunker near the Blue Ridge Summit and much closer.

Agent Johnson was a big man. Standing, he took up almost the whole aisle. He shook his head once, forcefully. "No, sir. You need to be off the East Coast. We're headed to Cheyenne." He hesitated, and the concern he radiated did nothing for the confidence of those watching him. "Reports say a second line of tsunamis is coming behind this quake. Bigger than the first. The waves could end up washing right up against the Appalachians. Orders are to get you as far away from the East Coast as possible."

"But," Tanner could hardly get the words out. "The East Coast is the financial center of the United States. New York City is the financial epicenter of the whole damn world. We can't lose the East Coast!"

"And over one hundred million people live on the East Coast." Mrs. Tanner interjected carefully.

"That too." Anger and confusion choked him, and he gesticulated in frustration. The red on his face deepened.

Hendricks was trying to get his attention. Tanner waved him off, but he persisted. "Sir, look down. The ground is still shaking!"

"How long does an earthquake last?" Tanner glared out the window, already refusing to believe any answer. Most buildings had already crumbled, and traffic was at a standstill. Fires peppered the landscape, and significant volumes of black smoke twisted, reaching for the skies and reducing visibility. They were too high up to discern any detail, but he could see the roiling movement of the ground and the enormous black fractures crisscrossing the Earth.

"Minutes for bad ones. But we've been in the air for at least 10 minutes. I think this is worse than bad!"

Both men watched as George Washington University buckled and fell as they flew past. Hendricks could only imagine the chaos on the ground.

Johnson was listening intently to his earpiece. "Sir, the Capitol building just collapsed. They were not able to evacuate before the earthquake hit. Both the Senate and the House were going to be in chambers today. The vice president is unaccounted for as well."

"Let's get to Cheyenne." Tanner looked sick. "We need to set up a base and start coordinating. We need to start contacting all emergency services in the Midwest and on the West Coast. We have to get help to the East Coast and help the survivors. I need information, damn it."

Hendricks quietly conferred with the two aides who had made it into the helicopter and then looked up. "Sir, I don't know how much help the Midwest or the West Coast will be."

"What do you mean?" Tanner almost growled.

"The earthquake is still shaking below us." Both men looked out the window at the ghastly damage of the still shuddering city. "And it's still spreading, sir. It's already hitting the plains states, and the USGS is warning that it is not stopping. They don't know what to expect from this or when it will cease. This is an unprecedented event, and no one knows what will happen next."

Furious, Tanner started planning. Somebody was going to pay for this.

Chapter Six

Emerson, GA: 9:30 a.m. local, 8:30 a.m. CST

Art took Highway 75 north; it was one of the fastest ways into the mountains and the quickest route to Holden. Fast was his goal today. He kept the radio on, and Marta manned the dial, trying to find any news updates available. They didn't have to wait long.

"The USGS just released another ShakeAlert message. This morning at 8 a.m. Eastern Standard Time, a massive earthquake erupted along the Mid-Atlantic Ridge. We don't have seismic measurements, but the message cautions that the eruption is thousands of kilometers long and the impacts will be felt heavily in coastal areas. If you are anywhere along the Atlantic Ocean, you must evacuate now! Tsunamis are predicted to hit any minute! Scientists are urging the population to move inland at least two hundred miles—."

"We have unconfirmed reports that overnight, a massive earthquake sank most of Iceland without warning. Hundreds of thousands are feared dead. Then, a few hours ago, we started getting reports that the Azores Archipelago, located along the Mid-Atlantic Ridge, was obliterated in an even larger explosion, blasting an estimated eighty cubic miles of gases, dust, and rock into the atmosphere. No survivors have been found. The European coast has suffered huge surges from the Azore's volcanic activity, resulting in a great loss of life. Casualties are anticipated to be in the millions—."

"There are additional unconfirmed reports of large landmasses rising out of the oceans along the Mid-Atlantic Ridge and heavy volcanic activity along that same ridge. While geologists believe these events are all related, the main priority is to get people to safety as quickly as possible. If you are within two hundred miles of the Atlantic Seaboard, you must head inland now!" The message was recorded and looped back to the beginning again.

Art wondered if that was because the radio team had taken their own advice, recorded the message, and abandoned the station to head for the hills. Maybe all radio stations along the coast were playing that message and running for safety. He wanted to drive faster but only dared push the speed limit slightly on these narrow mountain roads. They had passed through the last little town, a dot on the map called Emerson, Georgia, fifteen minutes before. Traffic was light; they had not seen another car in the last five minutes.

It turned out to be a good thing he wasn't speeding. Without warning, a white-tailed deer burst across the road. Marta screamed a warning; Art slammed on the brakes, skidding sideways, barely missing the colossal animal. With a bound, it was gone, vanishing in the massive pines on the other side of the road. Before he could catch a breath, they were suddenly inundated by animals of all types, following the first across the road and through the forest walls. Raccoons, deer, foxes, weasels, and coyotes streamed past the car, jostling it to get past them and run away.

"Is there a fire?" Marta gasped.

"I don't see any smoke—." Art rolled down the window just enough to try and catch a whiff of smoke. All he could make out was the musk of the fleeing animals. "I don't smell anything—."

"Those animals were terrified of something."

He agreed with her but didn't know what to suggest. They waited a few minutes for the last animals to clear, and he pulled the car back into their lane. Before he could accelerate, a strong jolt shook the ground in a sideways snap. It faded away, and Art released the breath he had been holding.

"Maybe that's what scared—" he started, and then the energy released by the Mid-Atlantic Ridge hit with a roar. The road pleated and broke around them, and they were thrown as the Honda sheared back and forth with the quakes.

Southwest Argentina: 11:30 a.m. local, 8:30 a.m. CST

Southern Argentina was all right in July. Having spent most of his deployments in rotting, slug-infested swamps or burning endless deserts over the years, Will enjoyed the dry, mild temperatures and a slight breeze cooling the morning sun's rays.

After a quick hike northeast, just over a mile and a half, Will stopped at a familiar stream, sides overgrown with clumps of bushes and trees. Partially covered with branches, his rented Ford Ranger was still tucked in the foliage off the dirt road. The babbling noise of the swiftly flowing water would mask his conversation if anyone did come along, though it was a relatively deserted stretch of land.

He squatted under a big ceibo, behind a mass of wild yerba shrubs, and pulled out his equipment—first the satellite tablet and then the satellite phone. Swiping through the screens, he used the news app to get updates. He was already aware of the twin catastrophes in Iceland overnight and the Azores Archipelago this morning. Max said Titan referred to them as tests and considered the losses simply the cost of doing business. Will gritted his teeth at the thought.

A few days ago, when he asked Will to go to South America, Ben had requested his brother to find and surveil a potential Mantle Cannon site here in South Argentina. The data MAC managed to strip off the Titan servers hinted at a facility nested at the antipode of Beijing, China. Using the drones, he searched over sixty miles before he found their lair. It was a good thing Hart and Newsom didn't build a bunker—he'd never have found them. Luckily, even criminals try to keep the costs down—at least when they themselves have to pay them.

He wasn't prepared for the news about the Mid-Atlantic Rift. The satellite videos flooding the news channels stunned him, which said a lot since he always expected the worst. The potential consequences scared him, and he wasn't a man who was frightened easily. He set the pad down and thought furiously, then picked up the sat phone.

Tapping on the screen, he worked on reaching out to his team, Dan Murphsen in the Tasman Sea and Aaron Blakely in the Southern Ocean off of Antarctica. The two men had served with him in the Rangers. He trusted them as much as he trusted his older brothers, which was saying a lot. When this crap with Titan International started, and he realized the global implications, he knew he was going to need help. He couldn't be everywhere. So, he recruited Murph and Blake, the two men he had served with his last eight years in the Rangers.

Murph answered almost immediately. "Murph, over. Encryption green, over."

Will checked his phone and was satisfied that the green bulb glowed bright. "Encryption green also. Sitrep, over?"

"Target acquired, Major. Monitoring underway. We're two hundred miles off of Sidney."

"What kind of activity you seeing?"

"Testing has commenced and been completed. They fired up their cannon and ran it for over an hour. As a result, there are lots of dead fish floating around here. Did you hear about Iceland and the Azores?"

"Affirmative. And the activity on the rift."

"We just got word about the Atlantic too. The news says the entire northern arm of the rift blew, not just some volcanoes along the vent. I thought this thing only impacted volcanoes."

Will snorted. "I think that's the big problem. The eggheads who built this shooter didn't really know what would happen. This is the type of catastrophe Max was warning everyone about."

"Well, what do you need next? Hey, wait a minute!"

The phone went silent, and Will waited impatiently. Murph was back a few minutes later.

"A helicopter just launched from the deck; it looks like it's headed for Sydney. I am guessing Hart and Newsom are on the move. What do you want us to do with *Titan One*?"

"Now we know the Mantle Cannon is the threat Max claimed. It destroyed Iceland and the Azores Islands and murdered millions. Even Titan doesn't know what destruction and loss of life are going to come out of the damage that freaking cannon has done to the Atlantic basin. We need to sink the ship and get rid of that cannon."

"I figured you'd say that. I have already perfected a plan with these gentlemen you arranged to help me. We will hole the ship from the bottom of the hull for quick sinking, swoop in with our fishing boat, and rescue the passengers. Nobody will have time to pack or grab anything; if they do, we'll also ensure complications wind up on the bottom."

"Tell Blake to make that happen on *Titan Two* also. Max is on his way here. We will destroy the core programming with a virus to ensure it can't be used again. We've got the home base here in Argentina covered. I hope they won't activate this cannon until Hart and Newsom show up. Let me know when your part is complete. And Murph, you and Blake need to get back to the States ASAP. I worked with our contacts in

Sydney. It's still possible to fly over the Pacific. They are going to get you two home. They have a jet waiting."

"I hear you, Major. Though Australia is a nice place. We've been in plenty worse."

Will signed off and took a swig of water from his canteen. He'd sit for a minute. It only took him another few seconds to realize the forest had gone silent. There were no insects or birds, and even the breeze seemed to have dissipated. On edge, he leaned forward.

Parrots suddenly launched from his tree in a colorful whirl. Cautious about being discovered, he pulled his gun and started to stand when the ground began to rumble, throwing him back against the iron tree trunk. Above him, the branches of the ceibo swayed sharply in time with the ground, and the bushes rattled in the onslaught.

The tremors got stronger. The ground bucked and rippled in a series of waves, undulating over to the stream. Water jumped and splashed, whipped into a miniature maelstrom strong enough to stop the current. Now on his hands and knees, Will attempted to crawl towards the Ford Ranger, bumped hard as he grabbed for the clumps of wild grass.

Will wasn't easily scared, but the quake's power was terrifying. The noise of the Earth was angry, a grinding, snapping sort of roar like nothing he had ever heard before. Dirt rose in the air, and loud cracks heralded falling trees as they broke in the grip of a monster. It occurred to him that this must be a residual quake from the rift splitting.

If it was this bad thousands of miles away, he was glad he was not onsite at the epicenter. Will held on for what seemed an eternity before the vibrations became less violent and the ground around him calmed. Trembling, he waited until he was sure it was finished and then checked his ride.

To his relief, the dusty Ford was intact and drivable. He needed to get back to Bahia Blanca and pick up Max tonight. That cannon had to be stopped.

Sydney, Australia: 1:30 a.m. local, 8:30 a.m. CST

Two successful tests. Newsom leaned back in the plush seat as the Gulfstream V left the tarmac with a happy sigh. He sipped the champagne the attendant had served. He didn't much like the bubbly, but it was time to celebrate, and this was how the influential and affluent partied. He was more of a whiskey man. Give him a shot of Macallan Scotch Whiskey, and he was good. No matter, he could wait. For now, he'd sit here and reflect on his good fortune.

When Hart approached him with the offer of CFO at Titan International seven years ago, he had vacillated. It amused him now to remember his doubts. He had not worried about the repercussions of using the Mantle Cannon even then. He understood that a few would have to pay the ultimate price to achieve the end goal—that was how science worked. His concerns were more practical; he didn't believe the weapon would perform.

Newsom wasn't an inventor. Hell, the only creation he had ever had anything to do with were his two avaricious, disappointing daughters who spent more time in his pocket than out. Their New York City condos, lavish lifestyles, and feeble significant others were bad enough, but neither one was likely ever to get a job and thus relieve him of their maintenance. His wife was no better. She lived in their multi-million-dollar Greenwich home, and he stayed in his penthouse apartment in Midtown East. She was only available when she wanted something. He didn't consider his marriage or progeny much of a success.

His career was where he poured his time and effort. It was not so much hard work, but more what he considered strategic positioning. He spent years at American Direct, which was part of their financial wheel. He made it to executive VP in his forties but could never get the next step up to the C level. It wasn't for lack of trying, and he didn't let morals or ethics get in his way either. The losers who took his promotions sure weren't any better than he was. There was just always something; another person got his opportunity, or the job was eliminated before it could be filled for some stupid corporate reason, and by the time Hart showed up with the Titan offer, Newsom was starting to worry that he would never get what he was owed.

So, while morally, he could have made another decision, he went with his gut and accepted Hart's proposal. And look where they were now. He smiled and twirled the stem of the crystal flute. In the front cabin, he could hear Hart snapping orders at Cynthia. He rolled his eyes, the expression pulling at the crow's feet that grew deeper every year.

He knew Hart wanted to get the general on the sat phone. After two successful tests, they were ready to run the big dog tonight in Argentina. If that went as expected, the payoff would be the start of billions of dollars lining Titan's pockets. He smirked and took a last sip. No one deserved it more than him.

Cynthia fussed over the equipment, trying to get a line out to General Wolfe. Her boss wasn't known for his patience, and she had no intention of losing this job. She wasn't working this gig for altruistic reasons, and wasn't fooled into believing they were helping the environment or anyone else. She was strictly interested in the payday.

Maybe that was cold, but Cynthia was a realist. With no family to fall back on and a deadbeat ex-husband in her past, she was determined to make the best out of these few years with Titan International. Her boss, Dror Hart, was egocentric, aggressive, callous, and tough-minded, but he paid well and on time. That was good enough for her.

Strands of light blond hair slipped from her chignon, and fashionable onyx-framed glasses covered her glacier-blue eyes. She cultivated a look of messy competence, knowing it worked for her here. Aware of the importance of this call, she exhaled with relief as it started to connect. Luckily, it went right through.

With his customary brusqueness, Hart grabbed the phone from her. "General Wolfe, can you hear me?"

Weird static and rumbling hissed on the line. Then suddenly, it cleared.

"Did you do this? Is this Titan's fault?" Wolfe snarled back at him.

Surprised, Hart looked at the phone. He put it back to his ear. "What are you talking about?"

"Earthquake—" the rest of the words were garbled. He heard someone shriek, and the line cut off.

"Newsom, something is happening in Arlington. Find out what is going on." He barked out the order. Jumping to his feet, he tossed the phone in her lap. "Cynthia, get the general back."

Newsom dropped the empty flute in the seat next to him and hurried to the front of the plane. "What's wrong?"

***

"Out! Out! Head for the parking lot!" General Wolfe yelled at the last of the crowd of people pushing their way out of the shaking building in the center of Arlington, Virginia. The Earth had roared for thirty minutes, and he had spent that time evacuating his people. He was starting to think the earthquake would never stop. He knew this had something to do with Titan International. That bastard Hart swore there'd be no impact on the United States. Wolfe should have known he couldn't be trusted.

A crash broke his thoughts, and he gaped as the glass entrance sheared and cracked. The front of the building sagged over their heads and started to lean. He stepped back as fast as he could.

"Sir, a helicopter is en route, ETA ten minutes." One of his aides—Miller, was the boy's name—nearly fell and he grabbed Wolfe's meaty arm. "But they want to extract you off the roof. They are saying it's impossible to land on the ground.

"Off the roof," Wolfe repeated incredulously.

"They'll drop a basket."

The building shifted again, and they turned and stood in shock as the main staircase folded into the elevator shaft with a massive crash. Clouds of shattered building material filled the lobby, the whole structure shook harder, and the entrance finished its collapse, entombing the last few that were too slow to get out of the way. Options were becoming limited.

"The back staircase, this way!" yelled his aide, pulling him north.

They stumbled and fell, picked back up, and struggled forward again. Wolfe had never ridden out an earthquake before, and he could not have imagined the power. As fear overwhelmed him, he found himself automatically bargaining with a higher being.

Finally, the shaking slowed as a popping sound filled the air and, with a few minor jerks, stopped altogether. Dizzy with relief, he paused to lean against the plaster wall, trying to regain his equilibrium. The path up looked insurmountable. Even with the quakes stopped, climbing the concrete steps wouldn't be possible without the help of his young aide.

Wolfe's arthritic knees and back made bending and ascending difficult. With the strength of youth, Miller charged up unimpeded, knocking away clumps of plaster, broken beams, and rebar, clearing a path for them both. Barely in his twenties, he grunted as he pushed and pulled the old general to the rooftop. Dust sifted through the air, making it hard to see and breathe.

Flinging open the door and falling through, they hesitated at the grim sight of a wrecked Arlington around them. Most buildings had collapsed, spilling brick and glass across the streets. Incandescent explosions from gas main breaks added to the cacophony of destruction. Miller held the general against the stairwell wall, not even attempting to move forward. It took all their effort to remain standing as their bodies tried to adjust to the lack of motion. Frantically, they searched the sky for any sign of the helicopter.

Miller saw the gigantic wave first. His youthful eyes took in the vast surge burying the city, block by block, in a glance. Desperately, he looked up, hoping to see the helicopter sweeping in for a last-minute rescue.

Only oily smoke crossed the sky. General Wolfe blinked as he watched the wave swallow Mosaic Park on the next block. He heard the screams of those in the parking lot as they realized their fate.

He stopped fighting the inevitable, straightening his stance, and waited. He thought about Titan International and wondered how much of this catastrophe was his fault. Probably too much, he decided grimly, as the wave surged up and over the roof. The heavy hit was the final blow to a building already fatally shaken.

The surge slammed into the walls like a runaway train, the force finishing what the earthquake started. The floors pancaked into one solid mass, and the current rushed on.

***

"About six thousand miles of the Mid-Atlantic Rift just blew up." Newsom looked up from his phone at Hart, who was standing, a guarded look on his square face. "So much energy was released, the East Coast has been hit with massive earthquakes and tsunamis. Washington, D.C. and worse, Arlington, where General Wolfe was stationed, were just wiped out."

"So, he's dead?"

"I think so." Newsom thought rapidly, trying to salvage the situation. It was tough; General Wolfe had been their only contact these last five years.

"We need to move forward with tonight's run." Hart narrowed his eyes. "The Chinese will take advantage of the destruction. The only way to stop them is with the cannon."

"Yes," Newsom waved a hand. "I don't disagree, but there has to be some way to get paid."

"How? It sounds like most of Washington, D.C. is underwater."

"Maybe, but we don't need Washington, D.C. or General Wolfe. The one person who you can bet was evacuated was Tanner. If the president of the United States can't get us our money, maybe we should let the Chinese have America."

"Tanner—," Hart rubbed his chin thoughtfully. He liked the idea. "Tanner hates the Chinese. He'd never pass this opportunity up."

"Exactly. We have to figure out where the Secret Service took him. Then we can contact him and make a deal."

They both looked at Cynthia. "Already on it, sir," she said hurriedly and started dialing. Luckily, she had made contacts in the military and political branches—knowing they would come in highly useful at some point.

"Good work, Newsom," Of course it was good work. Newsom was aware that Hart was damning him with faint praise, but said nothing. "We may be able to salvage this deal after all."

Newsom continued to ponder the alternatives. This would all work out fine. For a minute, he considered New York, Greenwich, and his wife and daughters. He waited to feel a pang of regret at their loss, but felt nothing. He wondered if insurance would cover the house or the apartments. He definitely felt a pang at the loss of property. The insurance companies would probably call this an act of God and refuse to pay. He'd find an angle. He always did.

Ben was a lanky guy with a bit too much body mass, though when he stood in front of the mirror, his T-shirt and shorts didn't bulge in weird spots. His smile charmed women, and children always liked his cheerful personality. But it had been too many years since he had spent time with either. Recently, he spent too much time in front of his monitor. He had been here all night, feeding probabilities to MAC and reviewing the outcomes with the AI. He was tired, but he couldn't imagine closing his eyes.

He rubbed a hand over his fading brown hair and glanced out at the double-slider windows in his office. The weather was nice this morning. Jake, his wife Randi, and their three kids, John, Pammy, and Cassie had arrived yesterday. Jake looked like Ben twenty-five years ago, so much that they could have passed for brothers, rather than father and son. Tall and sinewy, both big men with oval faces, dark eyes, and strong chins. His other son, Josh, looked and acted more like his late wife, Mary, slimmer, with light-colored hair and hazel eyes. Both boys had grown into men of whom Ben was proud.

Ben appreciated Jake and Randi's difficulty realigning their schedules and getting time off work at the last minute. But Jake hadn't complained when he called him yesterday morning and suggested a weekday visit. He listened silently and then agreed to head up to Nebraska immediately. His oldest son may have looked like him, but both boys had inherited their mother's strong intuition.

His granddaughters were playing with a blue ball in the yard, with Randi keeping one eye on them and one on her book from the lawn chair. With her blond hair pulled up in a messy style, she looked relaxed in a sequin-sparkly shirt and shorts. He wondered what she thought of this last-minute trip to Holden.

He liked his son's wife. She didn't ruffle easily, and she had a pragmatic way about her. Of course, he knew she was pacifying both him and Jake. If it hadn't been July, getting her to drop all the school and home responsibilities and visit Jake's doomsday dad at the last minute would have been impossible. Still, she had greeted him with a hug last night and didn't mention the clutter overflowing his office. She would be a great asset if things got as bad as he was afraid they could.

Staring out the window didn't clear his head. He could picture the activity in the Atlantic. MAC's simulations looped a running commentary of destruction through his cerebral cortex. Obsessing over the data in front of him just aggravated his heartburn from yesterday, and being up all night soured his stomach. He grabbed an antacid, chewing as he mulled over what to do next. The framed picture at his elbow caught his eye, and he sighed, letting it pull him into the past.

Ben's wife, Mary, had passed away from cancer more than five years before. The grief of losing her had upended his life, and twenty-five years of marriage had gone overnight. Mary had always been outgoing and energetic. Because of her, their free time was spent traveling, socializing, and trying new hobbies. Somehow, none of that appealed to his introverted, solitary nature when she was gone.

So, he dove deep into his first love of geology. First, he spent his personal time off, and then, once the USGS let him go, all the rest of his time researching anomalies and running data, trying to understand geological mysteries still unsolved by his peers. He was curious by nature and liked puzzles. But the amount of data he was forced to manage in pursuit of his goals was staggering. This pushed him to hunt down affordable technological improvements for his setup, and that, of course, led him to Max.

Talk about life-changing moments. The second he impulsively decided to help the boy, his world changed forever. The kid was a smart-ass, no question. But his intellect was beyond genius. Max's cutting edge was so sharp he might as well have been an obsidian blade. Titan recognized the threat and kept hounding the whistleblower, even when Max could not get anyone to believe him.

So, after that night, the hacker/cyber engineer and geologist became friends after a fashion. Or maybe colleagues since Max wasn't the friendly type most days. However, the more Ben learned about Max's other projects, the more fascinated he became with Max's quantum computer build. He knew enough about the technology to understand the difficulties in a broad sense. Max solved most problems through the design and build stages using his own quixotic ideas and combinations. With no one to tell him where he was wrong, somehow, he had somehow made it work. Ben came along while Max was constructing the shielded case to protect the quantum computer from atmospheric radiation and heat to avoid qubit errors. It was all a genius design, and Ben was very excited to help. Together, they built and refrigerated the box just above absolute zero, where it was set today. It hummed while he worked. It was weird, but he found the sound comforting.

It wasn't until after it was done and running that Ben understood why Max had spent the time and effort creating the quantum system in the first place. More prodigy than practical, Max had hoped his phenomenon would solve the risk with Titan. Basically, he planned to use it to infiltrate and destroy the Mantle Cannon, like the plot of a great cinematic movie.

The quantum computer was unique in its ability to chew through complex data in seconds, tackle optimization challenges to improve efficiencies, and revolutionize thinking in almost any field. Still, Max could not program it to do more than spy on Titan International as a whole. He was foiled by the most basic of network requirements. The engineers working on the Mantle Cannon took the whole system offline. To reach a cannon, you had to be onsite and wired in. Ben pointed out that it was a compliment to Max that Titan had gone so far in protecting their weapon, but Max was furious.

A few weeks later, the hacker bequeathed the quantum computer to Ben and left for New York. He went to lurk the busy sidewalks and find an anti-government reporter from Rolling Stone magazine, hoping they would hear his story.

Before he left, Max suggested incorporating artificial intelligence into Ben's research system. It only took him a few days to program it, and as an added benefit, he gave the artificial intelligence full access to the quantum computer. Max thought Ben was lonely and could use someone to talk to. When it was up and running, Max named the new team member MAC, short for "My Amazing Computer," so Ben would remember whose idea it was. It was pretty corny, but that was Max, a strange combination of sentimentality and obsession.

Ben's own research had started with modeling the planet's system processes with mathematical equations. His model was a complex tool, identifying and quantifying data to isolate drivers in nature. The variables represented the initial climate conditions and the subsequent climate changes over the last several hundred years. Endless repeated variations simulated potential outcomes to show how matter and energy interact in the ocean, atmosphere, and land.

Even before meeting Max, Ben bought better-performing computers, increasing cache, processor speeds, and large amounts of RAM as his model devoured more power with its calculations. That was why he shopped at the dubious equipment store in which they met. The equipment was pricey, and he needed the best. Ignoring the steep costs, he subscribed to the most potent geology and seismic software he could find.

However, MAC and the quantum computer Max built were the keys to unlocking his model. With quantum computing at his digital fingertips, MAC took Ben's model in a new direction. The AI didn't just use sophisticated algorithms and innovative systems; it interpreted interactions in ways Ben had never considered, including what potential effects a Mantle Cannon could produce.

Soon, he had a system hundreds of times more powerful than he used at the USGS. With the ability to perform one billion or more computations, MAC could try variations a human researcher could never get to. Max's last act before heading east was to help him move and set up in Nebraska. They both felt Titan closing in on them in the west.

Ben had bought this semi-ranch off the internet under an assumed name for cash, more for the refuge and anonymity than any other reason. The bedrock in this part of the country was ancient and stable. As a geologist, Ben liked the feeling of permeance. Max wanted a home base in the middle of nowhere in Nebraska.

Since all they could do was spy, Ben and MAC monitored Titan over the year as the self-proclaimed technological environmentalist company designed, built, and fitted *Titan One* and *Titan Two* with the weapons. The PR department told the world they were building sound probes that would unlock the secrets of the inner Earth. They claimed their intended goal was geothermal energy, enough to end the need for fossil fuels. It sounded great, but there was no truth in their promotions.

MAC hacked into their systems, raiding project plans and seeking test dates and places while trying to identify an end game. Last week, the AI discovered memos ordering Titan's two ships and a facility somewhere south to be appropriately stocked for the CEO's visit.

Hart never visited any of the sites. MAC and Ben took this as the sign that Titan was ready to test, and Hart wanted to be onsite. Ben was so sure he had sent out alerts over the weekend to Max and his family to be ready in case the shit hit the fan.

Everyone took his warnings to heart except his youngest son, Josh.

Josh and his partner Del were still in Chicago. Earlier this morning, Josh listened to Ben's assessment, but it was clear his mind was elsewhere. After he laid it all out, Josh said, "Okay, let me know if anything changes."

"Josh, I think you and Del should head here today."

"All this happened in the Atlantic and overseas, right? Even if there is a surge, it will be on the East Coast."

Frustrated, Ben tried to force the issue. "I'm not asking, Josh. I'm telling you. There's going to be impacts in Chicago, too. I'm in Nebraska for a reason. It will be a safer place to ride out this storm."

"I get it. But I have three jobs underway and can't just walk out. If something else happens, let me know."

Ben gave up, having no other choice. Thinking about the conversation, he slammed his desk with an open hand. He could not convince Josh to budge. Almost as if answering his failure, MAC started speaking.

"Catastrophic fracturing of the transform faults along the Mid-Atlantic Ridge has commenced. A seismic swarm is affecting the entire length of the North Atlantic ridge. Unusual thrust mechanisms and locations occurring as far as one hundred miles from the ridge. The swarm is attributed to magma intrusion, triggering up to magnitude ten earthquakes with multiple epicenters."

Swiftly, he pulled up the current satellite views, wondering if they'd reach far enough south to see the eruption. To his utter amazement, he had barely brought the equipment online before the mega eruption filled the screen. Switching satellites, he tried to find the end of the explosive mass pouring from the ocean, but the farther south he moved, the more disastrous the picture became. The more he saw, the tighter his chest knotted up.

He sure hoped neither he nor Josh would regret Josh's stubbornness. Then, he decided he better find Jake and warn him. He was probably in the barn with John. They both liked the horses.

"Alert!" MAC's modulated tones grabbed his attention before he could stand.

"Seismic shockwaves of magnitude nine and higher were produced and continue to be produced at the epicenters, 65 km below the Mid-Atlantic Ridge. Body waves and surface waves are spreading. Energy waves have reached the continents and continued to pass through. Earthquakes are imminent in this location. Repeat: earthquakes are imminent in this location."

MAC was still speaking when the ground beneath the house jerked in a sharp snap, and the Earth began to tremble. The walls started to vibrate, and equipment rattled on the desk. Suddenly, his model flashed red on the screen, and an unexpected shrill warning tagged "Real-Time" rang furiously.

He pulled his chair over, hands gripping the desk, trying to read the results. Stunned, he suddenly realized what was happening. MAC's unhurried voice confirmed what his eyes were seeing.

"A magnetic reversal is in progress. The poles are flipping and continue to move at abnormal speeds."

"No, that can't happen now." Dismay froze him. But he knew it could happen now, and agitated, he let go of the desk.

Luckily, Ben had retrofitted all his expensive computers and monitors, securing them tightly and even fastened the desks to the floor with braces and bolts. He had not done the same for his chair and regretted that instantly as a colossal jolt sent the wheels spinning violently across the rocking hardwood and bounced him with a crash into the wall. As the vibrations increased, he found it impossible to stand. The shaking grew so much worse that he fell out of the chair and slid to the floor. He could hear the girls screaming outside. The rumbling and pitching increased again, and Ben curled into a ball, hoping the roof and walls wouldn't collapse and the earthquake would end soon.

He couldn't see Randi reach the girls and pull them into her arms, trying to shelter them from the blows. He did hear the terrifying booms from blowouts, spraying sand and water more than thirty feet into the air. He knew what they were. He prayed they were erupting well away from his family.

His animals in the paddock shrieked and ran, stumbling away from the explosions. When the slurry was expended, the boils left craters behind, and soon they pockmarked the enclosure. Grains of sand and dirt shivered in the quaking air, adding to the chaos. The goats huddled in a tight pack against the fence, their terrified bleating a discordant undernote to the harshness of the earthstorm.

Ben didn't see Jake pull John away and outside, but he recognized the gunshot sound of the beams in the back part of the stable crack and give way, crushing the horses in those stalls. Their equine screams of fear were cut off abruptly as half the barn collapsed. John howled and fell, trying to run back to help, but his father would not let him go. They knelt together in the dirt, Jake holding John tightly, trying to balance until the jolts grew so strong that they knocked them both over where they huddled on the worn path.

And still, the ground shook, and the earthquake roared.

Sacramento, CA, USGS Office: 7 a.m. local, 9 a.m. CST

The seismographs' warning that a massive quake was heading their way didn't make the experience less terrifying when it tore into Sacramento. With this earthquake, nature had indeed released the planetary equivalent of the Kraken. Nothing this widespread had ever moved the ground in recorded times.

A quake that crossed the globe and rang the Earth like a bell for over thirty minutes was unheard of; Frank told himself as he hung on. He was witnessing history.

He was terrified.

After what seemed like hours, the tremors finally subsided with diminishing booms; the vibrations felt through the floor faded with eerie moans until it was just the creaks of settling debris.

Frank's ears rang from the roaring. Dust and drywall particles churned in the emergency lighting. He felt nauseous and lightheaded. Trying to blink away the dust on his lashes, he waited to see if the shaking had really stopped. After a few minutes of stillness, he heard others start to stir.

Coughing, Frank picked himself up, reluctantly letting go of the steel desk leg he had been hugging for the last half hour. Paper, equipment, loose objects, and ceiling tiles littered the tile floor. He brushed hard bits of something from his hands and rubbed the back of his head. Leaning against the table for a minute, he looked around. His colleagues were also picking themselves up. Some were crying, and a few were hugging each other. Several were pointing at the walls, but he couldn't make out what they were saying. He assumed they were astonished that the building still stood. He couldn't believe the walls had held through that monster either. There must be some mega steel beams framing this building. He couldn't believe he was alive.

Suddenly, he remembered his wife. He thought she would still be home, but he lost track of time and wasn't sure. He found his cell still in his shirt pocket, so he had some luck, but disappointment quickly followed. The phone wouldn't dial out, and, in the gloom, he could see he did not have a signal.

He went around helping others off the floor. Some of the more badly hurt he helped into dusty chairs. While he worked, the monitors that still hung on the wall flickered back to life, one by one, thanks to the automated generators that kicked in.

"Frank!" Someone was calling from the other side of the room. In the dimness, it was hard to see who. Carefully, he nudged the junk tossed along the aisles aside and made his way over. It was one of the program analysts; his name was Mike. It was hard to tell in the muted light and all the particles floating in the air, but Frank thought the tech looked more excited than scared.

"Are you ok, Mike?" he asked as he got closer. He could see blood or something smeared across the young man's face.

Mike waved his concern away, trying to get him to look at the monitor still braced on the desk. "Look, it's happening right now! It's a magnetic reversal, and it's happening right now!"

Frank gripped the chair before him as he studied the hastily wiped screen. He was sure multiple sensors were destroyed after the quake, but enough real-time data remained to see what Mike was trying to show him. The North Magnetic Pole and the South Magnetic Pole had switched. The magnetic field over both was weak, less than ten percent of its usual strength. If this data was correct, the ongoing volcanic activity in the Atlantic, maybe working in conjunction with the pole reversal, also disrupted the magnetic field over the Atlantic.

The magnetosphere continued protecting the Earth's surface from solar flares and storms by reflecting some of the activity back into space. Still, if these numbers were correct, much more energy was getting through than expected. Frank wasn't even sure how that was possible.

But the waning magnetosphere and fluctuating density and temperature numbers crossing his screen told him they were still in trouble. With the destruction around him, tech wouldn't provide the answers they needed. Even so, he knew in his gut. The planet was still in jeopardy.

He started looking for Albert.

Chapter Seven

After one last vicious jolt, the Earth stilled. Ben, his eyes glued to his wristwatch, stayed on the floor, curled against the wall. Thirty-two minutes! There had never been an earthquake recorded that lasted much over ten minutes. The longest was the 1960 Valdivia earthquake in Chile, with a magnitude of 9.4. Or maybe the 2004 magnitude 9.1 quake that rocked the Indonesian island of Sumatra. But thirty minutes! He imagined a potential earthquake could be extensive, and he still had no idea how bad it would be. The sheer energy released to reach from the Mid-Atlantic Ridge to Nebraska was unbelievable!

Shaking, he pulled himself up, leaning on the chair to regain his balance. He crossed the room, trying to understand what he could see out the window. He needed to find Jake and his family. Broken glass from the sliders crunched under his dirty sneakers as he tried to make sense of the yard. Even from here, he could see the mess that used to be the old barn. The air was hazy, and the sun, still shining, overlaid a weird orange cast to everything. Debris suspended in the air.

He glanced at his equipment. The green light that indicated MAC was online was out. The screens were dark, and there were no lights anywhere. It was no surprise that the electricity was down. Mary's picture was on the floor, face down. He left it for now.

Impatient with himself, he crossed to the back porch door on unsteady feet. He took note that the door, left open before the quake, was now off plumb and hanging crooked. The windowpanes in the kitchen were broken on the floor, as well as everything that used to sit on the table and counters. The can opener hung by its cord, but the heavy mixer and coffee pot hadn't been so lucky. Smashed parts made them look like candidates for replacement. Everything was so quiet after the roaring quake that he could hear his heart slamming in his chest.

He got through the warped door and stepped on the screen door, which was lying flat on the porch. Randi's lawn chair was on its side, but past there, he could see her sitting on the grass, comforting both little girls. All three were caked in dust. Small sprays of sand cratered the yard. He hustled through the debris as fast as he could and knelt in the grass beside her. Randi was trying to wipe Pammie's dirty face.

"You, ok?" he asked anxiously. "Girls, ok?"

"We're fine, just shook." She gave him a searching look, her face streaked with grime. "I think that's an understatement."

He nodded, already scanning the property for Jake and John. Helping her up, he was relieved to see both of the boys heading towards them.

"Grandpop, the barn, the horses!" John wailed inconsolably.

"I know, I heard." Ben squinted in that direction. "I don't know how sturdy the rest of it is. We need to move any of the livestock that made it through."

Now that the poles had reversed, he wondered what the model would project. He itched to check. But the animals had to come first.

"Randi, the house seems to be fairly solid. I reinforced everywhere I could when I was preparing for the worst. It's probably better for the girls out of all this dust. But there's glass and broken stuff everywhere in there. We have to take care of the animals out here. Can you start inside?"

"Yes, I've got it." She started forward with the girls, then stopped, frowning. "What about Kansas City? Did this quake reach that far? What about our house?"

Ben avoided her eyes, looking at the orange coating on his sneakers, then looked south. As far as he could see, the land looked as if it had been picked up, shaken forcefully, then dropped again, landing where it fell.

"I haven't had time to look at anything," he dodged her question. First, the animals—we're going to need them."

She nodded, taking Pammie by the hand; she carried Cassie to the house. Both girls had sticks and leaves in their hair, and their sunsuits were rumpled and stained. Pammy had reverted to sucking her thumb, and Cassie just hid her face in her mother's shoulder. It was going to take them a minute to get over the quake.

It didn't take too long to assess the barn. Only half of it was still standing. Ben was warned that the barn was old when he bought this place. He had lost two of the horses in the back stables. There was no sound or movement in the back, and he didn't think anything could survive the roof coming down like that. They would have to move the broken beams and tiles to get to them.

The other three horses he had placed in front stalls where the walls still stood. Though still terrified, rolling their eyes and stamping their feet, the black and two brown mares looked to have come through with no injuries. Two brown mules and five big goats in the pasture huddled together but also seemed uninjured. The chicken house had collapsed almost entirely, but the chickens had escaped and found new places to peck for lunch. The dirty dozen had already forgotten their terror and were complacently looking for bugs. There was more damage than he anticipated, but hell, the quake was more significant than any he had expected by a wide margin.

"We've got this," Jake told him as they surveyed the coop. John and I will put up the walls and a roof and herd the chickens back in."

"We're going to need those chickens and their eggs," Ben said soberly.

"How bad is it?"

"It's bad. I don't know geographically who was hit, but Jake, I think those earthquakes may have affected the whole Northern Hemisphere!"

The two men stared at each other, with John watching uncertainly.

"At the least, there will be widespread destruction and loss of life. Buildings, infrastructure, and homes are severely damaged or destroyed, and I am sure there are major transportation, communication, and power systems disruptions. We don't have electricity here, which is also probably widespread. I think there were significant landslides and tsunamis off the Atlantic, and hundreds of miles of the coast were also displaced. I know several huge surges hit the East Coast! I could see it on the satellites before the earthquakes."

"What about your equipment? Is it still running?"

"I think so. I locked everything down. If we can get the generator started, we should be good. It's a big one."

"Well, that's something. What about the horses that made it? Should we remove them from what's left of the barn?"

"Yeah, put them in pasture for now. They'll probably appreciate the open field after this morning." Glad for something to do, John headed for the horses, his father's tall shadow following. Ben could hear him asking questions and was pleased the boy was thinking and making plans. Twelve was old enough to be responsible. Those horses were still spooked.

Ben crossed over to the big solar Genny in the back shed. It was relatively new, and he had only used it once or twice. He hoped it didn't need much coaxing to get started. Flipping the energy valve to the on position and switching the battery on/off switch to on, he pulled out the handle to the on position. Pushing the start switch, he held it until the Genny coughed to life. After some preliminary spluttering, it began to purr smoothly.

In an excess of caution, he had fitted along the generator's bottom with natural rubber elastomeric isolators. Best on the market for vibration dampening. It looked like the machine had survived the quake well. A year ago, he had been doubtful that an earthquake would actually be a possibility in Nebraska, but he was glad he had not taken the chance.

Back in the house, he found the girls sitting silently on the table and Randi sweeping up the glass. She gave him a wan smile.

"Go ahead and check with MAC. We could use some good news. But when you're done, we need to talk about supplies."

He nodded. Knowing how much he had put away "just in case," he wasn't too worried.

MAC's light was blinking a steady green. He released a breath he didn't realize he had been holding.

"MAC, can I get an update?" he tried, fingers crossed mentally.

"Yes, Ben. The dipoles have reversed. There is an eighty-eight percent chance they will reverse back to their original hemisphere as projected in the next two hours. Volcanic activity along the Mid-Atlantic Ridge continues. Earthquake activity continues locally in the Atlantic, but ongoing energy releases have less than a twelve percent chance of reaching the continents. Ground displacement impacted all coastal regions with ruptures, landslides, and liquefaction. Tsunamis have also impacted the coasts. The ocean floor continues to rise as sections of the

continents break away and sink. The earthquake that impacted Holden, Nebraska, had a magnitude of seven point four."

He gaped at the pictures MAC displayed, captured from different satellites. The whole coastline was underwater. Here and there, skyscrapers rose above the waves, lonely gray sentinels left of what only a few hours ago were thriving cities. He could make out the Empire State Building in New York City, but where the Hudson River should have been, he could see no sign of the Statue of Liberty. Over three hundred feet tall—was it possible that much water had been sent into New York City? Or maybe the statue fell over?

"The quantum computer is in successful working order despite the quake and the brief loss of electricity, as there was no loss of refrigeration. I am working through the government and scientific agencies to get you the most recent updates, but the East Coast agencies have gone silent. Even the news and radio outlets are down. The potential for damage and destruction is high."

Fumbling, he tried the cell phone. As expected, there was no signal. He imagined cell towers were down everywhere and guessed it would be a long time before that was resolved. Until they showed up on his doorstep, he would have no idea how his brothers or his other son had fared in this catastrophic quake.

Trying to distract himself from that problem, Ben picked up his chair and rolled it back to the desk. It felt weird not to have the floor moving beneath his sneakers after this morning. Okay, the generator was working, the brackets had held, and his equipment was still running. He sat down and tried to understand what MAC was showing him. The various monitors warred for his attention as MAC showed him one astounding thing after another.

New York City: 10:30 a.m. local, 9:30 a.m. CST

The Empire State Building had held its ground through the quake and the massive waves. By Rob Smith's estimate, a restless sea at least sixty stories deep now surrounded the iconic structure. There did not seem to be much structural damage. The steel-framed skyscraper, made up of Indiana limestone and granite, had so far seemed impervious to the water. At 102 floors, the businesses at the top were still dry. The buildings around it, however, were submerged.

He stood, white face pressed against the window, shock muddling his usually rapid-fire thought processes. The city was gone. Water covered everything. A few buildings rose like islands, but other than the Chrysler Building to the northwest, which still jutted a good ten stories above the waves, the rest were aquatic tombs. He squinted, trying to make out any survivors over at Chrysler.

He couldn't see anyone.

Carefully, he kept his eyes averted from the water below. Plenty of bodies had floated by in the last hour. He sure didn't want to see any more. Twenty-five floors were high enough to guarantee he wouldn't be able to identify anyone he knew, but just the same, he didn't want to watch the macabre parade as the current carried them, God knew where.

He expected the rest of the city to be the same. He felt a quick pang of gratitude that his parents lived in the Midwest. Even his ex-wife left the city last year and headed for the West Coast when the ink on their divorce papers was dry. Somehow, his luck had held out; he was still alive, and his personal losses were minimal.

As the senior business planner for Titan International for the last three years, he liked his job even if he didn't like his bosses much. He very much valued the fast-run elevators installed in the Empire State Building. Regular speed elevators would make for a tedious ride-up, totally miserable each day, and he wasn't a fan of heights overall.

For the first time, he reflected on Dror Hart's hubris with appreciation: leasing the highest office space he could find to lord over the city had proved providential. He was a jerk, but that jerk inadvertently saved his life.

Titan International rented the entire hundredth floor. The offices were roomy, if a bit old-fashioned. He knew it made for a prestigious address. The atmosphere was usually quiet and professional, especially if Hart was elsewhere. Not on this momentous day, however. Outside his office, he could hear people arguing.

One of the women in the main bullpen, probably an analyst, started yelling about her kids. Other people tried to calm her down. From the sounds of the crying and swearing out in the main office, most of them weren't as fortunate as he was. Everyone was worried about family. He thought about joining them, but what could he do?

The air conditioning had stopped, and the familiar hum was replaced with silence. Already, the air seemed heavy and wet. He tried to think of something to do, but nothing came to mind. Idly, still in shock, he wondered if the building could fall and how much damage the saltwater could do. Did saltwater affect limestone?

The building shivered. Accustomed to the slight swaying on windy days, Rob ignored the motion. It occurred to him that with Hart and Newsom out, he was next up in seniority. As if acknowledging his thought process, the crowd outside his office started filtering in.

"What are we going to do?" one of the engineers asked plaintively. "Joe went down the steps. They're flooded at sixty-one."

Joe, one of the electrical engineers, rubbed his face, his mournful expression curdling Rob's stomach.

"Most of the windows are broken, probably from the earthquake, but the whole building below sixty-one is underwater. I talked to a few people from other offices in the stairwell. Nobody knows what's going on or has a plan. We could try getting out of here if we had something that floats. But where would we go?"

"I don't live in New York City. I live across the river," someone in the back spoke up.

"I live in New Jersey. Maybe the wave only hit Manhattan," said another, and then everyone spoke at once.

"Wait, wait," Rob held up his hands. 'We don't know anything. Does anyone's cell work?"

Everyone looked at each other, shaking their head; a few shook their devices, but no one had a working phone.

"The landlines are dead too." Rob rubbed his head. Maybe twenty people stood in his office. "Is this everyone on the floor? Where is the rest of the staff."

"This is everyone who made it in." Jenny, the receptionist, offered.

"Everyone else was on their way here," said one of the project managers. She started to cry, understanding the fate of their colleagues who hadn't made it to work yet.

"The subway," someone murmured.

"Not just the subway—everyone on buses, walking, driving. No more rush hour traffic," said Stan Abbot, who had been leaning against the doorway throughout the discussion.

"There's a satellite phone in Mr. Hart's office," Jenny said suddenly. "It came in after he left, and I put it on his desk. Maybe we could call for help on that?"

Rob's face brightened. He wove through the crowd and out, almost running to Hart's corner office. He found the box sitting in the In Box and tore off the wrappings.

"It might have to be charged up?" Jenny had followed him.

"They run on batteries," he grinned as the device powered up. "Look at this. The contact list has Newsom's name in it." He pushed the button and listened to it ring.

"This is Newsom," an annoyed-sounding voice answered.

"Victor, this is Rob Smith." He heard Newsom grunt in surprise, so he plunged forward. "You'll be happy to know that some of us in the New York office are okay. We made it into the office before the waves hit New York. But we're stranded on the top floors of the Empire State Building, and we need a rescue. Maybe a helicopter could land on the emergency helipad on the roof?"

Newsom recovered quickly. "Of course, Rob. I'll get with Hart, and we'll get something sent right away. You folks hang tight for now."

He hung up before Rob could say anything.

"Well?" Jenny asked anxiously.

Rob shook his head. "I think the bastard is going to leave us hanging. Let's see if we can get the Coast Guard, the Army, or someone else to help."

An hour later, with rescue on the way, he and several others worked to move everyone who remained in the building to the Observation Deck on the 102nd floor. Out of the thousands who would typically be in the building on any given day, the early hour of the catastrophe limited the number of people who were actually above the wave height when the water struck. In the end, Rob counted less than three hundred of his colleagues making their way up the staircase to the 102nd floor.

The stiff wind and shock kept most behind the observatory glass, but no one wanted to wait below. Rescue helicopters from Syracuse headed their way. Rob stared west over the water. He couldn't distinguish the Hudson River from anything else, and couldn't identify the few buildings in this direction that he could see. Shuddering against the chill in the wind and praying for rescue, he remembered something his father, a plumber for forty years, told him a long time ago.

Water always goes where it wants to go, and nothing can stop it in the end. His father had been right.

***

Victor Newsom moped in his plush airline seat. Hart and his mouth—always thinking his opinion mattered most. Well, he had news for Dror. The days when he took orders from a pompous, domineering asshole were almost over.

The cannon had worked! Sure, it had been Hart's project, and Brecken had actually conceptualized and designed the tool. But the actual execution was thanks entirely to his team. He brought the right experts together, and they were all loyal to him, not Hart. He negotiated the money out of DARPA, he overcame obstacles like latent bad press and that miserable little whistleblower, and he pushed the team to deliver. He didn't let anything stand in his way. Not Rob Smith, lead business planner whining about costs and budgets. Not disloyal employees or the stress of hiring new staff when the old staff didn't play ball. Not even ethical or moral concerns because, let's be real, you can't spend ethics or morals. Nope, this was all him.

He flicked through his phone, bored and restless, pausing at an old picture. In the frame, Katherine Manning, EVP, stood at his side in some American Direct function eight years ago. What a bitch.

Well-respected industry-wide and one of American Direct's most valuable executives, Katherine had hired him into the Customer Operations department with promises of promotion to her top spot when she retired in a few years. She claimed he'd be her successor. He thought he had it made. He actually worked hard for her. And then, when the time came, and she left the company, the job went to her boot-licking, stick-up-the-ass ex-military vice president, that jerk Chad Holiday. God, he hated that guy.

Well, Katherine retired to New Hampshire. Her house and the America Direct offices in New York were now underwater. He smirked, looking at her smiling face. Didn't see that coming, did you bitch?

Women. They had no place in business and no worth at the executive level. They just needed to shut up and do what they were told. He snorted softly. Not a chance before today. But maybe the cannon could help change the status quo. He could only hope.

He thought about Rob's earlier call for help. That guy, did he think Newsom had nothing better to do than spend hours on the phone trying to arrange rescue? Rob would figure out something; that was why they hired him. And if not, or the Empire State Building collapsed before their staff were pulled out? Well, he was ready for a new team anyway. Operations people were a dime a dozen.

Trying to get his attention, Hart snapped at him, interrupting his thoughts. Carefully arranging his expression, he got up and moved forward. This pact wasn't going to last forever.

Scottsbluff Regional Airport, Nebraska: 10 a.m. MST, 11 a.m. CST

"There's another airport northwest of here." Augie studied the map carefully. "Scottsbluff."

"With the damage we've seen so far. . ." Dave didn't continue, but he angled the plane left and north in the right direction. No one needed to point out how dire their situation was.

The airports they had already flown over were destroyed. The collapsed towers and hangars, smashed planes, and vehicles were terrible enough. But the runways had settled and cracked, breaking the pavement surface and rendering them unusable for landing a plane. Even if the streets and highways hadn't met the same fate, the enormous congestion of abandoned vehicles removed these as an option for landing as well.

"Augie," once he had his passenger's attention, he quietly tapped the gas gauge. At some point, we are landing. If Scottsbluff doesn't work out, we have to find somewhere flat, hard, and long."

Augie nodded once in understanding. "We could go on to Chadron," he offered.

Dave dropped lower so they could study the landscape as they flew over. He tried to be careful how low he flew because of the dust still floating above the ground. Clogged engines were a big concern today.

Broken highways led to collapsed bridges. Everywhere was littered with castoffs, snapped trees, and collapsed infrastructure. The further north they flew, the more buildings remained standing, but even those had taken a beating. Finding someplace safe to land seemed a remote possibility. He flew around Kansas City to avoid the black smoke choking its air space. Frantic light guttered through the pall, and Dave was afraid to chance where it was coming from. The fires and fissures were terrifying.

But leaving Kansas City behind didn't improve their situation. The ground between KC and Scottsbluff was a mix of devastation and desolation. Dave was beyond worried about their prospects and starting to get anxious. He kept one eye on the gas gauge and the other on the ground.

"Here's the problem," he finally answered, careful to keep his voice low. He didn't want to scare the ladies. "Even if we make it to Chadron Airport, which I know is where you wanted to land. Even if we get there, and the ground is like this: with no place to land, we are too low on gas to try anywhere else. And Chadron is a pretty hilly elevation. I wouldn't say I like our chances at all. I think we take our shot before we get to the hills because once we are there, our options are limited."

As harrowing as their takeoff had been, witnessing the earthquake's ongoing destruction below them really panicked Augie. Now they had no choice but to land in this mess? Fear clutched him tightly.

Scottsbluff was coming up on the left. A mass of black smoke served as a marker; the city was hidden under the inky cover, blowing like a long veil toward the north.

"According to the map, the airport is on the right side. We should start to see it soon." Augie strained to catch a glimpse. "There!"

Dave followed his pointing finger. He liked Scottsbluff airport already; the smoke was being pulled away from the airspace, increasing visibility.

Then, as they drew close enough to see the airstrips, his heart crashed. All three of the runways were rippled and puckered. There was not a chance he could land on any of them and remain in one piece. He shook his head gloomily, glancing at Augie, who could also see the damage. Augie looked stricken.

Then, Dave sat up straight; his emotions flipped again. "Look!"

Augie peered out, trying to see what was adding a note of hope to Dave's voice.

"You want to try and land on that!" Shocked, Augie fell back. "It's too short!"

The last third of the northernmost runway appeared to be intact. Dave ignored him. As he flew over low and then came around again, they could see some minor cracking, but overall, the pavement did appear unbroken.

Dave whooped and readied himself to land. "Get your seatbelts on, ladies; we are coming in for landing!"

Kay and Lily scrambled to comply. Augie gulped and pulled his seatbelt tighter. "Can you land us on that little strip?"

"Yes, sir!" Without any more discussion, Dave lined the plane up and descended. He steered the aircraft to within a few feet over the broken pavement, following the smashed runway until the moment he was past the worst of the breakage, and then he dropped and started braking. They bounced hard once, twice, skidded, and then the plane started slowing, hitting some minor bumps as it rolled. The end of the runway came up fast. Augie's hands rose as if to protect himself, and then, just as the pavement ended, the aircraft coasted to a halt, rolling a few feet onto the uneven, hard-packed dirt at the end of the tarmac. Dave shut down the engine, then he whooped again, raising his fists in celebration.

"Now, how's that for a landing?" he asked Augie.

"Great job," Augie managed, trying not to throw up.

Dave just laughed and released his seat belt. "It's a long walk back to the terminal, but I'm going to see if anyone is around."

"Ladies," he said, tipping his hat in their direction with a big smile. Kay tried to smile back, but her lips were still trembling uncontrollably. Dave dropped the steps out of the plane and, whistling, walked off.

"Is he brave or crazy?" Lily rolled her eyes at her mom.

"Are you guys okay?" Augie released his seatbelt and moved to the back. His two girls were still holding hands tightly, their eyes wide with terror.

"Yes. I've had better flights." Kay finally started breathing again. She let go of Lily's hand and rubbed the girl's back, pushing her own long braid over her shoulder.

"But not more important flights." Augie gave her a little smile of reassurance, even though his stomach still had not settled. "Our pilot has gone to see if he can find anyone to help."

He pointed through the window over at the black curtain cloaking Scottsbluff. "I don't know how much luck he will have, but we'll see. I am going to get out for a few minutes."

Augie shook his head and pulled at the collar of his shirt, sweating as he stood on the tarmac and surveyed what was left of the airport.

The excess of smoke-born molecules scattered orange and red light through the clear day. It was like looking at the world through a dirty filter. The sky to the west was covered in burning, rising clouds from the ground to as far up as was visible and spreading. He had never seen anything as black and ominous as the shroud that covered Scottsbluff. He wondered how anyone could be left alive.

Dave loped up, his spindly arms and legs making him look like a chicken. He'd been wound up since the earthquake started on Merritt Island, and the subsequent flight out here had done nothing to help. He was talking before he stopped running.

"There's no one back at the tower. I can't find anyone around. I'm guessing they all headed to the city to get their families out. Is that fire something?"

They both looked to Scottsbluff, black and ominous.

"I can't say for sure, but I think it's headed this way. The line seems closer than when we landed."

"What are those fires?" Augie pointed to the remains of the smaller fires that had burned out, dotted over the runway and by the garages.

"Pretty sure that's the small stuff that caught fire in the quake. Done now." He brushed his messy hair back and pulled his Florida Gators cap back on. "Okay, boss. What next? If I could get her gassed and back up, is there any point in me flying home to Florida?"

"I don't know," Augie prevaricated, unsure how much to share. But seeing the skeptical look on Dave's face, he flushed and confessed what he knew. "I think Florida's gone, or most of it, at least. I don't know anything concrete, since I left the house this morning. My brother is about an hour northeast of here as the crow flies. Through the mountains. He has a place we are headed to." He hesitated and then plowed ahead. "I bet we could use a pilot down the road. Why don't you come with us?"

Dave stretched his long arms above his head. He stared back south like he could see Florida. He shook his head, and just as Augie thought he'd refuse, he turned back and said, "We're going to need some transportation to get through those mountains. And I want to see if I can secure my plane somewhere away from the fires before we go. You may be right that we need it for something. I can only hope."

Augie smiled for the first time that day and held out his hand. Dave grabbed it and shook it vigorously. Now, they needed a truck.

Tennessee: 11 a.m. CST

Art wasn't sure if it was due to the bedrock under the mountains or something else, but once the seemingly endless quake had passed, the road destruction was not as bad as he had feared. The Honda had taken some hits; a few of the dents would be considered significant by a body mechanic, but the engine was still operational, and he took that as a win. The radio had stopped during the quake.

"Probably a wire pulled out," he said to Marta when the quaking tapered off. He knew she was smart enough to guess that something had happened to the radio towers in Atlanta, but he didn't want to go there—and thankfully, neither did she.

Neither wanted to speculate about what lay behind. They picked their way north around Chattanooga as far as Highway 75 could take them. Perched across the river, between the Appalachians and the Cumberland Plateau, the city raged with fire and streamed traffic as people fled the inferno in cars and on foot. The bridge still stood, and Art hoped that it was as structurally sound as it looked. By the time Highway 75 had turned into Highway North 24, they were both strung out by the impatient horns, reckless drivers, and near misses.

The broken highway struggled through the mountains. Others had stopped and pushed chunks of asphalt and fallen trees out of the way, opening a path. It was a rough, bumpy two-way road, snarled up bumper to bumper. Marta managed to get a signal on her phone, but she could only pull up local podcasts as they maneuvered around Murfreesboro and then Nashville past that.

"I've got something here," she finally said, raising the sound on her phone. "It's spotty. . ."

"Report Room out of Tennessee. We released this podcast today to help others keep up with the news. We think all the local radio and television stations are down from the earthquakes this morning. At least we can't raise any of them. I repeat, multiple earthquakes or one huge earthquake rocked the continental United States this morning. There is no one to tell us what has happened. We don't know the magnitude or severity of the damage, but if just some of what we have heard is true, it is bad.

"Many thousands are believed to be dead with catastrophic damage to the East Coast, which is still under water. In Nashville, most of downtown and the freeways have collapsed, and multiple buildings are burning. People are trapped all over the Metro. Emergency rescue is overwhelmed, and we ask for help from anyone who hears this broadcast.

"Additionally, multiple dams failed during the earthquakes. The communities of West Fork and Waterhill were washed away, and those casualties are going to be brutal also. Nashville General Hospital and Ascension Saint Thomas Midtown are both destroyed. Do not go to either of those hospitals if you are seeking medical attention. Ascension Saint Thomas West is still standing and taking patients, but they are overwhelmed. Do not head to Ascension West unless you are in dire need of help."

The podcast continued, but the rest was a mix of conjecture, opinion, and sometimes prayer. The Report Room was more feeling than fact. Art stopped listening as he edged forward past Nashville.

"It sounds like Tennessee is caught between fire and water." Marta pushed her shoulder-length hair back. "We are still four states away. Do you think we can make Holden?"

"Yes, we're going to get to Holden."

She bit her lip but did not argue with his flat statement. There was nowhere to stop anyway. She thought about her hospital and her patients. With her head turned, Art could not see her tears slip free. His heart was heavy, too, as he considered what might be left of Atlanta. Yet, what could they do but keep going?

Chapter Eight

Cullman, AL: 3 p.m. CST

Freney Peterson shifted the old black Mazda again and inched forward another few feet. They had been at this for hours. "Highway 68 is a parking lot. It is really bummer to bummer," she announced glumly.

Her friend from the assisted living group home shook his dark head, the unruly mass of his white hair bobbing up and down. Even now, Freney could make the jokes.

Tigh Hayes had called Alabama his home for eighty-nine years. He had buried two wives, a son during the war, and all of his extended family before deciding to spend his last days at the Shady Gardens Retirement Home. Meeting Freney at poker night—a short, skinny black woman of ninety-one who could both clear a straight and make him laugh—had been a bonus.

"It was a good try," he told her.

"I would have liked it better if we had succeeded. Especially since we had to go to all the trouble of sneaking out."

Shady Gardens Retirement Home in downtown Birmingham was a fine place to spend your last days, but not so much if you decided to escape.

Out of the blue, he had been forewarned before today's catastrophic event started, at least in a crazy, roundabout way. Early this morning, just as the sun rose, Tigh received a text from one of his old Army buddies, Joe. It was a muddled message, but it went something like "This morning, my grandson in the Navy warned me something bad was coming so to get safe so, I am texting all what's left of my squadron our old *get to high ground* alert". Perplexed by the words, Tigh wasn't sure if Joe's warning was sound, but after all these years, he didn't bother to second-guess it.

He found Freney at early breakfast, and they put their heads together over eggs and sausage. He thought she'd laugh at him when he told her something was going to happen and they should get to high ground, or protest that they were not supposed to leave the home without prior notice and arranged transportation. (Transportation—he hadn't even thought of how to work that?)

Instead, Freney rubbed one little finger over her chin. "Do you have a driver's license?"

"Nope, I gave it up when I came here. Didn't think I would need to go anywhere."

"I don't either. When mine expired, I figured it was time." But she smirked at him with a wink. "I have a car. It's old, but it runs."

"Where is it?"

"Next door on that old lot. I keep it gassed full up, too." Her bright hazel eyes met his. And just like that, he knew she was in. He didn't know if she believed him, but she was ready to have some fun.

"But where should we go? What's safe?" she hummed thoughtfully.

"Joe lives in Cullman, Alabama, north of here. Let's go north up Highway 65. We can start there. We can stop by and see what he knows. Look," He pulled his wallet out from behind the table and showed her the bills inside. "I've got bread, but we should go now."

That decision got them moving. They'd needed to devise a strategy to get out to her old Mazda and away before one of the aides could question them. They'd leave notes in their rooms. There would be hell to pay later, but, as Freney laughed, "Better to ask forgiveness than permission."

First, Tigh had to distract the director while Freney filched her bright red key bob out of the main office where they were stored on pegboard. It helped that the few keys on that board were rarely used, and nobody paid attention to them. Considering her age, she was good at this, in and out with the keys before he had barely started his lame distraction of questioning the air conditioning in his room. When he stumbled to a stop, the director patted him on the arm and let him go. She was used to forgetfulness around here.

The actual sneaking out was more stressful. "Over here!" Freney had whispered loudly, waving the key. She still wore her gray dress from breakfast, but she'd added a dark brown coat over it. Clean white sneakers finished the runaway ensemble.

Tigh, dressed in jeans and a tee, had his boots on. He flinched when he saw her gesturing and hastily peeked down the corridor. No one was looking at them. The halls at Shady Gardens were busy in the mornings with visitors, aides, and room cleaners, not to mention the congestion at the front desk in the lobby. Everyone was occupied with their own business. One at a time, they both hurried through the hall (though, in his case, it was more limping) past the people facing the desk and out the door, trusting the crowded space to cover their escape.

The car was parked on an old lot next to Shady Gardens. It was black and dusty and had seen better days. Luckily, it was parked near an entrance secured with just one flimsy piece of old brown wire hanging from crooked posts. Tigh took care of that while Freney got the key seated and turned. Seconds later, they were on their way, Tigh's phone taking care of the directions.

Before the earthquakes started, it had been quite an escapade, and they congratulated each other happily. "At our age, you take what adventures you can get," Freney told him, peering over the dash and watching for the signs leading to Highway 65.

"It's a nice day for it too." Tigh gazed out the windows. It might have stayed that way if the earthquakes hadn't kicked them around a little later.

Being slammed around by the quakes you weren't expecting was terrible enough. Freney, who in truth wasn't going that fast, slid to a stop at the first jolt, resting the car in a large, flat emergency area along the highway. They clung to each other against the seat cushions as the ground shook and jumped, and the Mazda did so along with it. Other vehicles slid against them and into them, and they all rocked together uncontrollably.

Neither knew how long it lasted, but it sure seemed like a long time. When the tremors disappeared, Freney let go and put her shaking hands back on the steering wheel. Waiting for the other cars piled around them to straighten out, she said, "Well, I guess your friend was right. He must have been talking about earthquakes?"

"Yeah, I guess so." Tigh picked up his phone, which had fallen on the floorboards.

"What now?"

He tried to make sense of what was on the screen.

"I think the cell towers are down," he said finally. "And the roads took some damage. I wonder if Shady Gardens got hit worse than here?"

She simply shrugged one shoulder in response.

"Unless you object, let's keep heading for Cullman. We can still find out what Joe knows. At the very least, we can tell him thanks for the warning. Let's keep going."

So, they had. And now, hours later, they were sitting in "bummer to bummer" traffic. That wasn't the big problem, in any case. The big problem, apparently, was ocean water. The news was patchy through Tigh's cell, but they heard about the East Coast. Then they heard about Atlanta. They exchanged horrified looks. And then, just a little while ago, they heard about the surge heading their way.

"How far from Atlanta to Birmingham?" Freney wanted to know, her lips thin with worry. "Like two hundred miles?"

Tigh agreed, still poking at his phone, trying to get more information from it.

"Tigh, I don't know if we're far enough away. Or even what far enough away looks like!" Traffic had started moving again, and she pulled forward, noting they were climbing onto Brindley Mountain. Thank goodness. Mountains had to be good compared to sea level. She held the car steady at twenty miles an hour. Still bumper to bumper but moving at last. A sign came up on the right: Cullman 3 Miles.

"I don't think it matters anymore, Freney."

She turned her head at the odd note in his voice. Her stomach clenched as she realized he had dropped the phone in his lap and was staring across the massive plateau they had just left below.

She hated to look but could not stop herself. Where the white pines met the ground, dirty water boiled through. From here, the water seemed as high as the trees themselves, maybe more than one hundred feet. The black trunks were ripped loose, caught in the waves, and tossed towards them in seconds. The surge plowed over the field, ripping up vegetation and sweeping everything toward the road—toward them.

Some vehicles tried to go around them, while others tried to drive up the side of the mountain and around the trees, only to get stuck, their occupants screaming. Tigh just reached over without looking and took her small hand in his. Multiple cars behind them were knocked off the road as the surge overtook them. They disappeared as the water gushed up the hill over them, always forward.

Seconds later, froth, seawater, and vegetation scoped the little Mazda up off the road and raced along the mountain. Freney waited for the water to pour over her, but suddenly, she realized they were somehow suspended atop its surface!

They could not see it, but due to the angle of their car and one very hoary old tree, the expanding energy moving along the surge forced the trunk under the car. It was so black, skidding along so fast they couldn't see anything, but they felt the crunch as the two fused, with the gears jammed hard into the wood under the Mazda's carriage.

The tree trunk carried them along the flow! The windows shattered, and spray filled the car.

Ocean water poured into the floorboards, and the smell of sea salt permeated everything. Freney choked and tried to clear her eyes, but it was hard to make sense of anything. She wondered how long this crazy ride could last when—

BAM!

The tree trunk they were tangled up in got wedged in some wild bushes and old boulders caught in a cleft, bringing them to a precipitous halt. Water continued to flow under it, causing the trunk to bob and holding it in place. The Mazda stayed firm, caught in the myriad branches of the trees.

Gasping, still held tight by their seat belts, Freney and Tigh just stared at each other.

"Well," Freney said finally, "at least no one is going to ask for my expired driver's license." They both burst into laughter. The jokes would keep them busy until the water went down or they figured out a way out of the car.

Cheyenne Mountain Complex, Colorado: 2 p.m. MST, 3 p.m. CST

"Okay, what do we have?" President Tanner dropped into a free chair at the wide round table, demanding attention. He was aware that the Combined Command Center was two thousand feet underground, and while he appreciated the security, he couldn't stop fretting about another earthquake event. While he'd admit this self-sustaining city had withstood the last monster quake with minor damage, he did not like taking refuge in a hole, no matter how big.

While shuttling them through the mile-long horseshoe-shaped tunnel, the airman driving the cart explained that the entire facility rested on 1,311 steel coils, each weighing 1,000 pounds. Built to absorb the seismic shock of a nearby nuclear bomb detonation or the longest earthquake in human history, it certainly seemed priceless after today. He explained that the complex trembled this morning but not to the extent that the land outside was jolted around. Still, despite his attempt to minimize the earthquake's impact, Tanner thought the kid looked a little pale. He bet it was worse than a few shakes.

He scanned the thirty or so faces of the people seated around the table. Another fifteen in uniform stood around the room and quickly filled the space. Most were strangers, but Bob Hendricks sat down from him with the two aides who flew in with them standing behind him. One of them, the young black girl Jen, had a phone to one of her ears and whispered in Bob's ear. Command Center clocks were arranged horizontally along a low wall above them, displaying the time in time zones around the globe.

Busy workstations filled the area. Banks of monitors covered the walls. Seven super-sized overhead monitors ranged around the room. Three of the big screens were grouped around the sleek steel table at which they sat. Presented on some of these were real-time, colorful, graphic maps of the United States, and it wasn't lost on Tanner that all the brightest colors identified were where the most significant cities sat. The Atlantic Seaboard was a band of muddy blue with no colorful graphics depicting the big cities. He scowled deeply, regarding it with ire.

When they landed, Col. Amos Stanely, command director of the 732nd Mission Support Group and the Cheyenne Mountain Complex, was waiting on the tarmac. After shaking hands, he explained that the MSG was responsible for Cheyenne Mountain's civil engineering, its physical and digital security, and ensuring that it remained "America's Fortress," perhaps Earth's most impenetrable command center. Tanner glazed over quickly. He wasn't interested in a tour. Stanely was a shrewd judge of character. From Tanner's reputation, he had expected little more.

Ready to report, the colonel stood erect with no expression on his long face as he took the lead and started talking first.

"Mr. President, I will first summarize what we know with certainty. Thanks to our satellites, we know most of the East Coast was flooded as much as three hundred miles inland this morning. The blue on the monitors indicates how far the water has inundated. The one-two punch from the Azores and the Mid-Atlantic Ridge hit us with multiple catastrophic tsunamis. The earthquakes between those surges made this a disaster of unbelievable proportions. It's all going to have to be mapped to be sure, but my people and the USGS believe that underneath all that new blue ocean, miles of land of the continental United States has subsided."

"Subsided? Where is it?"

"Sir, that will be a question geologists work on later. We don't know why it started or if it is still happening under the surface where we can't see it. The forces involved are beyond our current understanding. For now, we know that New Hampshire, Massachusetts, Rhode Island, Connecticut, New Jersey, and Delaware are completely submerged. New York City and Philadelphia are also underwater. The rest of the states along the East Coast are partially or mostly flooded. All the seaboard along the ocean is gone, but some of the bigger states still have real estate on their western sides."

Tanner had paled and then flushed red.

Colonel Stanely's baritone remained steady. But his ordinarily ruddy face was pallid, and he gripped the stack of papers in front of him so tightly they trembled. He was nauseatingly aware of the catastrophic nature of this briefing.

"Most sea level elevations of Virginia, North and South Carolina, Georgia, and Florida are also gone. That includes all the big cities like Washington, D.C., Wilmington, Charleston, Savannah, Atlanta, and everything on the Florida Peninsula. It is all under water."

Tanner seemed furious, and his eyes darted around the room, looking for someone to blame. The room had gone hushed as Stanely continued to read from his report. Even the workstations seemed muffled.

"Sir, this next part is difficult to explain because we don't know why it is happening. The ocean continues to move across the southern states. Where it runs up on the Appalachians, we have a natural barrier of sorts that is expected to stop the incursion. Maybe not drain back out, but keep it from pushing further west. However, the water crossing Georgia, in particular, is not slowing down or washing back out. With no mountain range to stop it, the effect is like water in a bowl tipped across the table, with the Atlantic as the bowl and the States as the table. We don't know how much or how long this surge phenomenon will continue, and we don't know what will happen with all this water when it is done."

"So, what are you saying, Colonel? Is the whole United States of America going to flood? What about all the people who live in the path of this surge? How deep is it?" Tanner stalked over to the monitor and watched as a dark line, indicating the surge, moved slowly west away from Atlanta.

Stanely shook his head. "It's deep," he admitted, choosing to answer the last question. "Corporal Abel, bring up the satellite feed of Atlanta."

"Yes, sir." A crisply situated young man quickly complied at the other end of the table. His fingers flew over the keyboard, and one of the monitors to Tanner's right blossomed with a real-time picture.

The ocean filled every inch of the screen. Here and there, a skyscraper rose above the waves like a lonely watchman. But nothing else marked where a major city had occupied this spot this morning. Not even debris floated on the waves as the powerful current carried everything away.

"This is Atlanta?" Tanner could not believe his eyes. "What happened to all the buildings?"

"It happened fast. The earthquakes brought much of it down, and before we could get in there, the second set of tsunamis hit, pushing further south. When we realized what was happening with the Atlantic, we sent out emergency warnings to get everyone in the east and the south zones a hundred miles away, telling them to evacuate north and west. The interstates that aren't underwater are logjammed for hundreds of miles with evacuees, and that's on the roads that are still drivable. Hundreds of roads were badly damaged or destroyed in the quakes."

Tanner slammed his hand against the wall. "Does anybody have any answers? Why were we caught unprepared? What about the earthquakes? How bad is the damage?"

"The earthquakes impacted every part of the United States, most of Canada and Mexico. Maybe deep into South America, we don't know yet. Major and minor U.S. cities are on fire. Roads, highways, and infrastructure like electrical and water systems are destroyed or at least badly damaged. That earthquake lasted over thirty minutes, which the USGS tells me is unprecedented and is what contributed to the major destruction. There's no count on casualties; it's just an overall consensus that it will be in the millions."

"Oh my God," Tanner whispered. "Where do we start?"

"Sir," said Bob Hendricks. His clothes were wrinkled, and his thin hair spiked up, but he had regained his composure. "Jen here has been on with the USGS out of Sacramento. Albert Longfield runs that branch. Longfield and one of his guys think they have a theory on what is happening. They are suggesting we are under attack!"

"Under attack!? From who? The Chinese?"

"From Titan International. They claim a whistleblower predicted something like this a few years ago. They didn't take it seriously, but now. . ."

"That is the most ridiculous thing I ever heard. Dror Hart is one of the most upstanding business leaders in the world. Stop spewing nonsense!" Tanner turned his back on Hendricks in disgust.

Hendricks plowed on. "Sir, Longfield and Robbins are also proposing we pull in a geologist in Nebraska who has modeled everything that has happened so far. They are suggesting we get him and his model out here to have some chance at predicting what's next."

"If he can shed some light on this, get him out here. But I don't want to hear any more bullshit about Titan International. Have this guy work with your scientists. We need answers." Tanner turned back to the monitors. 'What can we deploy to help some of these cities? Who can we get to help? What's happening with the other countries?"

"Mr. President, I have an update on the other heads of state."

Tanner swung around fast, looking for some good news.

Captain Laura Anson looked up from her electronic pad. Her expression was bleak, and Tanner's heart dropped even before he heard what she had to say.

"What about Russia?" He narrowed his eyes.

"Vladimir Putin is alive and, by all reports, somewhere safe. We have not been able to contact him or his cabinet. Russia suffered much damage from the quakes in the cities. With all of those old stone buildings, Moscow has suffered widespread destruction. Some casualty figures from the metropolitan areas are fifty percent or worse."

"Humph." For the first time, Tanner didn't look angry, which sent a shiver down Captain Anson's back. She hurried on.

"In London, the prime minister and most of parliament didn't make it out before the tsunami hit. The royal family did not get out either. London is flooded, but I can confirm that the only helicopter that could get off the ground was for one of the princes. I haven't identified which one yet. Both the president of Ireland and his deputy are deceased, and Ireland is in some political upheaval at the moment."

"President Macron in France was killed in the earthquakes. He and his staff were in an automobile, and quakes brought down a whole side street worth of buildings on the car. It's still buried, but there is no hope. There is still no word about Belgium or the Netherlands. Queen Margrethe of Denmark and her whole family died when the Royal House came down during the earthquake. Most of Denmark is underwater."

She took a deep breath and continued. "The presidents of Germany and Italy are uninjured and have been moved to secure locations. We can arrange contact when you are ready. The president of Portugal, his entire family, and his staff are missing. Most of Portugal was flooded, so we believe he did not make it out. The president of Spain is alive but was injured in the quakes. His staff moved him to the mountains in the north.

"We don't have any information from China, Korea, most of the Middle East, Africa, and South America. There is too much interference with communications, but we hope to overcome some of this and get you better updates."

She stopped and waited for him to ask questions. Already thinking of how to turn this catastrophe in his favor, Tanner had nothing to say to her. He waved her away without thanking her, instantly forgetting she was there. He had some ideas and needed to think.

Chapter Nine

Hours later, Ben was still sitting numbly in the same place. He called Jake and Randi in to watch the recorded satellite feed of the destruction and drowning of the Atlantic Coast. The mega blast along the Mid-Atlantic Ridge changed the oceans, shifting them into new areas as parts of the crust along the United States and Europe sank below sea level.

It looked like the United States had lost the largest amount of dry acreage. But many coastal European cities were also drowned. Paris was underwater, with just a few buildings, hills, and the Eiffel Tower sticking out of the waves. London was gone, as was the whole of Wales, and countless small English towns had been washed away; not even the London Tower or Buckingham Palace had withstood the assault. The earthquakes had leveled almost every city or town along the ocean, returning dry land to the sea.

Ben could not stop scanning the damage to the Eastern Seaboard through the satellite feed. He fiddled with the controls, but the picture refused to come into a better resolution because everything was still covered in water. The surges continued to rise and push west. Now, they were sluicing up against the Appalachians running north and south through the eastern states. So much water! Working with MAC, he started formatting the variables.

There was a lot of new data to load and run. He barely noticed Randi sweeping around him, and later, Jake and John were filling the broken office window with wood panels. The unfolding patterns changed every few seconds as he added real-time details from the satellites. He had made considerable headway through the specifics associated with the events of the last twenty hours. He moved carefully, checking to ensure that every step was built on the data before with no omissions or duplicates. Once his base was in place, he unleashed MAC on the new background to identify projections and outcomes.

He didn't know how long it would take, so he stood, wanting to check on the others.

"Well?" Jake said when he walked into the kitchen. His son leaned against the counter while he talked with Randi. Jake was a big guy like Ben. Over six feet and two hundred pounds, he carried it well.

"MAC's chewing through the data. I'm listening for his alert. How about you guys?"

The girls were playing in the corner with blocks. Their blond curls were brushed and tied in ponytails, and they giggled with each other as they slid around on the cool tiles. They'd already put the morning upset behind them.

The rest of the room, likewise, was now shipshape. He could hear the refrigerator humming in the corner. Except for the patched windows and some cracks in the plaster, things did not look too bad.

John was sitting at the table, sketching the horses in a canter. He looked up. "Grandpop, we put all the chickens back in the coop, and the horses are in the corral."

"Thanks, John." He ruffled the boy's hair, which was cut in the same style as Jake's dark strands.

"You already know the electricity is out," Jake said as he sat at the table and motioned his father to do the same. "Water's out, too; the pipes probably broke in multiple places from here to town in that earthquake. We filled all the tubs and sinks and every container we could find. I filled all the outside tanks and barrels for the animals. The pressure dropped off an hour ago. There is no telling when it will be back."

"Thanks, Jake, and you're right; I should have thought of that."

"Do you still have that portable potty? We need to set something up."

"Like an outhouse or something? Yes, it's in the basement." Suddenly grateful, Ben became aware of how much organization Jake had taken on while he worked at his desk.

"The wind is blowing from the south. The air is getting worse—plenty of smoke. We covered the windows to try and keep it out. I don't think we will be at risk for fire here, but we'll keep watch. You have that pond on this property on the other side of the barn, past the paddock."

"It's fed by a spring!" Ben held up a finger. "It's not huge, but if that spring keeps producing, that will be a big help."

"Yuck, you want to drink that old, green water with weeds in it?" John looked affronted.

"We'll boil it," his mom said with a smile. She tried to hide her worry from the children, but John was old enough to catch the creases around her eyes and understand where they came from.

Randi showed John another book on the table: "Recipes. Those weeds floating in the water, like watercress, lilies, and mint, can make some good dinners."

John didn't look convinced, but he didn't argue anymore. He knew today was momentous, and the adults were trying to strategize.

Jake continued where he had left off, "Your propane tank is in one piece, but it was bounced around pretty hard, and all the piping was pulled free from the house. It's July, so it is not a big deal today, but another thing I need to look at. I don't think the tank leaked, but it took some dents. We also need to check your chimney. Looks like you lost some bricks. I checked your bunker, too."

Last summer, back under the sugar maples and white pine trees past the far end of the barn, buried back in the hillside, Jake and John had found the partially blocked entrance to an old cavern. Some ancient geological fault had created this space on Ben's plateau. Excited, they had excavated enough of the cave to camp and stayed there several times.

After they went home in the fall, Ben spent additional time exploring the cave. To his surprise, it was a big area, nearly the diameter of the hill covering it. He cleared out loose rocks and rubble, disposed of piles of dirt and animal remains, and opened up coves and spaces large enough to qualify as rooms. He enjoyed the work, and had a great emergency shelter when he was done.

He had spent a long week fabricating a "stone" door on a fulcrum to keep the outside locked out and the inside safe. If you didn't know better, the slab looked almost like it had been there for thousands of years, he thought with satisfaction when he was finished. It was a good fit, and he was confident it could keep the weather and animals out.

Ben added shelves and tables near the front and loaded the place with provisions. That was one reason he wasn't worried about supplies. He needed to share that with Randi.

"Everything was on the floor, but no damage. John and I cleaned it up. After the quake this morning, I was glad to see what you did with the place. I was surprised at the size of it. I don't remember it being so big. Do you have a log of what's in there, or do we need to create one?"

Ben stood and reached above the refrigerator. He pulled down a green notebook that he handed to Randi.

"B is for basement, and C is for cave. It's not much of a coding system," he said, sheepishly. "Did you check the basement? I put all the bottled water down there. It was too heavy to move all the way to the back of the pasture."

"I did," Randy looked up from the notebook. "It was still stacked between the wall and those heavy shelves. Its weight must have held it in place. I also saw the water straws and chlorine tablets. I put them back on the shelves."

"There are UV lights in the cave, too. One of those will help with the pond water. I'm trying to think of everything." Ben rubbed the stress wrinkles on his forehead. "Now, we'll find out what I missed."

Jake started back up. "So, the cell phones don't work. They charge off the generator but can't pick up a signal. Towers must be down everywhere. You don't have a landline. I don't know if the wireline would work or the wires are all down, but it doesn't matter. We haven't heard from Art, Augie, Will, or Josh."

Ben's stomach felt hollow, but he refused to succumb to despair. "I know. I hoped one of them would have shown up by now, but with those quakes, everything must be a mess. Will is in Argentina. I don't expect him soon. Augie and his family were flying here in a private plane. I talked to him just before the quakes hit. Hopefully, they are close. Art and Marta were driving from Atlanta, so getting here may take some time."

"Well, while we are waiting, Randi wants me to try to call her folks in Denver, and I'd like to check in at work and see how the quakes impacted them." Jake worked as a manager at the Kansas City International Airport. He held up a hand as Ben started to protest. "I know it's probably bad. I want to see what I can find out."

"I checked; my Jeep and your truck both started up. I'll take the Jeep and see how far I can go. Your next neighbors are a few miles down the road, right? The Loungs, I think? I'll stop and check on them first."

"Yes, Davis Loung and his wife, Betty. I don't see them very often, but they're nice folks. It'll be ten miles west on Highway 20 to Holden, the closest town. The roads could be bad. Holden is a pretty small town, though. Maybe that played into its favor, and it wasn't badly damaged. Maybe I should go with you?"

Before Jake could answer, MAC's alert chimed from the office. It must have completed its analysis. All three adults and John jumped up and headed for the office. Ben leaned into the monitor, trying to read the updates. "What?" he mumbled, pulling the chair underneath him as he dropped.

"What's wrong?" Jake picked up on his anxiety right away.

"This can't be right. This here," he waved his hand over the top part of the projections, "this is what happened so far, Iceland, the Mid-Atlantic Ridge, the tsunamis and earthquakes." He started mumbling as he read further.

"Okay, that's good, right? The model was right and . . ."

"No! I mean, yes, the model was right, but . . ." He paled. "It's continuing with its projections! The model is still projecting! *This isn't over yet.*"

Northwest Nebraska, Highway 29 North: 3 p.m. MST, 4 p.m. CST

Kay put her back into it and shoved as hard as she could. She had lost count of the number of times they had stopped to push debris off the road. The three drivers that had slammed into each other here had left their rides behind and fled. She could see why; the escarpment at this curve pinched tight, narrowing the road. These vehicles were all old models, and the damage to each was extensive.

The white Impala lying on its side would never drive again with that hood crushed into the engine. Salvage probably wasn't worth the effort to whoever left it here. The other two weren't much better off. But if they could move the crumpled blue sedan over on its flat tires by maybe three or four feet, they could squeeze by without damaging their ride.

Granted, the short truck they had found in the airport hangar wasn't much to look at, more rust than paint, and it was sheer luck they had seen the keys in the broken glove box. But it ran a solid fifteen miles an hour, and that was better than walking.

The sedan finally gave, slipping over a few feet. Kay pushed her brown braid back over her shoulder as she stood up. Augie stepped around the back of the broken car, eyeing the open space left in the road. "I think we can fit through there," Augie said.

He gestured her back towards the little truck that looked as if a giant had taken a knife and sliced off the rear cab at a thirty-degree angle. It was an odd design, something Augie remembered from airports as a boy. It had been a long time since he had seen a truck like this towing luggage.

Masked and waiting, Dave sat at the wheel, and Lily sat in the abbreviated back. She had said very little since they left Scottsbluff. A wet cloth to minimize the fumes hid her face, but Kay knew she was struggling. Lily hadn't brought Grady home to meet them yet, but losing him and all of her friends was a big blow. While flying, the girl had whispered about her fight with Grady and how she had left things. There wasn't much Kay could do but offer comfort and time. She didn't want to admit that, deep inside, she was thankful to have her husband and daughter safe from the deluge.

Augie waved Dave forward.

"How much farther do you think?" Kay asked.

He looked up at the dim sun, now vermilion due to the vast amounts of smoke produced by the fires to the south.

"I don't know, maybe a couple of more hours." He held up his face rag. "Do you need more water?"

"No, I'm good." She tied the rag over her nose. "Hoping no more quakes."

Since they left Scottsbluff, a few tremors had passed, scaring them all. They were just aftershocks, but any earth movement was too much.

They stood to the side while Dave worked around the blue sedan. The edge of the brush guard scrapped some blue paint off, but then they were through. Augie and Kay jumped back on the truck, and Dave took off.

Hendron, KY: 4 p.m. CST

The Honda died just outside of Hendron. One minute, they were picking their way along Highway 24, and the next, it choked and stopped. The air was terrible here, tainted by the smoke and toxins from the hundreds of fires. He grimaced as the wind blew fumes across the interstate.

Art was no mechanic, but he tried looking under the hood. The air filter was clogged, so he banged the plastic piece sharply against the car. As Marta got out to join him on the side of the road, he noted her uncharacteristically wrinkled clothes. She had taken the time to fix her hair. It was pulled back in a neat clasp, as always.

They should have left sooner. If he had known before the early morning show, he could have had his co-anchor take the news. He shook his head.

"Is it bad?" she asked.

"It could be anything. The air is full of smoke and crap. There's a lot of tire and battery manufacturing in this area. The news is always full of rubber and chemicals burning around here. The air filter was clogged, but I think whatever's wrong is worse than that."

They were both tired, but it didn't matter. The orange sun was hot, they were sweating, and he had a headache from the fumes. He fitted the air filter back in its slot. Cars passed them sporadically, but no one was stopping. Art wouldn't have stopped, so he didn't blame them. He did not know what to do.

Just off the road, about three hundred yards away, he saw a cross and realized he was looking at a church through the dim light. There were cars in the parking lot and some damage to the building, but all in all, from here, it looked sturdy.

"Let's go there." He pointed.

She squinted doubtfully. "To a church?"

"Maybe we can get some help, maybe give some help." She brightened a little at that thought. He handed her the bags she had carried from the hospital and then pulled out their go-bags from the trunk. Swinging one over each shoulder, he balanced himself. He locked the doors, more out of habit than any genuine expectation of coming back. They cut down the overpass, careful to stay off the road. Hours after the quakes, people drove erratically, and Art feared it was because people were running, evacuating badly damaged areas. He could see fires all around, but the area surrounding the church seemed clear for now.

Praying somebody would be at the church, they picked their way over the train rails and across the street. No lights were on inside, but the quake had taken down the electrical, so he wasn't expecting anything else. Art knocked tentatively on the big double door, and then, when there was no response, a little harder. It swung open suddenly, and an unexpected smiling face popped out behind it.

"Come in, come in!" The man, in his middle twenties, had plain brown hair and eyes. He was dressed casually in jeans and a scruffy stained shirt. He waved them in. They followed him through the door, grateful for the help.

"You two look exhausted. Come to the nave and sit down." The nave was shadowy, but the air was much better. Art breathed in, trying to relax his scratchy throat. The overstuffed chairs against the wall looked fabulous, but they both hesitated to sit, filthy from the day.

"No, they'll wash, don't worry." He urged them down, then retrieved some boxes with straws from the stack on the table and put them in their hands—warm fruit punch. He smiled anxiously at them as they examined the little white boxes with cartoon animal heads on the front.

"Thank you, Pastor." Marta rested her hand on his arm in gratitude.

"Oh, no, that is not me; I am not the pastor." The man laughed; his round face merry. As he chuckled at her mistake, she realized that not only was this young man not clergy, but—on the basis of his distinctive syntax—he was probably slightly autistic, too.

"My name is Ed, Ed Wilson. I am just like you, lost and looking for a place to put my head tonight. My Jeep was crushed when the earthquake hit. I was over at the campus when it started, and the whole side of Emory Hall came down on top of my car. I am just grateful I was not sitting in it at the time. When that terrible shaking finally stopped, I walked here looking for help, and Pastor Don let me in. He is in the sanctuary with the others who do not have anywhere else to go. I have been answering the door all day because some of those who came here are injured and need him to help."

Marta stood up. "Injured? I'm a doctor. Can I help?"

"I would say yes to that! Come on. I will show you." Ed hurried to pull them through the wood doors and into the sanctuary. The room was vast and rectangular, the ornate ceiling at least twenty-five feet high. All the candelabras were lit, casting a subdued yellow light over the room. The dull-colored glass reflected a little of the late afternoon daytime, but a lack of vivid sunshine robbed the windows of their bright tints. The air was heavy but much sweeter than outside.

There must have been thirty or forty people lying on the pews and another dozen or more trying to help. People murmured as they talked quietly among themselves. Marta dropped her bags and approached two men working over a crying boy. The taller of the two held a flashlight on an injured limb, and the blood glowed a deep red in the white light.

"Hey Ed, has anybody checked this place? Do you know if it's going to stand? What if we get more tremors?" Ed was nodding before Art finished talking.

"Yes, yes. We checked. There's a lot of stuff knocked down, including the cross over there." Ed motioned towards the front of the big room, and now Art saw where the ivory white cross with Jesus reposed was leaning awkwardly against the altar wall.

"Don't worry, it's not broken. We put it there to keep it safe. But we did not find anything that seemed risky. That guy over there," he pointed to a tall man in a jean jacket, holding a cap while he talked to the woman next to him. "His name is Greg. He said he worked for the city and knew what to look for. He is the one who said we looked okay. He said, 'These old churches were built to last.'"

Marta was already examining the young boy with a bloody arm. She and the shorter man Art assumed was the pastor started discussing what the church had available for first aid, and he tuned out. There were other ways he could help. He reached into his go-bag and pulled out a flashlight.

"Hey Ed, there's a lot of people here."

"Oh, my yes, there are a lot of people here." Ed agreed, watching him move the light around the walls. "Do you have another one of those flashlights?"

"The flashlights? Sure." Art pulled one out of the second go-bag and put it in Ed's eager hands. "How about food? Do we have any? Can I help prepare anything?"

Ed stopped fumbling with the flashlight. For the first time since they'd encountered him, he was at a loss for words. "I am passing out juice boxes," he said, with uncertainty. "I don't know about food."

He looked over at the pastor for help.

With the flashlights leading their path, Art went to check, assisted by Ed and with the blessing of Pastor Don. Though the church kitchen had big windows, the light from outside was muted. All the windows were broken, and sweeping up the glass was the first order of business. Art could see smoke swirling through the orange hue around the building, wafting into the kitchen. He was grateful for the flashlight.

The shelves held canned goods, some boxes, and a big bag of rice. The refrigerator was dark, but the interior was still cool. Odds and ends filled the fridge. Maybe he could make this work.

"Ed, I'm a pretty good chef. How about you and I whip something up that will put a hot meal in everyone's belly?"

"I am not a good chef," Ed declared, looking very uncomfortable. "And the stove does not work. Nothing works because we do not have electricity. We do not have electricity because of the earthquakes."

"Gotcha, buddy. But people have to eat. Let's see what we can do. We can start with this." He pulled a one-burner camping stove out of the go-bag. "Let's find a pot that will work on here."

Ed brightened up and picked up the flashlight. Art was a smart guy.

While they worked, they talked.

"Is your family going to be worried about you?" Art asked as he mixed ingredients.

Ed cleaned the few vegetables at the sink. "I have no family," he answered, carefully examining the green peppers for dirt. "I live by myself in a room at the YMCA since my mom went to heaven. I work at the college. I keep the rooms clean for the Library, the Science Hall, and the mathematics classrooms. I was getting done yesterday when the ground started shaking. It scared me to death!"

"Me too." Art agreed.

"I wanted to check the library when the shaking stopped, but it fell down! It was a pile of bricks. There wasn't anyone to ask what I should do next. I waited and waited. So, I came over here. The church is a safe space, and it did not fall down. Pastor Don was really nice to me and said I could watch the door and pass out juice drinks."

Ed chatted on while Art thought about Nebraska and his brothers. He hoped everyone was all right. He thought about Marta's mom and dad on the West Coast and wondered if the earthquake had impacted the faults in California. She hadn't mentioned them yet, but he knew she had to be thinking about them. He added more salt to the pot and worried as he worked.

Chapter Ten

The Loungs and Reynolds were okay. When Jake saw the Abe and Pearl Reynolds talking to Davis and Betty, he remembered that the rotund couple owned the next property up the road on the north side. When he pulled his Jeep aside from an old Dodge truck parked on the driveway, Jake found all four of them in Davis Loung's pasture, discussing the quake damage.

"Hey, Jake Stone. Is everything okay at your dad's?" Davis leaned on the fence to talk, slipping his hammer into the belt he wore. Jake noticed some fence poles were leaning and a few braces were at an angle. He figured Davis had been out here repairing the damage.

"The barn took some damage, and the windows are all broken, but we're okay," Jake said. "You guys are all right, too?"

"Fence damage. The shed came down, and so did the tack room when the ground opened up underneath it, but the house and shop are standing," he waved a hand toward the rustic log retreat. "Broke windows, just like yours. No electric and water pressure from Holden is kaput. The big wrap-around porch fell off the front part of Lem Reynolds' place." He thumbed back at the couple standing with Betty. "They were just telling us. It was an almighty crash, he says. Man, that was some earthquake. I thought quakes only lasted minutes, not hours!"

Jake started to answer when they heard a deep growling sound in the distance. Immediately, he turned west, expecting to see the ground shaking.

Nothing moved.

Then, almost right away, he recognized the mechanical edge of the growl and knew it for what it was.

"Is that a helicopter?" Davis shaded his eyes with a hand, trying to see in the glare of the orange setting sun. "That's the first chopper we've seen since the quake. I wonder if they're with Urgent Response."

"They sure don't seem like they're responding urgently." Walking up, Betty twisted her nose in a sniff, her hands held up before her eyes as the helo flew closer. Jake remembered she could be a little tart. "The earthquake was this morning. Where were they then?"

"Those markings look like a military chopper." Jake twisted his neck, squinting, trying to read the white and black letters in the bad light.

"Hey Jake, that helicopter is headed for your place. Didn't your dad work with the military?"

"No, he worked for the U.S. Geological Service," Jake corrected him, then stopped and frowned at the dull gray copter as it flew closer. It did look like a Sea Hawk. The helicopter whooshed over and past them a minute later, still heading for the Stone property. "I was going to try and get to town, but I better get back."

Jumping in the Jeep and starting the engine, he spun the wheel, rounding another of the endless sand blow patterns tearing up the ground, and sped up the drive.

Minutes later, Jake pulled into the Stone driveway. The helicopter had already landed, but more than one surprise was waiting for him when he arrived. Parked in front of the house sat a weird half-truck with a tall, skinny guy leaning on it. The guy saluted him as he hurried past. Jake promised himself he'd find out about that next.

For now, he focused on the crowd surrounding the landed helicopter in the right-side pasture. Luckily, the horses, mules, and goats were all grazing in the left pasture. He walked through the gate to stand beside Randi and the girls. John was with Ben, who was talking to an earnest-looking guy with gray hair and a pencil protector in his short-sleeved shirt. Standing by listening was another man in a light gray flight uniform with his arms behind his back. They both looked pretty serious.

Jake smiled when he realized who was on Ben's other side. His Uncle Augie, wife Kay, and their daughter Lily had made it!

"What's going on?" he side-whispered to Randi.

"Navy helicopter from the West Coast. They're looking for your dad," she whispered back.

He stepped forward, wanting to hear what was being said. The older man was talking, the one who looked like a scientist.

". . . magnetosphere changed shape multiple times since Iceland failed last night. It's lost more than ninety percent of its strength in the last twenty-four hours, and so far, it is not recovering. When we checked the recordings, we found pulse activity through the Earth for over an hour before the Azores Archipelago, and then the rift let go. It is too coincidental that the pulses you described happen, and all this catastrophic activity occurs immediately afterward."

Frank intercepted the look Ben exchanged with Augie. He pulled Ben's attention back, and held it with fire in his gaze as he continued to talk.

"Whatever those pulses are, they had some effect on the planet's inner core. That impacted the magnetosphere negatively. As bad as that would be any time, it is worse today. If this was last year, it might be different because the solar activity last year was historically low. But this year, we've seen a big rise in activity from the sun. In terms of solar storms, the last dozen years have been volatile. In the last few months, we've had multiple massive solar flares and potent ionizing cosmic rays hit the barrier. We both know the sun's normal energy is enough to cause havoc here on Earth if that barrier is not shielding the planet, let alone any combination of factors that have a multiplying effect."

"The rate of decay could increase exponentially." Ben looked past them across the field at the setting sun. "Ozone holes are already starting."

"But that's not all?"

Ben looked back at Frank and shook his head slowly. "No, that's not all. Frank, somehow—and I haven't had time to work through it—too much cosmic radiation and solar particles are slipping through the magnetosphere. That energy is heating the atmosphere. I can't explain how it is happening, but the model is projecting severe disruption in the climate models, maybe catastrophic results if this cycle continues. The poles reversed this morning at 7:43 AM CST. But since then, *the poles have flipped three more times!*"

Frank stared at him. "Will they flip again?"

"I don't know. We have never postulated this as a possibility. But at some point, they need to reverse back to their original hemispheres and stay there. Until they do, I think we will see some adverse climate reactions."

"Ben, President Tanner's team contacted the Navy to get Lieutenant Mitchell—," he indicated the young man in flight fatigues,

"—and this helicopter to fly you to Cheyanne Mountain Complex. They need your data and you out there right away."

Ben started to protest. His brother stepped up, and Jake pushed forward, also complaining.

"No. Stop." Frank held up his hands, waiting for them to quiet. They stopped, though Jake grumbled a little.

"We need help, Ben." Frank's face was lined, and the exhaustion he felt was evident. "Millions are dead . . ." he choked for a moment. ". . . including my wife. If the government is going to try to save the people that are left, we need information. With your model, you are among the few scientists left alive with relevant data that might save lives. I know you better than this. You will not let all those people down, no matter how you were treated in the past."

"Ben, the goal was to get everyone here for safety, not have anyone take off." Augie pulled on his arm. "And I just got here. But this is what we've seen from just the quakes and the tsunamis. This is worse than we ever could have anticipated."

"I know. Give us a minute," he told Frank, pulling his brother and son to the side.

"I need to go. The model is growing; the algorithms are spinning up links between factors and figures, which yesterday I would have said did not correlate. Some of the outcomes the model is suggesting are catastrophic—even worse than we've already seen. MAC is making leaps, and I don't understand. There are intricate layers here, and I need experts in other fields to keep up. I don't know what I can give them, but maybe we can work with their techs and figure out what's going on for all of us." He took a deep breath. "Augie, you know MAC almost as well as I do. I can't take MAC or the quantum computer with me. I need you to be my technological go-between here. Jake, that leaves you managing the property with the women until I return."

"I brought some help," Augie said. "Dave over there by the truck is our pilot. I told him we could make a place for him, at least for now. With Florida covered in ocean, he agreed. He's a good guy who could help while you're gone."

Jake exhaled. "Are you sure about this? How are you going to get back here?"

"I'll figure it out. More importantly, how are we going to communicate? I sent everything Max developed with Will so he and his team could remain in touch. If I find something, or Augie does, I sure as hell want us on the same page."

Lieutenant Mitchell was able to help with that. He handed Jake a silicone terminal, all black and glass.

"This technology is amazing. It is called Laser Communications—invisible infrared lasers. It's faster than radio frequency, more secure, and cheaper, too. We used to have a lot of problems with direct-line-of-sight requirements and operational distance, but the guys in the lab worked all that out. Now, we can transmit huge packets of data at unprecedented speeds. If Dr. Stone needs to reach you, he won't have any trouble if you have this receiver."

While Ben collected his laptop from the house, he gave Augie and Jake a quick tutorial on the handset. Ten minutes later, they were flying away.

Randi took the girls, Kay and Lily, into the house. Jake sighed and then walked with Augie over to the weird-looking truck. "Jake Stone," he said, extending his hand in greeting. He received a firm shake in return.

"Dave Skinner. Where is your brother headed?"

Augie rolled his eyes. "Cheyenne Mountain Complex. Presidential request. It looks like this mess isn't over yet."

Dave's gray eyebrows popped up like two caterpillars. "More earthquakes?"

"I don't know. My brother was working on answers before the military showed up. I told you about his model."

"Yeah, sounds like science fiction, but whatever. It got me out of Port St. John before the island pulled an Atlantis and disappeared underwater."

Jake showed Dave the laser phone. "This is more science fiction. This is some kind of Star Wars communication. When my dad figures out what's happening, he is supposed to call us on this."

They all studied the device, and then Jake shrugged.

"I don't know how long he'll be gone, but I could use some help. Augie will be working on the computers and communicating with my dad. In the meantime, I haven't had a chance to check the stove in the house, so I thought we could make some burgers on the grill. At least for tonight."

Dave was already nodding. "We better check the connections."

Cheyenne Mountain Complex: 7 p.m. MST, 8 p.m. CST

"Tell us where you've discovered so far, Dr. Stone." Men and women of assorted ages filled the room, all dressed in military fatigues, waiting attentively.

Ben couldn't help but compare this to the last time he tried to share his model at the USGS Think Room. From the quirking on Franks's forehead, he figured they both remembered the same thing. Frank gave him a hard look, and he knew his friend was warning him not to refer to Titan International by name. They didn't need all of this to get back to President Tanner yet.

"You are aware that the poles have shifted multiple times today?"

Ben's question received affirmatives, and while a few looked scared, others seemed uninterested. One young man spoke up impatiently. "The earthquakes and tsunamis weren't the results of pole shifts, Dr. Stone."

"Well, that is not entirely true, Corporal." He ignored the disdainful twist of the military scientist's thin lips; glad the man's service training kept him from arguing further.

"Give me a few minutes to explain. I'm going to give you the background first. Five years ago, I wondered how likely a break on the San Andreas fault might be. I wondered if I could predict something like that." The group grew restless, murmuring at his words. Ben nodded, understanding.

"I get it, but as a geologist, predicting earthquakes is the Holy Grail of seismology. I had the time, and I wanted to try. So, I ran multiple simulations. The more I contextualized the data, the more I added to the analytics. It got pretty big, and the data soon overwhelmed my basic computing ability, which led me to search for better equipment. I never found a way to predict earthquakes, but something else happened. While I was pursuing my goal, I chanced on a young man, a genius, really, who held data about a potential catastrophe so large it would impact every man, woman, and child on this planet. I started looking into his claim, and one day soon after, I realized this risk was real."

Nobody said anything. Maybe all the death and destruction in the last twenty-four hours bought him some credibility.

He plowed forward, hoping to keep them interested. "This person was an employee of a large corporation in the United States. During his employment, he was assigned the job of creating the software for a machine capable of mutating pressure and heat waves that could be shot through the planet like William Tell shooting an arrow through an apple. I know what you are thinking." He held up a hand to stop all the unbelieving comments coming his way.

"It's not impossible. Not only was it possible, but they built it. They call it a Mantle Cannon. The first test run was overnight. You have already seen the results. They aimed it at Iceland, hoping to break the mantle under the landmass and release some magma. I doubt they intended to destroy the island, but that's what happened. Instead of being horrified by the loss of life and designating the whole thing a failure, these people deemed the exercise a success."

"So, they turned up the power and tried it on another target. The Azores Archipelago was one more test. It probably seemed an acceptable loss out in the middle of nowhere, not very populous. Again, from their perspective, aside from the loss of life and a beautiful paradise wiped off the Earth, it was successful. The Azores Islands were destroyed. The cannon works. And there is no way for anyone to link it back to them. It is the perfect weapon."

"But this company didn't anticipate the pulses' overflow impact on the Mid-Atlantic Ridge. I don't understand why either, but I am guessing the ocean floor was already weakened along the rift. Those pulses cracked the mantle under the ridge like an opera singer hitting the right note and shattering crystal—not just one crystal flute in this demonstration, but thousands of them."

"How do you know this?" someone asked doubtfully. "How do you know what they're thinking? Do you know someone who is working there now?"

This was the part Ben was hoping to skim over. "So, that young man I mentioned, well, before he left this company's employment, he built a back door to their systems. And we've used it to keep tabs on this company ever since."

"Hacking?" Disapproving voices rose again. Ben held up both hands.

"Please. Let me finish the story. I think you'll agree that in this case the end justifies the means. I worked extensively with this young man over the last few years. Using artificial intelligence and quantum mechanics, he developed dozens of new techniques to prepare a model that would help us track the results of the damage caused by a potential Mantle Cannon. We were worried about unprecedented volcanic activity, possibly thousands of people affected."

"Why didn't he report this to someone before it was too late? Before there was damage?" an angry voice shouted out.

"We tried," Ben said simply. "I can't tell you how hard we tried, but no one believed us. And then, a few months ago, our AI postulated a new theory, and everything we researched said the new theory could become a reality. Our computations suggested that the mutated pressure and heat waves from the Mantle Cannon might actually slow down the movement of the outer core, reducing the magnetic field and causing a pole shift. And that is how we get to shifting poles. As you know, the planet's molten core dictates the magnetosphere's strength, the magnetic field that protects the planet from solar activity. The magnetic poles are thought to reverse every three hundred thousand years or so, and the process is believed to take centuries, if not longer. Current science tells us that the magnetic field would weaken dramatically during a reversal."

The group stared back at him. He was losing them, but this was so damn complex.

"So that was the research we started following. We couldn't stop the company from building a cannon. We couldn't get anyone to believe us. So, we needed to understand what could happen and what we could do to be ready. The idea was not to limit potential outcomes. If we could determine what happened during prior pole reversals, maybe we could prepare for this one. Using the structure of Earth's two magnetic poles, I reconstructed Earth's dipole moment for the last ten thousand years. I used the paleomagnetic data in sediments, lava, and artifacts to interpret geomagnetic field reconstructions. I had the most up-to-date archaeomagnetic data compilation and paleomagnetic directions from the sediment records, strategically selected based on data quality and geographic location. I just started digging with scalable patterns. And the model we created gave us a picture of what could happen if we experienced a pole shift.

"So far today, we've experienced pole shifts and their results. By studying those results, we can see that my model's outputs were accurate. But the Mantle Cannon is still out there, and my information suggests that everything that has happened so far was only a test. This would suggest it hasn't been at full strength yet. Well, testing is completed, and from the corporation's point of view, it was a success, with some minor unanticipated issues arising. As in, the planet was wounded, and you and I know we will pay the price of those wounds."

"Why would any company create a weapon to destroy the planet? That's insane; they have to live here, too. What company are you talking about?"

Ben spread his fingers wide and then clenched them again. "I can't tell you that right now. But you're right. It is insane. They intend to use the cannon to reorganize the political and financial power distributed worldwide into one bucket. By crushing our enemies, the United States becomes *the* world power. For some people, such an outcome would be worth the sacrifice of millions of lives."

He stopped and sighed. "But it gets worse. This company underestimated the abilities of the cannon. They were as surprised as anyone when it took out Iceland and the Mid-Atlantic Rift. But worse, they seem to have completely ignored the pulse's effects on the planet's core. It doesn't fit in their model, so they have disregarded the data. They intend to move forward with their plans. Maybe the only good news I have is that there are people out there working to stop a full-strength deployment of this weapon. Good people, dedicated people trying to stop this madness.

"While they are doing their part, I need other help from you. I hope you can help me run the data and analyze the fact that the poles have reversed not once today but three times. I don't know if this ever happened before in the planet's history. I don't know if my model can keep up with the impacts. I don't know if it is going to happen again—or, if it does happen again, what the outcomes will be. How much of this can the planet and the magnetosphere take? Just today's events have had cataclysmic results. What else is going to happen? This is what I am hoping we can work on together. Because even if the cannon is stopped and dismantled, we still have to live with the damage already incurred."

"I have millions of terabytes of data backing up everything I have shared. You are welcome to review everything; unfortunately, you don't have enough time to catch up. Events are moving too fast. Until this week, I thought all of this would play out over months or at least weeks. Not hours. You'll have to take all this at face value and move on to the next step."

He rushed on, ignoring the sour looks.

"The potential pole shifts are just the first problem; truthfully, there isn't much we can do about it except monitor and predict what's next. Even if you don't believe what I told you about the poles shifting, we have other problems. So far, the northern arm of the Mid-Atlantic Ridge has taken out a good chunk of the Atlantic basin. The way I see it, we've got twin issues from just that event alone. The first issue is the pyroclastic material pouring into the stratosphere. The model projects that, within less than two weeks, the ash, soot, and rock will circle the planet. There will surely be longer-term effects too. We can all agree that these products will spread to higher latitudes a few months from now, choking out even more of the sun. The volcanic dust veil created by such huge amounts of the planet will act as a solar radiation filter, lowering global temperatures in many areas for several years. In other locations, the temperatures will rise dramatically due to unprecedented amounts of radiation passing into our atmosphere.

"Our models are projecting a temperature decline of up to 10°C in the Northern Hemisphere. People are going to freeze. And it will take years to repair the electric grid," agreed a dour-looking technical sergeant seated closest to him.

"We aren't going to be able to grow enough food," added another sergeant, a slender woman with high cheekbones and slightly slanted eyes. "It could be years before we can coax up fields of wheat, barley, canola, rice, or soy again. Maybe potatoes can stand the cold temperatures. But we don't have anything near what we need to be planted. The livestock is going to have to be rationed. I have no idea what the activity in the ocean did to the fish stock, but maybe we can harvest algae and some other nutrients from the sea."

"That's all true, but it's still only the second problem," Ben said, taking back control of the conversation. "The third issue is the ocean itself. The oceans have shifted. They are still shifting. If my model is right, we aren't getting back most of the East Coast. That land off of the Appalachians is now the sea line." He pointed to the monitors circling the room, stabbing a finger as he called out the states. "Florida's underwater. The surges from the Atlantic rolled over most of Georgia, Alabama, Mississippi, and Louisiana and took a big bite of Texas. The Gulf of Mexico is gone; now it's just clear blue ocean."

"We don't know that water won't recede," someone called out.

"True. However, part of the projections included much of that land destabilizing and the sudden sinking we saw during the earthquakes, so I am not very optimistic. But either way, right now we need to worry about the land and the people who survived. And now you are caught up, that's why I am here. We're seeing activity no one expected. We need to figure out what the results of this activity will be. We need to prepare people as much as possible. So, let's get started."

***

"Sir, are you able to take a call from Dror Hart?" Asked the aide assigned to assist him as he caught up with Tanner in the hallway.

"Yes, I am." Tanner grabbed the device and then looked around. "Where can I have a private conversation?"

"In here, sir." The young man led him to a small office and then left, shutting the door behind him.

"Dror, is this you? Where are you?" Tanner asked, heartily despite the circumstances.

"President Tanner, good to hear your voice," Hart was jovial. Both men were full of crap, but neither would ever admit it.

"Please, call me Ron. I told you before." They both laughed, but Tanner got serious fast.

"My people are telling me that today's global events might have originated with Titan International. What do you think about that?"

"Ron, let me explain what you have to gain before we start discussing blame. And if you don't see this as the best opportunity for making America great again, then I am prepared for any feedback you have for me."

"Fair enough, but this better be good. The loss of the East Coast is no small prospect."

Hart chuckled, hiding his unease. "Sometimes we must pay a big price to get what we want. What if I told you that by the time the sun rises tomorrow, I could completely solve your problems with China? No more economic PRC bull, no more disregard for human or religious rights, and not a peep out of Beijing for the foreseeable future. We kick China back to the stone age tonight. I could make that happen, Ron."

Dead silence answered him. Hart knew how to play this game. He waited, letting the possibilities and repercussions run through Tanner's brain.

"And what would you get in return?" Tanner asked finally, his tone cautious.

"I already had a deal in place with General Wolfe over at DARPA. Unfortunately, the side-effects of our testing have taken him out of the playing field. I'd like you to honor his end of the agreement. Keep in mind, Ron, Beijing is watching everything we do. If they perceive any weakness, well, we both know they'll be across the Pacific and moving in before we can do or say anything. And America was hit hard today."

He didn't mention that it was Titan International that had hit it. He figured Tanner understood the score and was looking for the strongest position.

"Other countries were hit today also. We could wait and see what China does."

"We could, Ron. But everything is in place right now. I can't say that will be the case even a few days from now. With all these earthquakes and tsunamis, everyone is at risk. Worst case, America is left exposed. Beijing will never pass up an opportunity like that."

"How do I know America won't get hit on the West Coast? After all, you didn't foresee the damage in the Atlantic happening and look at New York City. I loved that city."

"I know. That was . . . regrettable. If we could have foreseen all eventualities, we would have done everything in our power to change the outcome. But wielding the cannon is like using a bulldozer to move a golf ball. It gets the job done, but there can be some unintended side-effects. Don't dwell on New York, Mr. President."

Tanner noted the sales job and how Hart switched back to his honorific title.

"New York is gone, but we can rebuild. Well, we can rebuild if we don't let Beijing get in the way. If left to them, they'll build great cities on American soil, but we'll all be subservient to another Mao Zedong. I don't know about you, but I don't want to become a communist after we fix the few things that went wrong."

"You're pretty glib about the destruction of the East Coast, but let's say you are right. Titan International will be a pariah when it gets out what caused this mess."

Well, sir, I would like to spin the story in a direction that benefits us all. The American people don't always have to know exactly how things happened. The victors have written some of the best parts of history. This could be one of those times."

"You've thought out everything, haven't you?" Tanner's tone was sardonic, but he wasn't pushing back. Hart thought he was beginning to glimpse a gleam of hope.

"Sir, I just want to help make America great again, and the way to do that is to eliminate Beijing. After that, we can talk about whatever next steps you'd be interested in. After all, the Middle East and Canada are still in the game. Maybe the world doesn't need them either." Hart's laugh was unctuous. Tanner couldn't help but think about the possibilities.

"Ok, you got a deal, Hart. But I don't want any more impacts on America. Keep all the damage on the other side of the world, do you understand?"

"Perfectly, sir. I will be in touch as soon as the run is complete."

Tanner hung up and stared at the wall. This could be a win–win. First, get rid of China, then pin everything on Dror Hart and Titan International. He'd be a hero who didn't have to deal with Beijing anymore. With all the damage and rebuilding, maybe he could postpone any general elections for a long time. Perhaps he could be president for life. He chuckled at the thought. There was always a way to win.

***

Dror Hart watched Victor Newsom through partially closed eyes. Seven years ago, when the Titan CEO offered Victor Newsom the CFO job, he had run a thorough background check on the little weasel. He had been made fully aware of Victor's lack of morals and greed. But Victor got things done, and he didn't let ethics or principles get in his way.

Dror needed this project completed, and he was under no illusions about the laws that would need to be broken, the money that would need to change hands, and, most importantly, the lack of regard for any negative outcomes that would have to happen.

In other words, people were going to die, and he didn't need a bleeding heart on his hands. Victor was aloof and detached at best. His predominant trait of being utterly indifferent to anything that didn't further his goals made him ideal for this project. Dror also needed a fall guy if he was going to come out of this squeaky clean. That was the real reason he hired the man as CFO.

Money and even power weren't enough for Dror Hart. He understood long ago that only absolute power would give him what he craved. His intense desire to control had motivated him for as long as he could remember. When he fortuitously came across Otto Brecken's research, he knew he finally had a tool that could make him endlessly wealthy and the most formidable man alive. All he had to do was ride Victor Newsom long enough to get the cannons built, placed, and activated. Then he'd collect.

Dror Hart was careful to maintain his ethical persona. Nobody would have trouble believing Victor had pulled this off under his nose.

After that, history had plenty of examples of little weasels who had accidents and were no more.

Chapter Eleven

Southwest Argentina: 11:45 p.m. local, 8:45 p.m. CST

"Ladies and Gentlemen, we are approaching Comandante Espora Airport in Bahia Blanca, Argentina. We should be landing in about fifteen minutes. Conditions remain clear despite the activity in the Atlantic. As always, thank you for flying Southern Airlines." The pilot signed off with a click.

Max struggled to contain his anxiety, ready to disembark at the pilot's announcement. But years of being hunted left him cautious. He had spent the flight reviewing the specs of the Airbus 300 and was ready to disembark most unconventionally through the cargo hold. He counted on the air hosts to be busy with deplaning and not tracking every individual. He'd see how well that worked in a few minutes.

As the plane dropped onto the tarmac, he caught sight of the terminal through his window, a two-story building with a lot of glass in the front. His spidey-senses tingling, he tried to make out the details of the people he could see, but it was too far away. Well, he already had a plan. He wasn't taking chances.

Backpack settled on his slim form; he edged to the rear of the plane once they came to a stop. No one paid him any attention in all the chaos to get off. The door to the cargo bay was latched but not locked. He was through in seconds and down the ladder. Tight quarters led to the storage area, and he waited nervously until he heard the doors clunk open. Moving fast, he crossed the small space, grazing bags and boxes, through the door and down the ladder before the ramp agents realized he was there.

"Hey! Détente!" Spanish voices hollered after him, but he didn't stop. The trick was to get lost in the people and vehicles, but quickly, he could see the problem with his plan. At midnight, there were few of either on the runway. Luckily, he was a fast runner. Sprinting across the deck, staying in the shadows as much as possible, he slid into a dirty alcove partially filled with pallet scraps and crouched under a big hunk of wood. This was one of those times his meager wardrobe came in handy, he reflected as he hid his face under his hood. The black hoodie, dark jeans, and pitch-colored sneakers were ideal for kneeling concealed in the darkness.

It was several minutes before he felt safe enough to stick his head out. The air was heavy with jet fuel, and there was almost no wind. Humidity was not as bad as he expected. No one was around. The ramp guys had gone back to the plane. Can't keep the other passengers waiting on their luggage, he congratulated himself. He moved out, careful to stay in the gloomiest areas, especially as he approached the terminal. He had no intention of entering the building. He just wanted to get close enough to circle around to the front.

He was starting to think there was no one looking for him and that his paranoia had gotten the best of him again when he saw several men loitering in front of the terminal. They moved with purpose, communicating with hand gestures. Suspicious bulges ruined the lines of their cheap clothes. The biggest one spoke into a cell phone. Max couldn't hear what he was saying, but he looked pissed. If these guys had been here for him, they would have been angry when he hadn't exited the plane with the rest of the passengers. He crouched in the bushes and watched.

"Do you think it would be smart to escape now before they catch wind of you?" The whisper behind him made him jump, causing the bushes to rustle. Will grabbed his arm and held him still while they waited to see if anyone noticed. Their luck held; none of the hard-looking men were facing their way.

"You scared me," Max whispered furiously.

"Come on."

They moved slowly and carefully out the backside, using the foliage as cover. Will led him out of sight to the Ford Ranger parked a half mile away. Max sighed in relief once they were clear.

"Your luck won't hold forever, especially with stunts like that."

Max scowled. "I thought I did pretty good until you snuck up behind me and scared the crap out of me."

"What if it had been one of them sneaking up behind you?"

"Well, it wasn't. And if you really found their building, we can take out the Mantle Cannon tonight and end this. I have the virus." He tapped his backpack harder than necessary, so Will knew he had been more scared than he would admit.

"I found it. It's about two hours from here. An hour and a half drive and then maybe a thirty-minute hike to the facility. But as far as this being the end . . ." he shook his head slowly. "I saw what happened in the Atlantic today. Even if we stop them before they run a full pulse at 100%, is it already too late?"

Max sighed and stared out the window. "It's too late for a lot of people. I spent a year in New York and Washington, D.C. trying to get someone to listen until Titan sent so many goons I could hardly move around. I left for Florida. Now they are all underwater—including all the people who wouldn't listen, probably."

"The eruption in the Atlantic sounds pretty bad. Can we recover from those two test pulses?"

"I don't know. But the chances have to be better than if Newsom gets off a shot at their real target."

"Beijing, China. That's why you knew the facility would be around here somewhere. This place is the point on the planet directly opposite Beijing."

"Yes," Max agreed. "Titan spent big bucks for decent encryption of their systems, especially after I left, but they were no match for MAC. He got in and figured out DARPA's first target and their whole wish list."

"I've been in many places the United States government would like to see wiped off the map. I wouldn't have expected Beijing, China, to top the list." He turned hard onto the gravel. The lanes got worse from here, and this morning's earthquake activity hadn't helped. Clumps of broken vegetation and clods of dirt made the road rough driving.

"It turns out that the political party in Beijing has been a critical threat for years. It just took the average American decades to figure that out. People used to believe it was Russia, but Russia doesn't have anything like the economic power China wields."

"It's always about money." Will's cynicism darkened his tone.

"I wouldn't have guessed China either. But having the facility built here pretty much confirms it."

"And if Beijing is destroyed?"

"I don't know politically, but another twenty-two million people live in the range of this Mantle Cannon. I couldn't get anyone to believe me on the last two. I tried for years before I met Ben. And all of us together couldn't stop what happened to Iceland or the Azores Archipelago, not to mention all the coastal communities that were wiped out today by the 'oops' activity in the North Atlantic. Millions and millions of people and children . . ." His voice choked. "I won't be able to live with myself if we don't stop them and make them pay. Whatever it takes."

They both fell silent, busy with their thoughts as they continued through the night.

***

Figuring he wouldn't find a better spot to park in the dark than the one he left this morning, Will pulled off the path and drove over to the ceibo tree. He worked the SUV back under cover and made sure it couldn't be seen unless you were standing right next to it. He used a broken branch to wipe their tire tracks away. The ground looked like it had gone through a grinder after the earthquake, with many bushes and trees uprooted and toppled. It was doubtful anyone would notice the faint tire tracks in the hardpan, but he'd rather be safe than sorry. He also strewed broken branches and leaves around, just in case.

Will was dressed all in black, matching what he guessed the mercenaries would think of as a security uniform. Five men had paced the hewn path around the facility when he was there this morning, all more or less indistinguishable in tight caps of onyx bristles over deeply tanned scalps, dark tees tucked into jeans, and blackened boots.

He pulled out tan dress pants and a nondescript beige shirt and handed them to Max.

"Why do I have to wear these?" Max's hair, the color of a raven's wing, fell over his face as he looked down. He could really use a trim to help him pass as an employee, but they didn't have time now.

"You need to sit at the workstations to gain access to the software. All the scientists are dressed like that." Will pointed to the clothes.

135

Max gave a long-suffering sigh but went around the truck and changed quickly. When he returned, they both pulled on their backpacks, and Will ensured he had his weapons and the explosives set and ready. Crickets sang through the night, reassuring the ex-ranger they were alone. The insects would shut down immediately if anyone were moving through the forest. Nature's best security alarm. Though he knew the answer, he asked the question that was bothering him anyway.

"Are you sure we can't just blow the place up like Murph and Blake are doing with the ships?"

"Nope, I told you, MAC and I think this is the last cannon. But if they have my software, there's always a chance they can copy it and carry it to wherever they build a new cannon. I need to destroy it at the core. The virus I wrote," he smiled grimly. "They won't be able to do anything. They'll never see it coming. As a bonus, my program will piggyback on any signal emanating from this place, using their feed to dump their database into every live computer system in the world. Then, everyone will have the proof needed to make them pay."

"Okay. We'll do it your way. The place is guarded, and they are armed to the teeth. But Max, this is pure risk. Hart and Newsom may be in that building. If one of them sees you, well . . . They left *Titan Two* early this morning. Murph saw them fly out. There's a good chance they came here. Here, take this."

He handed Max a Glock 17. Max's face wrinkled, and he gingerly held the gun by its handle. "I thought you would do the shooting, and I would do the hacking."

Will suppressed a sigh of frustration. "Max, this is not a joke. These people will kill you just as soon as look at you. If something happens to me, that gun will be all that stands between you and a painful demise. By the time the sun comes up, this will all be over one way or the other. I'd like at least one of us to walk away from it."

"Okay, okay," Max slipped the gun in his backpack. "Don't get shot, Will," he added soberly. "I need you."

"Likewise. I am not a computer geek and have no idea how to hack into their system. You need to be ready to take care of that."

"I just need a few minutes to cable in and start the virus. It will load in less than three minutes. After it loads, we need about thirty minutes to let it run and send. Then, you can blow the whole building off of the continent, hopefully, with Hart and Newsom inside."

"Three minutes once we are in is a long time, let alone thirty minutes. Let's hope it goes that easily." In Will's world, military operations rarely went according to plan. As if to prove him true, vibrations suddenly rippled under his feet. He jumped, assuming another earthquake.

They recognized the difference right away. This wasn't an angry Earth, shaking and breaking everything in its reach. This was a pulse with a definite pattern, and they looked at each other, anger and fear across both faces.

"They started the cannon," blurted out Max.

"Come on," Will said, pulling him south. "We might still be able to mitigate this if we get there fast."

***

The closer they got to the building, the more powerful the vibrations became. Max was nauseous from fear at what they were about to try—or perhaps because the ground reverberated like a tuning fork. He wasn't sure which, and Will did not give him time to dwell on it. They knelt in the undergrowth, heads together. He tried to focus on what the ex-Army Ranger was saying, but the armed mercenaries pacing around the building kept distracting him.

"There's only one door that isn't covered by cameras. I found it last night—probably an error, but it's a lucky one in our favor. We can get to it without being picked up by the security system, but you have to stay close to me and walk in my footsteps. I picked the lock last night and got in. It opens into one of the rooms they use for storage. A rack was up against it, but I shifted it enough for us to slide through. The storage room opens into a long hallway. There's a big glassed-in chamber about one hundred paces from the storage space. This is the room where they built the cannon, which is sitting in the middle of the area, and multiple workstations circle the perimeter. If we can get you to one of them, you can access the system and upload the virus. Stay low and quiet, and hopefully, no one will notice you. What are the repercussions of uploading the virus while the cannon is operational?"

"I don't know." Max's teeth chattered. He realized he was sweating, and it wasn't hot. He was scared.

"Well, it would be good to know if it was going to blow up or something, but I guess we'll play it by ear. I am going to be setting my explosives while you work. I am giving them a forty-minute timer. We need to be out in thirty-five minutes if we want to survive, so work fast." He looked at Max's white face. "Don't worry, genius, you got this. It will be fine."

Max appreciated the support, but he didn't feel any more confident. He followed Will through the trees, each step pulsing back at him. Only the heat of his rage at Titan International kept his feet moving.

***

Darkness filled the storage room. Will shaded a flashlight with his hand after pulling Max into the small place's center. It smelled like machines and oil in here.

"Thirty-five minutes, we have to be out of here. If I don't get back to you, don't wait. Head back here and get out to the forest. Understand?"

Max nodded. Outside, he had just wanted to get inside and out of sight. But now that he was in Titan's building, his stomach knotted with tension. The walls and floor vibrated every ten seconds, with each pulse of the cannon.

"Leave your backpack here. It would look conspicuous to walk around with it. Just carry your laptop. Put any adaptors you need in your pockets. We have to get this right the first time. Slide the gun under your shirt and in your waistband." He helped Max get situated, then took a deep breath. "Ready?"

"Not even a little."

Will clapped him on the shoulder. "This is where we say 'HOOAH!' Just stay calm, one step at a time, and keep your eyes open."

Max lived his life in front of a computer, and he experienced life from the other side of the screen. It took everything he had to step out of the darkroom and into the lighted hallway. He kept his eyes on Will's back as they walked down the hall. They reached the glass in seconds, and Max got his first look at a completed Mantle Cannon.

It was enormous. Easily twelve feet tall, the machine's circumference was like that of a city bus. Painted bright red, a pumping chamber dwarfed the rest of the assembly, crude parts jumbled across the oppressive body. The whole thing gave off a weird cyberpunk feel, Max thought with a shudder.

Multiple tubes twisted around the base, some thick and some thinner, where they joined the chrome-plated hardware. A motor the size of a van ran hot, driving steam or smoke through the manifold outlets— he couldn't tell which. A group of men stood around it, talking rapidly and gestating. Others were at workspaces, presumably monitoring the monster.

Off to the right side stood Newsom and Hart. One looked bored, and the other looked pissed, and neither paid any attention when Will pulled open the door. Max hurried through, careful to look away. Will's big frame blocked most of Max's entrance, and he slipped around to the opposite side from the Titan executives. The pulsating cannon kept everyone focused in the middle of the room.

Will took note of the terminal Max chose and then left. He only needed a few minutes to set the explosives, but he wanted to get them out as quickly as possible.

Max also worked fast. He connected and started his download, keeping his head low and listening for trouble. All he could hear were the pulses of the cannon. Three minutes were up, and he activated the program from his screen. It flashed twice and narrowed to a pinpoint of light. That was the sign it was running. Now, he just needed thirty minutes to execute.

While the program ran, Max looked around. He could not see around the cannon but could hear conversation between pulses. A musty, sour smell layered the room. He wondered if the chemical odor was hazardous for those working in the big room. Newsom and Hart certainly wouldn't care. The desk felt damp under his fingers. He bet the ventilation in this facility left a lot to be desired—he assumed there was no OSHA or health department in Argentina. Then, a sudden glimpse of a dizzying perspective brought him up short. These were mass murderers; he reminded himself: workspace hygiene was presumably very low on their list of priorities.

The first part of the virus—the part to shut down the cannon—was up and running, yet the cannon kept pulsing. The second half of the code to capture Titan's criminal fingerprint and send it worldwide was still loading. Nothing was working fast enough. He stared anxiously at the monstrous device, wondering if it had run long enough to impact Beijing, China.

Beijing, China: 2 p.m. BST, 12 a.m. CST

Top members of the Chinese Communist Party and the National People's Congress met once a month in the Fujian Room in the Great Hall of the People, on the west of Tiananmen Square. The meeting started hours early this Wednesday, as no one had gone home since the day before.

Yesterday's strange global earthquakes prompted runaway paranoia among the few bureaucrats in this war council. The generals of the armed forces, who understood the costs of war, sat immobile in their seats. Their faces implacable, the soldiers watched the tide of sentiment among their political peers shift radically with each new piece of information. No one here believed the land and life losses over the last twenty-four hours were due to natural causes, and the unbelievable catastrophe of the Mid-Atlantic Ridge only confirmed their suspicions. But there was no proof that America or anyone else was attacking.

Frustrated with the lack of knowledge, General Yichen Zhi Peng growled softly. As the ranking officer among his comrades, he knew they waited for him to speak. He paused, allowing Minister of National Defense Guo Jun Hie, a senior party official but a bureaucrat with a cold heart, to finish his ranting.

"Too often, we have looked the other way from America's insults. It is obvious this activity is part of the West's strategic plan to take out the strongest nations, and they will be coming after us next." Zeal burned in his eyes, and Minister Hie was clearly ready to retaliate with all measures of force.

"Why do you say that?" Peng asked, his words clipped. "All the damage is on the other side of the planet. There has been no threat against the east at all."

Minister Hie shot to his feet, his face turning purple. "No other country received warnings either. Coastal Europe and Africa are decimated. Something must be done. The military needs to act now. *You* bury your head like an ostrich, waiting for your tail feathers to burn!"

His words challenged the group, stirring up agitation and hate. However, with decades of experience in military strategy and history, Peng understood how big of a step retaliation was. To strike at the United States was to be willing to start a conflict that would most certainly blossom into a world war. He did not have enough evidence to condemn his country to the misery that would inflict, at least not yet.

"The United States suffered heavy casualties and destruction as well," Peng reminded them.

General Secretary Chau Hu Liu stirred restlessly, silencing the others as he made his opinion known. "Minister Hie is correct. We cannot be sure that this is not some plot by the Americans and that we are next in their strategy. We have only heard from a few of our informants, who had no information. The rest have been silenced, whether by the Americans or some act of nature; we cannot know. To hear the other nations speak, this event is simply an unprecedented natural disaster. Our spying satellites and balloons corroborate the damage, but not the cause."

Wong Haoyu, Chairman of the Central Military Commission, waited a moment, his lips compressed. "Even if we believe this is in some way a threat from America, how can we respond without more information? A first strike needs a destination, and we cannot just spray the American continent with nuclear arms. The rest of the world would condemn us and side with the Americans. Even worse, we would not know if we had stopped the threat or missed it completely."

Minister Hiu sputtered angrily and launched into another diatribe about fearing the dragon. He slammed his hands forcefully on the table before him, his voice rising several octaves.

A small man with a narrow face sat at the other end of the table, staring out of the window. Speaking so softly that almost no one heard him, Lio Chaoxiang, the Chairperson of the NPC Standing Committee, said, "Do you feel that?"

Next to him, Comrade Hsu Zixin, concentrating on listening to Minister Hie, shot him a sideways glance, not understanding what his peer was referring to.

Abruptly, the room shivered.

Minister Hie desisted from his diatribe in mid-sentence, his last word ending in a gasp. His face was swollen with emotion and surprise. The others held their breath. For one long moment, silence hung in the air.

Outside the Great Hall of the People in Tiananmen Square, tourists and citizens alike walked through the sunshine in airy T-shirts, shorts, skirts, and sandals. July was always hot, but this afternoon seemed more stifling than usual. The main conversation and thrust of discussions were of the earthquakes and tsunamis destroying the Atlantic coastline. The screaming headlines were terrifying.

And then the ground shook ever so slightly. Hardly anyone noticed. A young teen in a white short-sleeved shirt and jeans recovered as his bicycle tire wobbled. Bringing the bike to a stop, Weng Xi pushed his black glasses back up his nose and frowned. Was that weird? Did the pavement move? He had heard the earthquake news reports from the west. Was that an earthquake tremor here in Beijing?

No one else seemed to notice. He waited several seconds more. Nothing happened.

Xi shrugged and started pedaling forward.

When the land moved again, he had just circled the Monument to the People's Heroes. This time, the vibration popped in a quick jerk, shooting a wide crack through the cement that split the stone halfway to the entrance. Xi's mouth dropped open in astonishment.

A rapid thought—there would be hell to pay for this, and then—all at once, hell really did break loose with a roar like an enraged dragon.

Strong tremors rattled the pavement. Citizens screamed and tried to run, but the walkway shattered like an eggshell and slumped as the ground sank away. He couldn't help anyone and watched, horrified, as folk dropped clean out of sight, swallowed in a gulp. Dust rose where the center of Tiananmen Square crumpled into a widening hole with no bottom. Panicked by the escalating threat, Xi backpedaled, trying to keep the bike upright and out of the growing mouth gnawing at the ground before him. He had barely touched the street when the Monument to the People's Heroes tipped dangerously forward, and then, with a crash, all ten stories of the obelisk fell out of sight. Aghast, he tried to scramble further away.

In the Fujian Room, chaos reigned. Some politicos ducked under the heavy table; others jumped to their feet only to be knocked to the ground by the jolts. Security burst into the room, guns raised as if the soldiers expected to find a crazed giant shaking the building. Glass shattered, cutting through the embossed shears and flying through the air like diminutive darts, burying themselves in exposed flesh.

Delicate pale-colored screens printed with ibises and flowering trees were hurled across the room to land in broken heaps. Heavy pots holding ancient bonsai banyans rolled across the floor, tearing the small trees out by their roots. Pictures smashed, and crystal chandeliers fell like bombs. The air heated fast as fissures split through the city, tearing buildings apart.

Waves of superhot gas, ash, and rock fragments rolled up and out of the cavity, consuming Tiananmen Square like the foul breath of some gargantuan prehistoric creature. Xi fled west on Chang'an Avenue, his bike skipping over the trembling road. The faults chased behind him as he pedaled as fast as his skinny legs had ever pumped. Whole slabs of concrete sheared in the tremors and folded away.

He gawked in awe and almost spilled as the Museum of the Chinese Revolution, the Ministry of National Security, and the Ministry of Textile Industry sank. The spaces they had occupied shimmered with boiling gas, and a sulfurous odor caused him to choke. Not knowing which direction to go, Xi concentrated on speed and dodging the running bodies, trying to escape the heat and destruction. Sweat poured off of him, powder and dirt streaking his skin. It was so hot that he grew dizzy and nauseous.

The mighty holes continued to grow as the vibrations ate away the stability, and now, as the ground underneath failed, the vast block-sized buildings, all glass, stucco, and brick, started to lean like they were melting. A train whistle screeched frantically off to his right. The Beijing

Railway Station buckled sideways, both train and building plunging into another hole. Cars and trucks were piling up on Jianguomen Avenue, their owners abandoning them and fleeing on foot. The congestion forced Xi to pedal slower, and he concentrated on his path ahead.

Shrieks of fear rose around him, and suddenly, he realized the screaming was in front of him and behind him. His glasses were streaked, and he struggled to see through the grime in the air. Wiping them rapidly on his dirty shirt, he cleared them enough to see what had inspired the cries. His heart nearly stopped when he saw where the shrieks were coming from. The emporium, packed with stores, clubs, and the post office, probably full of hundreds of people at this time of day, was free falling into another pit. This one was growing exponentially, eating yards by the second, and headed right towards him. Running out of options, Xi swung southwest, dodging the sinking Ancient Observatory and streaking across a broken Gloria Plaza.

He was breathing in great gasps now, his chest heaving with a lack of oxygen. His throat burned from the firestone and ash, and he blinked, trying to clear his sore eyes. The road was clearer here, as the still trembling ground had less to knock down, but he was coming up on the Dongbiamen River. He risked a look back and was instantly sorry.

Most of the familiar landscape was gone; in its place rose fires and smoke, but most terrible of all, Xi realized that the orange and red glow tinting the city came from magma—lots and lots of flowing, spilling, and spraying lava. For the first time, he thought about his family, fearing the reach of this monster.

His ma and ba and all his sisters and brothers were somewhere in the city behind him. He pulled up to the sloshing river and stopped, tears rolling down his dirty face. The dragon had destroyed Beijing, and as he watched the great holes still growing, he knew it was now devouring the remains.

Southwest Argentina: 4 a.m. local, 1 a.m. CST

Max rechecked his smartwatch. Thirty seconds had passed since the last time he had looked. Altogether, twenty-eight minutes since he had sat down. Still, the cannon pulsed. It sounded like a cross between an elephant bellowing and a car crash, setting his teeth on edge.

He wondered where Will was. Edgy with nerves and never good at sitting still, his slim form shifted in the cheap plastic seat, bending round to maybe see something on the other side. He dropped to the laminate flooring and crawled forward a few feet during the next pulse—finally, he saw some activity. Hart and Newsom were gesturing and talking loudly to each other.

Heads together over a tablet, one black and one gray, they were clearly pleased with what they were looking at. Noise suppressors covered their ears, and he wished he had thought to bring some. Even though they were yelling, he couldn't hear what they were saying. He contemplated moving closer when he realized the assistant, Cynthia Whatshername, was looking at him with wide eyes. He scrambled out of sight just in time to hear her start shouting something—he was pretty sure he knew what—as another pulse shook the room.

He reached the desk and jerked the laptop free, praying that the program was completed. There was no time to check. As he headed for the exit, hand outstretched, aware they could see him now several things happened simultaneously. The door swung open, framing Will, alarm darkening his face.

Guards started yelling behind him. He couldn't understand the words, but he tried to move faster. Then Newsom yelled his name. He'd recognize that angry voice anywhere; he'd certainly had to listen to it enough when he worked for Titan. A second later, a gun roared behind him. Something punched him hard in the lower back, propelling him into Will's arms. The pain was excruciating, and he stumbled, clinging to his laptop desperately.

Max saw stars, his world black at the edges. Will was shooting back, cursing, holding him up with one hand and firing with a big black gun in the other. The noise was incredible. Now, the group behind him was really screaming. There were more gunshots, but thankfully, he took no more hits.

A deafening, recorded voice cut through the babble, repeating its message in clipped tones. "This facility is in destruct mode. Please leave the building now."

Chaos, colors, and lights circled them as Will pulled him down the hall. Confused, he tried to speak up, sure they were going in the wrong direction. Will ignored him, and then they were through a door and outside, back in the night, running over concrete. Automatic weapons fire chewed through the dark. Something big loomed in front of them. Another door opened, and Will was shoving him onto a seat. He heard the door slam, and he had one more crazy thought, concerned about his blood-soaked clothes staining the fabric underneath him, and then he passed out cold. When the facility blew three minutes later, he missed the whole thing.

Finding a doctor in an Argentinian forest at night, while being chased by mercenaries, was about as easy as it sounds. Will was able to stem the bleeding from Max's gunshot wounds. Luckily, it was a through-and-through, entering in the lower right back and coming out on the right side. Always anticipating trouble, he carried first aid. He poured the antibiotic powder into the holes and packed them with field dressings. He hoped that nothing had been nicked because he couldn't do a thing about it if Max were bleeding internally. The hacker did not regain consciousness.

The darkness hid them while Will performed first aid. His only choice after that was to abandon the battered old truck he had stolen from the parking lot, using loose brush and branches to conceal it in the underbrush, and then pick his way through the night with Max over his shoulder.

He hiked until dawn. It wasn't much of a sunrise, he noted. The rosy glow of morning seemed muted today. He was not sure if it was his mood or the Earth vomiting up the mantle into the atmosphere that could impact the skies this far south, but he guessed it didn't matter. What mattered was finding medical help for Max.

Stopping to catch a breath, he laid Max down gently. Soft exhalations moved the kid's narrow lips, so he was alive at least. Will had a decent idea of where they were, but if he was right, they were basically in the middle of nowhere as far as finding help went.

He tried to get Max to drink a little, disappointed when the water ran down his chin. Max sure looked young, he thought. He didn't even have a shadow of whiskers. Rubbing his chin, Will felt the bristles. He was tired, hungry, and angry that Max got shot. He knew Ben was counting on him to keep Max alive, despite the kid's headstrong nature. He had to do something. He needed a plan.

He pulled a scanner out of his bag. Holding the square box first one way and then the other, he tried to identify any human-sized heat threats moving in his direction. The forest fairly shivered with motion, but everything was small, at least for the surrounding twenty-five miles. It looked like he'd lost Titan's hired guns in the chaos of their facility going up in flames.

He coughed and wiped his mouth. Next, he pulled out the satellite phone. The green bulb glowed brightly, so the encryption still held. He dialed Murph but got no answer. He tried Blake next.

"Encryption green, go," Blake said urgently.

Will prepared himself for the bad news.

"Encryption green, go. Report, Blake."

"Major, we took out *Titan One*. The ship is at the bottom of the ocean. We pulled all hands onto our ship before it went down."

"Good job. However, I hear a but in your voice."

"Yes sir, one of the, *ah,* survivors is the lead scientist, inventor, whatever of the Mantle Cannon. He is talking up a storm. Seems like after *Titan One* released the first pulse set, this guy realized that his new toy had some unintended side-effects besides blowing up Iceland. He tried to warn the bigwigs at Titan International not to run the second test until he could sort out the potential consequences, but no one was in the mood to listen. He says that just before their ship started taking on water, he had the medical staff in his cabin trying to slip him a mickey or something."

Will groaned. "Assholes. What were the unintended side-effects?"

"I'm not sure about all the scientific jargon, sir, but basically, the cannon slows the core of the planet, which impacts the magnetosphere. That's the field surrounding the planet, keeping all the space junk out, like radiation."

Will leaned back and exhaled. This sounded a lot like the conversations his brother Ben and Max used to have. His stomach twisted in fear. "I know what the magnetosphere is."

"Well, this doctor says the damage compounds every time they use the cannon. We sank their ship, so he didn't have any instruments to detect anything, but when we told him Titan had used a cannon twice in the last twelve hours, he nearly wet himself. He keeps babbling about the end of the world. The rest of the scientist types just seemed confused, and the few security guys aren't talking."

"Well, this is a freaking cluster." Will's eyes dropped to the motionless body of the one person who could give him an idea of what to do next. "What about Murph, did he take out *Titan Two*?"

"Yes, and they were able to do it without any casualties. A chopper will pick me up in the next fifteen mikes, and we'll grab Murph on the way back to Sydney. You have great friends, Major. I was able to work out a jet standing by on the runway, waiting to get us back home. We should be there tonight. Were you able to eliminate the cannon in Argentina?"

Will snorted and closed his eyes, wishing this would all go away. "Yes, but there's more bad news. A third ship, the *Titan Three*, anchored about six thousand clicks off of South America in the Pacific. It has an operational cannon, and it's aimed at the Middle East. I don't have any reason to believe Hart and Newsom aren't on their way out there right now."

"So, we still have a live cannon." Blake was silent for a minute, and then he continued soberly. "Major, if this doctor knows what he is talking about, the core may not be able to withstand another run. We might be on the precipice of a disaster we can't recover from."

"I hear you. I'm working on a plan right now. When you and Murph are together, call me back. I think we are going to need a two-pronged approach this time."

"So, we're not headed back to the States," Blake chuckled. "Well, Murph will be happy. He has been bored stateside since we retired."

"With everything that has happened over the last twenty-four hours, I don't think we will ever be bored again, no matter where we are."

"I hear you. No problems. We got your six. Tango Mike." The connection went dead.

Will hung his head. Now, he really needed a plan, and he was getting really tired of sitting in the dirt.

He had a few more cards he could play here. He had hoped not to use them, but it looked like he had no choice. He dialed, his plan taking shape. He was still in the game, but the costs were growing exponentially.

Chapter Twelve – Day Two

Holden, NE: 5 a.m. CST

Dave tucked his hands under his armpits to keep them warm while he waited for Jake to join him in the backyard. Lightning danced across the sky in the distance, the thin, bright strands winking in and out against the dark sky. He had not visited Nebraska before, but why was it so cold before dawn on a July morning? If this were a sample of Nebraska weather, he'd need more than a T-shirt. He'd have to ask one of the ladies.

He had been too tired to worry about anything last night, but now he thought about the clothes in his closet in his condo. It was not much, but his jean jacket, the three or four pairs of blue jeans, and a handful of T-shirts were all underwater now. He had left his old Chevy parked at the airport. Gone now. And everyone he knew, including his neighbors and his landlady, was dead. He thought about Mrs. Petroff. She had managed his building for the last ten years, and while they did not talk much, he liked her despite what a stickler she was about collecting the rent on the first day of the month. Well, that wasn't going to be a problem anymore.

He wanted to convince himself that some people survived, but in his mind's eye, he could see that churning, foaming avalanche of water engulfing everything familiar to him. The speed of those surges! The water buried the buildings in a single surge. No one would have had time to react, even with a warning. He shook his head mournfully.

Well, he still had his plane, and she was his most prized possession. He tied her up in one of the smaller empty hangars at the airport where they landed. He left a note explaining the situation, hoping that was enough, because that plane and these clothes were all he had left.

Jake came through the door before his thoughts could spiral further down. "Hey, here's a long-sleeved shirt. Probably too big for you, but it is chilly this morning."

"I noticed. Is this what mornings in Nebraska always feel like?" Dave pulled the shirt on. "Kansas City Chiefs?" he asked wryly, indicating the red helmet on the front.

Jake chuckled. "I left most of my clothes at home. I don't know when we will get back or what we'll find when we do. And no, this weather feels pretty unseasonable to me. I wonder if this is because of what happened or is a taste of future things."

Dave got serious. "You think we could have winter in July?"

"I don't know; my dad and uncle are the scientists here. But we should plan for the worst and hope for the best while waiting to hear from them. The first problem is to button this place up." Jake grabbed the broken back door and attempted to push it back into the jamb. "And we better figure something out for the animals, too. The barn is in rough shape."

The wind had picked up while they were talking, and a weak sun had pulled up over the horizon. Yesterday's dust swirled. He could still smell smoke in the air. Jake didn't want to say it out loud, but he was worried about the weather. He wished his dad would call.

Hendron, KY: 6 a.m. CST

Art peered out the broken kitchen window. He was glad to see the faint glow was from a reluctant sun rather than a fire. Soot clung to the frames, but he saw no live fires. Maybe they had burned out while it was dark. A chilly breeze pushed the curtains, causing him to shiver. He fingered the layer of grime across the counters and frowned. They had wiped the counters down last night, but ash had already piled up in just a few hours—the air stank of burn.

He had gotten a few hours of sleep early this morning but still felt exhausted. There had been so much traffic in and out of the sanctuary as refugees from the city and off the highway stopped for a safe place to hole up for the night. The number of those seeking shelter compared to last night had tripled by daybreak. They had gotten rowdier, too. It would get worse, with no food left and the water rationed sparingly.

Art turned as Pastor Don entered the hall doorway with a tired "Good morning."

"Good morning, Pastor. Is everything OK?" he asked, noticing the awkward angle at which the pastor held his arm.

"Please, call me Don. 'Pastor' is for church. I banged my arm in the earthquake yesterday. Just a bruise, but it's sore." He looked around the room while rubbing the ache. "Some of our visitors are asking about food. We finished what we had on hand in that meal you made last night, right?"

"Yes, everything was gone by midnight—down to the last cracker. I know that means the people who arrived after that have had nothing to eat. The water is going fast, too."

"People are scared. They're hungry, and they are getting restless. The big question is when will help get here."

"Or will help get here? There isn't much traffic on the highway. I'm thinking if rescue were coming from a bigger city, they would be here by now." Art shook his head. "We can try to get to a store. Do you know where the closest one is located?"

The clergyman nodded.

"There's a small neighborhood convenience store two blocks over." He lowered his chin and narrowed his eyes. He looked speculative and nervous, with his light-colored hair pulled to one side and the round glasses. "Art, this isn't the best neighborhood to walk around."

"Yes, I figured." They didn't need to say more. They both understood what he was trying to say.

Thirty minutes later, Art and three other volunteers were walking through the empty streets of Hendron. The air was saturated with smoke. An acrid odor wafted on a slight breeze, something putrid like sewage contaminating the morning. Deserted cars littered the fractured road. Signs from the earthquake were everywhere. Deep cracks ran up the walls of buildings, and flapping curtains filled broken windows. Bricks piled in the street, and signposts lay on their sides. Traffic lights were smashed on the pavement, and electric wires curled like dead, black snakes. Art tried to see if any people were peeking out of what was left of the structures, but he heard and saw nothing.

So, when two loud cracks of a rifle split the air further down the block, they all jumped in fear. Instinctively, Art crouched down, looking for something to hide behind. The derelict cars on the road seemed his best bet. He waved at the others to follow, and they ducked below the hood of the nearest one.

No one could see anything from here, so the four men crawled and slid up the street in single file, hiding behind one abandoned wreck at a time. He heard the rough talk before he saw the group of men speaking. Their voices were not reassuring. They didn't sound professional like the military or law enforcement. They sounded angry and impatient. Brutal orders were barked out, and the silence from whoever they were aimed at told its own story.

He stole a glance over the hood of a dusty Dodge Durango. The convenience store they were searching for was directly in front. A removals truck was parked off to the left. Multiple men clutching rifles stood outside. Other people were systematically emptying the store. Everyone looked frightened and rushed. A dead body lay on the sidewalk. The bright red blood splattered across it left no question where the gunshots had gone.

Art signaled his men back. Scrambling up the street and around the corner, they all sucked in air, panting from stress and exertion. None of them had guns, and Art wasn't willing to take chances with their lives.

"What are we going to do?" the biggest of his team asked. He was angry and sweating. Art thought the guy would like to return and pick a fight with those thugs despite the guns.

"Not that. Whoever those people are, they already shot one person this morning." He tried to speak calmly, but he was still shaking inside, the sight of the bloodied man seared in his mind's eye.

"We need guns," another of the men said, trying to sound harsh.

"We need food," the last one said softly. Art thought the guy sounded scared until he added, more loudly. "We're going to have to take it."

Stunned by the violence and having a hard time believing how fast society was deteriorating, Art shook his head slowly. "We don't have guns. Let's go back to the church and figure out another move. Do any of you have cars that are operational?"

Before anyone could answer, a peppering of shots snapped through the air. Art swung back towards the convenience store only to realize the shots weren't coming from that direction. The reports came from behind them. He rotated so fast that he nearly fell.

"They're coming from the church," the big guy cried out, and he took off in a run. Art stayed low, trying to run at a crouch and keep up with the others. Muted semi-automatic gunfire filled the air as they got closer. It was coming from inside the church. Even muffled, the noise was terrifying.

The oversized double doors burst open, and people started pouring out, running in all directions. Some were screaming, and others fled in silent panic. Their skin was sallow, their mouths gaped in shock, and broad, fearful eyes dominated their faces. Parents held children or pulled them along, trying to shield them as they ran. No one looked back. Art pushed his way inside, trying to find Marta under pressure from people fleeing. He banged through the nave, intent on reaching the door to the sanctuary, when a hand snatched his elbow, yanking him hard.

He jerked away, then stopped when he realized it was Ed refusing to let go. "No, no, come with me," the young man hissed.

"Marta," he started to say, but Ed pulled him harder, almost off balance. "She's back here," Ed whispered loudly. "Come with me."

Someone opened fire at the front of the church by the altar. It took a moment for Art to realize they weren't shooting at him, and he took the chance to duck away after Ed.

They slid down a dark hallway through a passage Art didn't recognize and then pushed open another solid-core antique door. It felt like it weighed fifty pounds, only the oiled iron hinges allowing it to glide open easily without creaking. His stomach was doing summersaults, so he took a tentative step into the room. Shadows and the weight of a hefty space slithered over his face until Ed snapped on the flashlight he had given him the night before, covering most of the radiance with his hand. The walls caught the glow, reflecting the white light at them. Art realized there were mirrors everywhere.

Nervously, Ed used his body to push the door shut behind them. Marta and the pastor stood in the center of the room, terror twisting their faces. They had clutched at each other when the door burst open. Then Marta cried out in relief when she saw Art and ran to him.

"Marta!" Art grabbed her, and they held each other for a minute. He could feel her trembling.

"What happened?" he asked Pastor Don and Ed over her head.

"One of the groups that came in early this morning pulled out guns." The pastor rubbed his arm, distracted. "Others tried to take the guns away. People were shot. Some ran. I think some are dead." Lines of sorrow creased his face.

"When the shooting started, I pulled Marta out of there and put her in here. Then I went back and got Pastor Don, too," Ed told him triumphantly. "I put your bags in here last night, too. I liked this room; no one else was using it."

"It's used for wedding parties." To explain, he waved at all the mirrors lining the walls. The pastor took off his glasses and wiped them on his sleeve.

"Guns in the sanctuary. It's terrible. The situation is deteriorating faster than I thought it would."

"They were rifles," Ed observed dispassionately. "AR-15s, a Colt M4 Carbine, and a Ruger AR-556. Bullets from these types of guns travel three times as fast as ammunition from a handgun. They are quite dangerous."

All three of them stared at him. Ed blinked, then smiled at their surprise. "I know things. I am smart, too." He patted the flashlight for emphasis.

Don shook his head, took a deep breath, and then another before putting the glasses back on. "Not now," he said. He looked Art right in the eye. "You need to get out of here. Here, take these." He handed Art a key chain.

Art looked at the silver keys and then back at the pastor.

"Marta told me last night you are trying to get to your brother's place in Nebraska. Those are the keys to my car. I don't need it. This is my church, and I am staying here."

He held up a hand as Art and Marta started to protest. "This is my home. I am not going anywhere. If you are worried about the car, you can bring it back one day. I'll be here."

"You don't have any food or water; there are crazy people in your sanctuary with guns! And anyway, if there are injured people, I should be the one to go back in there," Marta insisted.

"No, you shouldn't!" Ed looked alarmed.

"No way," Art jumped in firmly.

"No. I'll do what I can for the injured. Most of the people ran out when the shooting started. It will be all right. I know what I am doing. But there is one thing: take Ed with you." Don pushed Ed in their direction.

"I think you need me here," Ed said doubtfully, resisting the push.

"I've got this handled. It will be easier without having to worry about you. Besides, they need you. Go with them, Ed." He threw Art a beseeching look.

"I think both you and Ed should come with us," Art said. "But Ed, I could use your help. Please come." It was his turn to pull on Ed's arm.

Reluctantly, Ed nodded.

They grabbed the bags from the floor and pulled an unenthusiastic Ed behind them down the hall and out through the back. They could hear shouting and arguing coming from the direction of the sanctuary, but no more gunshots. The back parking lot was empty of people. Pastor Don showed them his older model minivan and motioned them to hurry.

"Thank you, Pastor," Marta said as she hugged him firmly.

"God bless," he whispered and disappeared back through the door.

Art said a prayer for the pastor as they pulled away.

Cheyenne Mountain Complex: 5 a.m. MST, 6 a.m. CST

Ben stared at the monitors. The videos looped between satellites, each of the views more terrifying than the last. Beijing, China, the center of a 3000-year-old civilization, was destroyed. No matter how hard he tried, he could not identify one manufactured artifact. Fissures miles long split a burnt Earth, and lava fountains sprayed hundreds of feet into the air. Darkness permeated the skies and rolled in gouts of smoke over the landscape. The false night was lit only by burning embers and running molten rock. It looked like Hell. He shivered at the sight.

The magma body under Beijing must have been tremendous. The scientists here were reporting a crater circumference of eight thousand miles impacted by what they were referring to as an unknown super volcano. No one had guessed the amount of molten rock under the city, but Ben knew better. The risk had been minimal until last night.

Desperately tired, Ben had stolen a few hours of sleep after midnight in one of the guest billets, only to wake to more bad news. He rubbed his face, thinking about Will and Max. There had been no word yet from either of them, and with the events in Beijing, his chest tightened, and a band of stress made it hard to breathe.

Trying to focus, he bent over the keyboard, syncing the areas he wanted to focus on. Augie had sent more data from MAC, and the team here loaded this most current data as soon as it came in.

It was time to run the model and see the projections. While he waited for the results, he ran a simulation. First, he pulled up the historical magnetic map viewer MAC had created previously. It tracked the northern dipole's shifts across Canada, more than six hundred and eighty miles during the twentieth century. During the 1970's, the rate of motion accelerated from five miles to thirty-two miles per year. In his simulation, you could see the rate of movement increase as the pole wandered over the screen toward Siberia. Now, he added the new data from the movements of the last forty hours.

The North Magnetic Pole skittered suddenly at the minute of the first reversal. Ben's mouth dropped open as he watched. The counter clocked it at fifty miles an hour! First southwest towards Greenland, and then jerking hard north, on the mark of the second reversal. The last recorded reversal sent the pole due west towards Norway. His data showed no slowdown in the dipole. It was still moving at fifty miles per hour. He could hardly believe what he was seeing.

"Dr. Stone, can you look at this?" Distracted, he looked up at the master sergeant holding a sheaf of computer printouts. The woman had almond-shaped dark eyes and a black cap of hair. He recognized her from the session earlier, where she had talked about the food that might be available if the planet cooled off. Her smooth face was set in professional lines as she waited for him to answer.

"Sure," he said. Trying to stand, he tripped, and immediately felt foolish.

She did not even notice. She spread the sheets on his desk with precise motions, then indicated specific markings. "The South Magnetic Pole is in flux as well. The south dipole moved at each of the reversals. It looks like both dipoles moved in the same pattern and the same distance. The South Pole is also continuing to move, which gives more relevance to your theory that this event is not done. See this here." She pointed to the numbers running down the side. "Something is causing them to coordinate."

She leaned past him and started typing on the keyboard at the next workstation. "Something else you need to see. These are temperature variations worldwide. Two days ago." She pointed to the first column. "Yesterdays. And today. The planet is down two degrees overall in forty-eight hours."

"That's impossible." She watched his emotions play out, and the stress lines deepened around his eyes.

"And here it is happening. Some of it can be blamed on the activity in the North Atlantic and maybe out of China. As we discussed earlier, there'll be repercussions from all the material forced out of the mantle. But this is too soon and too much."

"I wonder," he sat down abruptly and pulled the keyboard over. He continued speaking while he typed. "Before your people picked me up, I worked with MAC to figure out this new data. In one of the sets, MAC found a large expansion of cosmic radiation and solar particles passing through the magnetosphere on the other side of the planet. We have spent years worrying about the ozone layer leaking into space, but I think we had the problem backward. Yes, the ozone layer is under attack from the sun; how much of an attack, I don't know, but after seeing your temperature data, I agree that the numbers are critical. However, we might not be around long enough to worry about losing the ozone. The amount of solar particles leaking into our atmosphere may be a larger problem."

She pulled up another chair and sat down at the empty workstation. "May I have access to your model?"

He faltered at her directness, but under the circumstances they faced, he recognized the foolishness of his hesitation. "Of course, Master Sergeant."

"Why don't you call me Min. It will be easier for both of us."

"Okay, but call me Ben."

She nodded briskly and then accessed his data, pulling up the grid of numbers and letters changing so fast it was impossible to read them. Ben showed her how to engage alternate searches while the model ran the main query. While they worked, he wondered how much she knew about this place.

He blurted out his question before shyness could stop him. "Min, how many people can this place hold?"

She glanced over at him. "Generally, around five hundred troops and scientists are working here. It depends on what is going on. But you could double that with some planning and keep everyone fed and hydrated for over a year. Why? Did you want to move in?"

Ben laughed uneasily. "No, I have a place to go. But there are so many people at risk right now. I wondered if President Tanner would bring some in here."

She snorted, surprising Ben with the unprofessional sound. "President Tanner only worries about President Tanner. I doubt he has even thought about sharing his shelter. But don't worry, Col. Stanel is a good guy. He takes care of his people. Right after the quake hit, when we realized how much trouble the country was in, he ordered the soldiers and scientists stationed here to bring their families in. We're at capacity."

"Is your family here?"

"I have no family. I've spent my formative years in the military. A spouse would have been neglected, and my parents have passed." She stopped typing and laid her hands on her lap. Ben noticed how long her slender fingers were. Now, I feel pretty lucky I had no one to lose."

He nodded in understanding. He thought about his parents and Mary. He was suddenly glad they weren't suffering through this.

They needed to help as many people as possible, and foreknowledge could do that. Ben had an idea where to start to find the answers they needed. As he worked, he hoped his suspicions about how bad things could get were wrong.

The laboratory Ben and Min worked in was on the bottom floor of the three levels. Just below them sat the giant coils designed to dampen the Earth's sudden motions. Further back, a tunnel led to underground reservoirs carved from solid rock, which were created to store drinking and cooling water. A spring uncovered during construction had been channeled to ensure fresh water.

From the perspective of the earthquake twenty-four hours ago, damage to the facility was minimal. Engineers had verified the stability of the mountain's internal structure through the night, and the reports were positive so far.

It was what they couldn't see that threatened them.

Deep in the Earth, a gaseous river of sulfur dioxide fed by the churning belly of the Dotsero Volcano, the only active volcano in Colorado, flowed deep beneath the mountains. Mixed with magma, it produced magnesium and high levels of carbon dioxide, and minor cracks in the crust allowed the gas to leak southeast of the crater, penetrating along a natural lateral fault under the mountains. Around one hundred years ago, the fault hit a granite wall and began to pool in a cavity. Less than a quarter mile from the western slope of the Cheyenne Mountain Complex and buried deep, no one knew it was there. With only rare earthquakes to change the topography and little activity from the Dotsero Volcano, the lake of gas and liquid would have stayed underground indefinitely.

Until yesterday's tectonic event.

The enormous granite barrier sheared in a mighty fissure during one particularly severe jolt. The ground above it heaved higher than the massive evergreens covering the hill, slumping back and unrooting every one of the giant trees. The billions of tons of stone, trees, and soil sealed off any escape up for the gas, but the vast spasms continued, slicing a new fault forward through the rock, allowing the gaseous river to roll under Cheyenne Mountain.

As the last of the big quakes vibrated the mountain, a crack pierced the rock shell through one of the reservoir walls carved to store water. Over the next few hours, the crack split up and down like spider lines on a cracked windshield and widened.

The reservoirs were monitored daily using a strict routine. However, with so many areas to check after the quake, no one had ventured this far back of the facility after the initial earthquake damage inspection. The usual bright lights illuminating the cavern were out, and the much dimmer backup lights were on emergency generators until electricity from Colorado Springs could be re-established. The two harried engineers didn't notice the new fractures in the shadows of the back wall, and they didn't kneel close to the water where they could have smelled the pungent and suffocating odor resting on the lake's surface. After a cursory exam, they rushed out to complete their checklists in other parts of the facility.

Malodorous fumes continued to belch through the fracture from floor to ceiling of the cave. Most of it poured into the pool of water, turning the liquid into sulfuric acid. But gradually, the air became saturated as well. You couldn't see it, but a veil of death filled the shaft from top to bottom.

Several hours later, the lake had turned acidic.

Near the center pooled a white and dark slick of shiny plastic on the water. The edges bubbled and fell away, sinking into the liquid. A plastic dime store duck had floated on this lake for years, reportedly left by maintenance divers looking for a way to orient themselves while underwater. If anyone had been paying attention, the absence of the duck would have strongly indicated trouble. In another hour, it had dissolved completely.

Chicago, IL: 7 a.m. CST

Josh Stone stood on the street, staring at the crumpled remains of the pricey condominium under renovation until yesterday. He and his partner Del paid just over three hundred thousand for the mid-unit Greystone condo. It was a crazy big bet for them, and they were so close. Just a few weeks from complete rehabilitation before the earthquake struck. He should probably feel better that it wasn't just them; neighboring buildings on West Briar Place had also been reduced to heaps of stone. Or feel worse for the hundreds of people trapped or killed by the debris across the city. But he was numb. All he could see was the disaster in front of him.

All of their plans and money sat in this pile of rubble. Sure, they had two other jobs in the works. Del was checking on those now. But it didn't matter because this was where he had bet their future. The ground trembled under his feet. A hard bump and then stopped. Another aftershock. Damn, how he hated the ground moving. And the wind was cold off of Lake Michigan today, he thought dismally.

"Josh." He turned to see Sam Raffa standing behind him.

"I expected you," Josh said grimly.

"Just want to be sure. You still owe the money."

"It's right there," Josh said, gesturing sardonically at the ruined building.

"This is how it works when you borrow outside the banks. You take on all the risk. Now, you need to make it work."

The first time Josh met Sam, he found him charming and sincere. What an idiot he was. Now, he felt the iron fist beneath the velvet glove.

"Just wanted to be sure you understand. Cash is always preferable. But if you can't work it out in the next few days, I have alternative methods for you to pay me off. Until you do, I own you." Sam placed his hat back on, carefully covering his tight curls. His expensive suit was the only thing not ruffled or ruined on this street.

"It turns out I have a little problem, too. A time-sensitive problem, you might say. Let me know when you are available. But don't keep me waiting." The jerk walked off, treading carefully so as not to dirty his fancy shoes.

Josh stared at the ground, angry and despairing. Why had he ever taken the loan? He knew the risk. But in a few more weeks, they could have completed the job, sold the condo, and finally been financially solvent. Sure, insurance would pay eventually, but Sam would not wait that long.

Sam didn't have the deep pockets of the Mafia behind him. He was using his inheritance to bankroll his very own loan agency. No credit checks, but high-interest rates and a very short lending period. He used his contacts through his family's real estate business to target willing marks like Josh and Del. Once indebted; there was no out until it was paid. And for those who fell behind? Well, he had since found out that Sam outsourced for wet work as needed.

He thought about his dad's phone calls urging them to go to Nebraska. Leaving Chicago would set Sam off faster than anything else. The loan shark would come after his money even with the quake damage blocking the roads. He couldn't bring that trouble down on his family. He had to stay until he worked this out.

He started walking. The L Train was back up and running between here and his place on Oak—one minor stroke of luck. Already, the city had people out trying to clear the streets, but it would be a while before you could drive any distance. A breeze caught him between buildings, and he shivered. It was pretty chilly for July, he thought, and he forgot the observation as fast as it crossed his mind. Crowded out by all the other trouble jostling for space in his head.

Chapter Thirteen

Southwest Argentina: 10 a.m. local, 7 a.m. CST

Hours later, Will stood in a fern gulley beside a small pond. The subtle beauty of the area was complemented by the light breeze moving the grasses with a gentle touch. Behind him, a small thatched house sat beside the dirt road. Matte-painted ATVs cooled off, with the four dark machines parked behind tall evergreens on the side, each fitted with exhaust silencers. Even the normal plinking sounds from cooling metal were absent. All he could hear were the dragonflies and bees zipping around. Will had been impressed with the stealth of the three-wheelers that had pulled them out of the forest, but he expected nothing less than top-grade equipment from the man he called for help.

The peacefulness around him contrasted sharply with what was going on in the rest of the world. He had spent the last forty minutes reviewing the news on his satellite tablet. The Atlantic Rift continued to spew Earth into the sky. Thousands of miles of shadows and death covered an area the size of a continent. He was no scientist, but he understood that just this one catastrophe was enough to cripple the world for decades. Unfortunately, there was more. Iceland was basically just *gone*. And coastal ports around the Atlantic had vanished under a displaced ocean, showing no signs of returning to where it came from.

The estimated number of dead was staggering. Unbelievably, America had seemingly lost the whole East Coast to multiple surges, and the current had not retreated. The earthquake he had ridden through yesterday slammed North America in a complex pattern, dismantling the big cities and destroying infrastructure in its wake.

The most heart-rending piece of news came out of Beijing. Despite their efforts, he and Max were too late, and the Chinese mega city suffered a horrible fate as a result. Beijing and the surrounding countryside were destroyed in lava and ash. The videos looked like the surface of a volcanic moon, gray and stark, with nothing moving except streams of molten rock. Millions more lost. He cursed himself for not stopping the cannon sooner. Clenching his fists, he paced and waited for some news on Max.

"You're looking stressed, mi amigo." An olive-skinned tank walked out the door with a big white smile. Dressed in camouflage pants and a white tee, Will still saw the soldier he had served with for five years. Lt. Marco Cruz was one of his most reliable men until he lost a leg in a firefight in Iraq. Will was glad to see that he had adapted well in retirement. He couldn't tell which of the limbs was a prosthetic from the soldier's gait.

"How's my friend? Are there any updates?" Will couldn't suppress his anxiety.

Marco's wife, Ana, had been a nurse in the States. When they moved to Argentina after Marco left the Rangers, she became the de facto doctor for many rural families outside the city needing care. When they arrived this morning, she was ready and waiting. Max's stretcher was quickly transferred to the house.

"Ana said you did a good job in the field. It went through and out, but it looked like only the meat was hit, nothing major. There is no sign of infection yet, and the lady sleeps normally. Ana says she will wake up soon." He stopped talking when he realized Will was staring oddly at him. 'What's wrong?'

"Why are you calling Max a lady?"

"After she cleaned and dressed the wound, Ana changed your friend's soiled clothes. She said the patient we brought in was a lady."

Will's mouth dropped open. "Max is a girl?"

Marco laughed, a resounding booming echo. "You didn't know? That is priceless! I knew you didn't have time for many women all these years, but I thought you could tell the girls from the boys." He clapped his friend on the shoulder and motioned towards the wooden bench. "Sit down, amigo. Ana does not need us underfoot while she tends to your friend. Tell me more about what brings you to the bottom of the world. I was surprised to get your call."

"I tried not to involve you," Will admitted. "But you were my wild card."

"I've been called worse. You said this has to do with yesterday's disasters?" Marco's smile slipped for the first time, and he looked worried.

"Titan International, you've heard of them?"

"Yes, an environmental company; something about geothermal heat or something?" His forehead wrinkled, the creases disappearing under his close-cut black hair.

"Yeah," Will scoffed. "Environmental as in destroying environments. They are responsible for Iceland and the rest of the damage in the Atlantic."

Marco's dark eyes widened. "They blew up Iceland?! I thought it was volcanoes?"

Will shook his head in disgust. "This is the craziest story. They created some kind of ground cannon. You point it at the ground and send mutated pulses through the Earth. It was supposed to target a few volcanoes, have them erupt, and take out the surrounding area. It worked too well with Iceland. Now, no more Iceland."

"What are mutated pulses?"

"Beats me. When Max wakes up, we can ask him—or her, I guess."

Marco looked at him sideways. "How did you get involved with this? You left the Rangers."

Will blew out a breath and rubbed his head. He was tired. "Through my brother. He and the *person* you have in your house are whistle-blowers. No one took them seriously, so I got involved, and here we are. We're a rogue unit. Neither the military nor the government is working with us, at least not from the point of view of stopping Titan. I don't know how much they even understand after yesterday."

"When you called, you said you took out Titan's installation south of here. It's on the news that terrorists bombed someplace out in the jungle. I am guessing that was you?" Marco avoided his gaze, staring out over the pond. He sat motionless, a mountain of strength.

"Yep. That's where Max was shot. I abandoned our first ride and ditched the one I stole; too few roads and too many mercs chasing us. Then I hiked to where you picked us up. If it had just been Max and me, I would have worked it out, but the way things always go, I stumbled over intel that reset the ballgame during the op. These clowns went old school, using paper instead of keeping everything digital, trying to keep their plans from being hacked. It backfired for them in a big way this time."

He pulled a wad of wrinkled paper out of his backpack. "I found this in the control room while setting the self-destruct. I stopped to read it. In hindsight, I should have waited; maybe Max wouldn't have put himself in the line of fire. Too much time working with professionals, not used to babysitting hotheaded kids." He shook his head. "Then this morning, Blake updated with mission creep."

He paused, hating to drag his friend into this mess but knowing he had no choice.

Marco straightened, giving him the look he remembered from missions they had shared when the outcome was less than assured— pretty much every mission they went on, on reflection. "Tell me."

"There were three cannons. Murph took out one in the Tasmin Sea, Blake took out the second off Antarctica overnight, and I took down the third in the jungle. Except, according to these papers, that isn't everything."

Marco groaned. "Let me guess, there's another cannon."

"Yep, nobody is as industrious as the bad guys. It's in the Pacific, a prototype off the coast of Chile, about three thousand klicks from here as the crow flies. Another ship-built cannon. And that's not the worst of it." Will held Marco's gaze as the ex-soldier braced for the coming blow. "Blake pulled the guy who designed these cannons off the ship they sank. The doctor had a sudden rush of conscience because, in his zeal to create and use his big weapon, he used poor judgment and unleashed it on the core of the planet, where the damage it is doing caused a reaction that would probably kill every person left alive on Mother Earth. He believes the damage is exponentiated every time the cannon is used. He claims they must be stopped before the fourth cannon can be fired up, or we—as in every life form on the planet—will pay the ultimate price."

Marco exhaled deeply. He understood the stakes. Hell, these were the stakes he was familiar with. He looked back at the house and pictured Ana working inside. He turned back to Will. "What do we need to do?"

"These papers give us the current coordinates of *Titan Three*. I called in some old favors to get a small jet waiting for us at the airport. It will get us out to the Pacific. I've been working with Admiral Maddocks on the side. He still owed us for that op in Venezuela a few years ago, where we pulled his son out of that POW camp. I don't know how much he believed about Titan International, but he pays his debts. I told him the whole story. He arranged a sub to meet the two of us, Murph and Blake. Luckily, it's within twelve hours of these coordinates if they hit the gas. We'll take down that ship with a torpedo before they can power that cannon up and try again."

Marco cocked his head and then flexed his arms, muscles popping. "Okay, as long as it isn't harder than that op we pulled in Yemen. That was some crazy times. I'm in. We're, we're going to need some equipment. I know a guy who can help. He has some great stuff."

Titan Three, Pacific Ocean, off coastal Chile: 10 a.m. local, 8 a.m. CST

Even after a few hours of sleep, his eyes still felt like sandpaper when he blinked. Not that you could really sleep while flying in a helicopter. In the first seat behind the co-pilot, Newsom sat directly across from Hart. Newsom rubbed his face fretfully and tried to listen to Hart's side of the conversation with the president.

"Thank you, Mr. President. I am glad we were able to deliver. I think it will be quite some time before China sorts out its mess and becomes a problem again. Yes, I agree, the loss of life is regrettable, but you can't make an omelet without breaking a few eggs." He rolled his eyes at Newsom. "Well, let's collect payment for this go-round, and then we can discuss other, *ah*, areas of opportunity."

He dropped the phone on the counter with little regard for breakage. "He wants to see what we can do with the Middle East or Korea."

"I knew he'd see things our way. I figured the Middle East would be next after China. That's why I sent *Titan Three* to its antipode a few weeks ago. We'll be onsite in ten hours or so." Newsom's satisfaction gleamed through his toothy smile.

"Yes, well, we only have this one cannon left on this side of the planet, thanks to the incompetence of your security team."

Newsom frowned at the dig but didn't argue back because, actually, the situation was worse than Hart was aware. Somehow, both

Titan One and *Titan Two* had sunk overnight. He didn't believe in coincidences, so that left sabotage.

The security teams on both ships claimed the cannons had somehow damaged the hulls. He knew that was bullshit. Partially because the facility last night was attacked in mid-pulse and partially because that worthless little whistleblower they couldn't catch up with ran out of the building just before the self-destruct blew. It all felt connected. Well, he fixed that problem and grinned, thinking about the feeling of the gun firing in his hand.

And even better, if the kid wasn't dead, he had finally hired someone to finish the job. That had been his mistake in the past: he wasted time employing security to stop the leak. This time, he went pro and hired an assassin with a stellar reputation. Lobo Gris would get the job done. The killer had already started looking for the little traitor today.

"Everything is set up; the cannon is aimed, and we just need to flip the switch. We don't even have to be there," he said instead.

"Let's get paid for China first," Hart grimaced. "I don't trust the president any more than I trusted that general. I'm not doing this for free. I want to know as soon as the money transfer is complete. And I don't want to hear crap about the banks being down. New York is done. I get it. Shit happens. Set up a new office on the West Coast and get the bank accounts fluid. That's the only way you and I will get paid."

Images from New York flickered through Newsom's thoughts. Pretty gruesome with all those bodies drifting around, banging into each other like that. He wondered if his wife saw the waves coming. He hoped so, enjoying the thought of her terror. Now, she could keep the house in Greenwich forever, a watery tomb fitting her haughty ass. His daughters might be gone, too. He hadn't given a thought to looking for them. Funny, he felt nothing when he assumed they were dead.

Newsom had also ignored Dr. Brecken's warning of a slowing core from the previous day. It didn't fit with sealing a deal through President Tanner, so he blew it off as if it never happened. Professionally, he knew better than to let facts get in the way of a good story. Just bend the story to make it what you need. This was why he was such a successful businessman.

As for the potential casualties in the sinking of *Titan One* and *Titan Two*, well, he couldn't worry about everything. You could always hire more help. As for Dr. Brecken, designer and builder of the weapon that would make Newsom millions, he assumed security would have taken care of the good doctor. They had all the specs and requirements in multiple locations. They didn't need Brecken anymore.

Hart shifted, uncomfortable in the vibrating seat. The helicopter was more than halfway to *Titan Three*. He knew the CEO had no family, girlfriend, or anyone he'd mourn today. No loyalties to anyone, and Newsom knew that better than most. All the big German cared about was lining his pockets. Newsom returned his attention to his boss as Hart started speaking.

"I want you to pull a team together as soon as possible. We're going to need a place to build more of these cannons. Now that we are on a roll, we might as well rebuild the planet so America stays strong. It's a good selling point." Hart stared at the water below, then turned back to his subordinate. "Let me know as soon as the money is transferred."

Newsom nodded and leaned back so Hart could not see him. A scoff twisted his mouth. There'd come a time when he didn't have to take orders from Hart either. He could wait. The key was to be ready.

Cheyenne Mountain Complex: 8 a.m. MST, 9 a.m. CST

Tanner brooded in his quarters. The room was okay, but it wasn't like his room in the White House. Of course, the White House was a trash heap now, and underwater to boot. That was a mark against Titan.

He was going to have to be careful here. There was a way to win in this situation, but with all the unknowns, it would be easy to misstep. Already, some scientist, geologist, whatever had pointed the finger at Titan. It wouldn't go away just because these executives wanted to be the ones to write history.

Damn Dror Hart! You would think he could keep his business private. Well, Tanner wasn't going down as the president who colluded with the guy who took out New York City. But the offer to kick the Middle East back to dust was tempting. Too many problems with those guys. They couldn't get along with each other or work with entrepreneurs like Tanner. Too fanatical, constantly worrying about other stuff like religious disputes, savage retaliation, and archaic traditions.

Suffice it to say he was delighted with the Beijing outcome. He had pulled a sorrowful face and made all the obligatory remarks about being so sad, too bad, but inside, he was as gleeful as a kid at Christmas. That jerk Hu Liu, China's most recent political leader, was a real piece of work. With any luck, he was at ground zero when the ground gave way, and he'd not have to deal with the little yellow creep again.

Being president would be much easier if he could say the same about the Middle East or Korea. He sighed. Why did everything have to be so complicated?

He thought about the money Hart was waiting for. Tanner wasn't in any rush to pay. Not because he wouldn't pay, but it wouldn't hurt Hart to wait for it. As a businessman, Tanner knew how to keep partners on the hook. Reel them in slowly; don't give them big expectations. Hart would get his money when Tanner was ready to fork it over.

As president, he should be spending his time worrying about conditions in the United States. Between the damaged infrastructure and misplaced citizens, it was a hell of a mess. But Stanely's team was all over it. He'd get an update soon. He thought about Beijing again and rubbed his hands together. It was worth every penny.

Southwest Argentina: 12 p.m. local, 9 a.m. CST

"Not too long. She needs to rest." Ana smiled at him as she partially shut the door, and Will knew Marcus to be a lucky man. The room was small and whitewashed; a window in the corner and a twin bed took up much of the space. The slight figure on the bed didn't move, dark lashes down over pale cheeks.

"I know you are awake, Max." Will tried not to sound accusing but figured he had failed.

Max's eyes popped open, and the mouth he was familiar with twisted in a scowl. "Fine. What do you want?"

"We need to talk. I need to update you and get your advice. But first, what the hell? Why did you let Ben and everyone think you were a man?"

She wouldn't look at him, just stared at the wall. "It's none of your business. I appreciate you getting medical help for me and helping me stop Titan, but that's all we have to discuss."

"Fine." Will was pissed, but he tried to move past it, knowing what was at stake. "But we didn't stop Titan."

She jerked and tried to sit up.

"Whoa, lay down; Ana doesn't want you to start bleeding again." He pushed her back on the pillow and sat next to her. She was strung like a piano wire, radiating tension.

"What do you mean, is the cannon still running? Did my program finish running?" Her words tumbled out, and then she stopped short. Her dark eyes got big, and a crease formed across her forehead. "We didn't blow up the facility?"

"No, just stop talking. I'm going to catch you up. I couldn't keep us away from those mercs and get you help, too. So, I called a friend who evacuated us from the forest. Ana, his wife, is treating you. We're off the beaten path here in a pretty rural area, about fifty miles due north from Titan's property. I don't think they can find us. You ran the program last night. I don't know if it completed running. You came running through the door and got yourself shot before you could say anything. But the pulse kept pounding until we blew the place, about five or ten minutes after you were hurt. That stopped the cannon, but . . ." he looked away, not wanting to see her face when he told her. "We were too late. Beijing, China was decimated. It doesn't exist anymore."

She gasped and went rigid as a board.

"It gets worse. Max, they have another cannon. They had four cannons, not three, as we assumed. There's another one in the Pacific on a ship, *Titan Three*, over three thousand miles from here. Hart and Newsom probably headed there last night after the evacuation alarms were triggered. We didn't stop them. It's a fully functioning cannon, which means they probably copied the software from the cannon here and loaded it long before we got here with the virus."

Her expression was stricken. "I need my laptop."

A few minutes later, he was back with it. He helped her arrange it on the side of the bed and move it so she could see the screen. As weak as she was, her fingers flew over the keys.

"Fifteen percent battery. Lucky it didn't die." Her voice was hoarse. "The virus uploaded, but it failed to shut down the cannon. You stopped the cannon in the forest only because you blew it up. Newsom has been one step ahead of us all along."

"There's more," Will told her quietly. "You and Ben were right. The cannons damaged the rotation mechanism of the Earth's center, and each use dragged the core slower. Another shot could stop it altogether. We have to take out that last cannon."

"Ben . . ." she started to ask, but he was already shaking his head.

"We lost your backpack in the explosion. I still have my sat phone but can't raise the States. Too much debris in the air must be blocking the satellite signal, or it may have been damaged last night. I'll leave you my phone, and hopefully, you can figure out a way to fix communications and talk to them back home."

Her eyes hooded, and with stiff lips, she said, "Leave me?"

"I have to go after *Titan Three*, Max. You know I do. And you are in no condition to come along."

"How do you know where *Titan Three* is?" she asked.

She took the sheaf of paper he held out to her. "I picked this up last night from their control room. It has the coordinates for *Titan Three*. I am leaving this with you in case some intel in there can help."

"You can't go by yourself," she said, giving him an indecipherable look. Then she stared at the floor, her hair falling over her face.

"He's not," The door had opened while they talked, and a big man filled the frame, muscles bulging from his arms and shoulders. He winked when she looked up, and Max involuntarily shrank back a little.

"I'm going to keep him company. He might get in trouble by himself." He gave Will a look. "I reached that guy I know. He is going to set us up."

"Good," Will pointed at Marco. "My friend, Lt. Marco Cruz, retired. He is going to help me shut down Titan once and for all. Max, we are leaving in fifteen minutes. I need you to walk us through anything you can think of that might help. We're only going to get one chance at this. We have to destroy that cannon before they turn it on."

St. Louis, IL: 10 a.m. CST

Art and Ed stood on the embankment of the Mississippi River as the mud squished around their shoes. Images of death and desolation floated downstream. Between the trees, poles, boards, and trash-shaped junk, eddies swirled fragments of buildings, roofs, and bits of broken everything. Bodies of bloated people and animals moved in the murky current. Here and there, clouds of flies darkened the air. The smell was awful. Ed turned away, tears in his eyes.

"The bridge is broken. We cannot drive across the bridge. All the bridges are broken. How will we get across the bridge?" Ed's flat statements rubbed him wrong, but Art bit back the words he wanted to say.

The Poplar Street Bridge collapsed during the earthquake yesterday. The railroad bridge to the south, Eads Bridge, and all the crossings as far north as they could see were also in the river. Shattered saplings, wrecked boats, and shards of unidentifiable debris bumped against the few stone and steel supports and girders poking above the water. A solid line of vehicles covered the road until it broke off abruptly and ended in the river.

Art imagined it looked much the same on the other side. Most stranded drivers had abandoned their cars and hiked back to town. A few determined souls camped overnight further up the hill on the plateau, trying to find a way across the river. With the bridges all mangled wrecks in the river, that looked like a tough ask.

"We got over the Ohio River. We'll get over this one, too," Art told him, trying to be patient. Ed didn't answer, but his doleful expression betrayed his lack of faith.

But when they reached the Ohio River, fortune was on their side. The bridge was twisted but not broken, and they could pick their way over to the other side. Avoiding most of downtown St. Louis, they drove through the suburbs to get here, trying to find a standing conduit along the river. But, like most of the other routes they had passed, Poplar Bridge wasn't operational: it wasn't just broken; it was gone.

"Look, the Gateway Arch didn't fall. It is still standing." Together, they studied the stainless-steel monument across the river.

174

Undamaged, as far as they could tell, the arch swept gracefully toward the sky. It was the perfect distraction to change Ed's mood.

Ed smiled. "The Gateway Arch is the tallest monument in the United States and the tallest arch in the world. It was designed by Eero Saarinen, an American-Finnish architect, and construction started in 1963. . ." Ed continued with his rote recitation of facts about the Arch, almost as if he were reading from a book.

"Ed," Art interrupted him as they climbed up the hill.

Ed stopped talking and walking as if they were connected. He turned to Art expectedly.

"Did you memorize the book on the Gateway Arch?"

Ed half frowned at him. "No, I read the book. I remember the words. Do you want to hear more?"

"Uh, sure. It's very interesting." They started climbing again, with Ed picking up the narration right where he left off. Since they were almost to the top of the hill, Art filed Ed's exceptional memory abilities away for now. He wondered what Marta would say when he told her about Ed's memory. It was like traveling with a library—which, come to think of it, was probably not a bad thing right now.

He half listened to Ed while he looked for her slender figure in all the litter. They found her sitting on one of the giant concrete blocks by the road. It would be blistering hot here along the river at noon on a typical day in July in St. Louis. Today, it felt pretty mild. The urban area behind them was still suffering fires if the great gouts of black smoke staining the sky were any indication. But the eastbound winds were taking most of the city smoke and heat with them, and the air here was relatively straightforward and breathable. Art decided to be grateful for small favors.

Marta held a toddler on her lap, letting him play with her fingers while she reassured the boy's mother sitting beside her. It was the most relaxed she had seen her in the last few days, and he was happy she had a moment to regroup.

"I always carry a small first aid kit. I'm glad I had it. Bobby's head will heal. The wound is clean, and those stitches will hold it." She told the woman. Art was reminded again why she was such a good doctor. People liked to talk to her.

The makeshift bandage from one of Art's shirts covered the wound while Bobby's curly brown hair fell over his forehead. His freckled face was relaxed, and there were no tears. He leaned against Marta contentedly.

"Thank you," Bobby's mother said, her cheeks dimpling. "When he fell and cut his head *after* that awful earthquake and the bridge falling, and everything else was all over, I just could not believe it. I knew he needed stitches, but where could we go?" She smiled tremulously. "Dr. Marta is like a fairy godmother, right Bob?"

"Yes," the little boy agreed.

"We need a fairy godmother to get us across the river. We cannot go around the river. It is too big. The Mississippi River is the second-longest river in North America. It flows two thousand three hundred and fifty miles from its source at Lake Itasca through the center of the continental United States to the Gulf of Mexico. That is too far to go around," Ed informed everyone.

"He's right," Art admitted. "And we won't find a way over any of these bridges. They're wrecked."

He heard the rocks crunch behind him as someone approached. "Maybe we can help." Art turned to face a rugged individual with the same taffy-colored hair and hazel eyes as Bobby, on a giant of a man.

"Daddy!" Bobby slipped out of Marta's arms and hopped over his father. He smiled and effortlessly swung the little boy up.

"Thank you for helping Bobby," he told Marta with a big smile. "Maybe we can return the favor."

He turned back to the river.

"See that barge?" He pointed a few hundred yards off the shore where several men stood. In front of them, sat a long, narrow boat with a flat bottom, half up on the bank and the rest in the river.

"It's seen some days, but it's seaworthy. It should be able to withstand the pummeling of all that crap in the river. We plan to load our trucks on it and push it to the other side."

"What are you going to push the barge with?" Art asked, bemused.

"That's the tricky part. See that outboard fishing board boat over there?"

Art looked, but the closest thing he could see to a boat big enough to push a barge was a partially swamped fishing dinghy. The whole front end was broken off and smashed into the mud. The back was hanging on by a few boards, bobbing in the shallows.

"You mean that wreck?"

"Yeah, it looks like that. But the outboard motor is in good shape. I'm a mechanic, and one of those other guys works on engines, too. We already got it started this morning. You're right, though; the boat is a loss. We will rig that motor onto something else we can use as a boat. We only need to push that barge across the Mississippi River. It doesn't have to last forever. Look, all those guys and me, we have to cross the river. We have family on the other side. I bet that river is not even a mile wide, and I am not staying here when where I want to go is less than a mile away. You've seen the state of that water. Swimming is not an option."

Art knew a good deal when he heard it. He held out a hand. "Art Stone. I appreciate you including us. This is our friend, Ed Wilson, and my girlfriend, Dr. Marta Jenson. How can I help?"

"Jack Mackey." Jack held out a big hand. "I'd like to leave my wife Angie and Bobby with your family while we work, if you don't mind."

"I can help. I know about the Mississippi River," Ed said instantly, worried about being left behind with the women and children. He moved closer to Art. He spoke fast. "On average, the Mississippi River along the St. Louis banks ranges from fifteen hundred feet to two thousand feet. The average depth is about nine to twelve feet, but the normal water level is approximately twenty feet in the center of the river channel. That can vary greatly depending on natural shoals and deep spots . . ."

"Thank you, Ed. We'd appreciate your help." Jack interrupted and clapped him on the back. If he noticed Ed's unusual verbal delivery, his expression did not indicate it.

"They can stay with me." Marta stood up and patted the cement block. "This area can be my base if anyone else needs medical attention."

"We have some blankets and stuff in our truck," Angie offered.

Jack handed a protesting Bobby to his mom, and the three men headed back down to the bank. They stopped at Jack's red truck long enough to pull out his tool chest. Ed reeled off everything he had read about the Mississippi River and barges as they picked their way down the slope. Obviously, he had read more than a few books on the subjects. It was going to be a long afternoon.

Chapter Fourteen

Moca, Dominican Republic: 10 a.m. local, 12 p.m. CST

Emilio Santos rarely left his hometown of Moca anymore. The trip was too hard, and really, everything he wanted was already here in his open balcony apartment. When there was a reason to leave, he sent his grandson Bendo. Two days ago, he received word of an urgently anticipated package waiting for him in the shoreside town of Gaspar Hernandez. Yesterday, Bendo had volunteered to drive the old truck down the mountain and pick it up.

Emilio wasn't a fool. He knew the attraction was the drive and seeing the senoritas on the beach. But he wanted the package, and Bendo was a good boy—most of the time. He had watched from his chair while Bendo combed his dark curls and straightened his collared shirt in front of the hall mirror.

"Eh, you look beautiful." Emilio waved, dismissing him. "How about my package?"

"On my way, abuelo," Bendo sang. He grabbed the keys. "I will be back tonight."

"It's a forty-minute drive—you could be back in two hours," Emilio pointed out.

"Yes, but I drive very carefully."

Knowing this to be accurate, Emilo let it go. Tonight would be soon enough for the package.

An hour after Bendo drove off, whistling and with a wave, an earthquake shook the valley. For the next thirty minutes, the valley trembled. That was a surprise; even though he was familiar with the island's movements, Emilio had never been through such a long quake. He assumed the culprit was the Enriquillo-Plantain Garden Fault to the south. He sighed as he stared in that direction. Things would be bad again in Haiti.

Despite the duration of the shaking, his apartment stood firm. Of course, they lost electricity. It was unreliable on good days. Things fell

179

over, some dishes broke, and the hall mirror Bendo had used fell and cracked, but overall, he came through it all right.

Only now, it was the next day, and still no Bendo or package. Emilio fretted and tried the mobile phone again. No answer.

He decided to go out and stand on the balcony to watch the street, hoping to see Bendo drive up. As he stood, it occurred to him that the room had darkened to a strange green color while he sat. The heat and hazy sun had disappeared. Weird shadows covered the balcony. But it was just noon, too early for a customary afternoon storm. Puzzled, he leaned on his cane as he stepped on the patio tiles.

An enormous lightning bolt unexpectedly ripped across the sky, thunder right on its heels. Half blinded, the flash so bright he felt his eyes burn; Emilio threw up an arm and fell back into the apartment against the wall. Without warning, wind gusts packed with dust howled through the wooden door, slamming it back into the wall. Above, electric bolts raged across a sprawling mass of black clouds, their light shocking.

Panting, Emilio stood inside the door, defying the cold current of air blowing through. What a storm! It was all wind and lightning. Not a drop of rain hit the tiles. Unwilling to wrestle with the gale, he left the door open and limped over to the narrow window. The glass shook in its frame from each blow of heavy air. Outside, it looked more like night had fallen than the middle of the day. The town was gray, and he wondered if the few store-owned generators had cut out when he could see no artificial light. A purple-black sky illuminated by hundreds of bolts of electricity seethed with a power that unsettled his nerves. He had never seen anything like it.

Another enormous bolt slammed into the street, and the concrete exploded, flinging chunks one hundred feet away. Blinking through the spots in his eyes, Emilio watched in horror as a young man sprang from a parked car and sprinted toward the nearest building. A second mega strike of brilliance slammed into the runner as if he was targeted, and he exploded just like the concrete, blood and body parts splashing on the pavement. More mega bolts followed each shot, obliterating what it struck. Roofs, vehicles, street lights, trees, and even people and animals that could not get under cover in time were annihilated, steaming, wet chunks all that remained.

"No," Emilio wailed, fearing for himself, the town, and Bendo. Icy air swirled in the room, and sparks flickered madly. Lightning continued its assault on the buildings and the streets. Each strike flared as the explosion of energy released chaos, and still no rain. The ferocious wind tore at the structures and whipped dirt over everything.

"Abuelo!" Between rolls of thunder, he heard someone screaming. The hall door flew open, and his grandson fell into the room. He looked awful, covered in dirt and disheveled, dried blood and sweat smeared over his face. He crossed the room in a second, pulling the old man away from the shuddering glass, across the room, and into the bathroom without windows. The door resisted the wind's push, but Bendo got it closed, and he fell, chest-heaving, onto the floor. The roar of the wind cut down noticeably, though the storm continued to rage outside.

"Bendo," Emilio's voice shook as he leaned against the sink. "What happened? Is it from yesterday's earthquake?"

Bendo leaned back against the door and closed his eyes. He could feel the clatter as the wind continued unabated. "It's bad," he stuttered. "After the earthquake yesterday, a giant wave hit the shore. In the towns, all the people were washed away. Everyone is dead. Trees, buildings, resorts, everything is gone. Just mud miles from the shore."

"But how did you survive?" Emilio struggled with the words.

"I stopped to pick up friends by Las Lagunas. I was there when the earthquake started. I would have been at the beach if I had driven straight to Gaspar Hernandez. The tsunami would have caught me. I'd be dead, too. While we were driving, we heard some alerts on our cells, something about a massive underwater explosion in the Atlantic, but we didn't believe it. Stupid!" He went to smack his forehead and winced instead when he felt an extended, bleeding cut.

"We barely missed it; we saw a five-foot wave of water and garbage rushing toward us just before Joba Bridge."

"That's fifteen miles from the shore!" A massive blast of thunder punctuated Emilio's amazement. Bendo had to wait for the roar to subside before continuing.

"When it hit us, the truck was pushed off the road and smashed into a mahogany tree. We were caught under piles of broken junk and bent trees. Luckily, we were at the end of the wave. Some of the water retreated right away. Our cells were ruined. Only a few people came behind us on the road, but no one had a cell. I couldn't call you. It took us hours to dig out and more hours to get back here. Just as we got to town, I saw the sky and realized this storm was blowing up. But I had no idea. I barely made it back here. That lightning is crazy! It's killing people!"

Emilio nodded as he pulled out the first aid kit. "I was worried about you. I am glad you are safe. Let me clean you up while we wait in here." He recoiled as another explosion hit close by, and thunder shook the building. "Then we will go out and see if anything is left standing."

Cheyenne Mountain Complex: 12 p.m. MST, 1 p.m. CST

"Ben," Min pulled his attention away from the monitor, where he was tracking the volume of space particles entering the Earth's atmosphere. "You need to see this."

Min had the weather radar up, and it looked like a strong storm was brewing somewhere in the Caribbean. Orange and red cloud bubbles covered a large island area. Hot pink centers suddenly blossomed as if in a time-lapse video.

"What's this?"

"Dominican Republic. I was checking the effects closer to the equator. They also felt the earthquake yesterday, and tsunamis swept in and took out the north and west coasts. But this is today. This thunderstorm just erupted out of nowhere. It's the tropics, and it's July, so you expect the instability. I checked, and the ingredients for something like this just weren't there even thirty minutes ago. Look at this. These winds are clocking in at one hundred miles an hour!"

"Like a hurricane?"

"Only if you have a hurricane blow itself up out of nothing in less than an hour."

"Master Sergeant! Here are the voltage test results you requested. The results are unbelievable." Min took the clipboard from the technical sergeant. The man tried to remain calm as Min read the results.

"The measured voltage in that storm is over two billion volts! Ben, this is more than your average summer day thunderstorm!" She turned back to the technical sergeant. "Do we have any drones we could send into that storm?"

The technical sergeant's thin face narrowed more as he considered the request. "No, not over the Dominican Republic. Nothing we could get there in real-time. But we have access to space-based lightning mapping. Let me show you."

Min was back in fifteen minutes. "Ben, you've got to see this." She pulled up a new screen on one of the workstation monitors. The background was black, but thousands of overlapping dots flashed and faded simultaneously.

"This is over the Dominican Republic right now. Huge amounts of energy are being produced here—maybe as much as one hundred times more than any storm ever measured!"

"What kind of energy is being measured?"

The technical sergeant answered before Min could. "These are particles with extremely high energy levels that came from space—cosmic rays."

"These numbers are fairly steady on a regular day. During a thunderstorm, they can change drastically and quickly. But this is insane. No one has ever seen numbers change like these." Usually calm and composed, Min's stress was evident in the higher pitch of her voice. "Another is blowing up over Jamaica, and we have identified the start of a third thunderstorm over Puerto Rico. It looks like the three might merge. There's no rain, only electrical and wind, like massive dust storms. We're getting reports from the Dominican Republic about hundreds of bolts striking randomly. Casualty numbers are growing. Do you think this has anything to do with the geomagnetic disturbance?"

"Yes, I think it does." Ben pointed to his screen. "The poles have not slowed; if anything, they are moving faster. They are still mimicking the same path, exactly opposite of each other. We have not had another reversal, but the number of particles getting through the weakened barrier is reaching a critical point. My model shows we are on the verge of new complications."

"What kind of complications?" People started drawing closer, listening to the conversation.

Ben hesitated and then started listing his concerns. "The ozone layer—this activity could create all kinds of symptoms. The truth is we don't know what could happen. These electrical storms could get much worse. I think unfathomable amounts of the solar wind particles, and maybe some debris we don't have categorized, are getting through to the atmosphere. We will surely see the impact on the auroras, but there are other much more serious hazards. Risks impacting the satellites and limiting the data we can access. Communication could take a mortal blow. But the thing I am most concerned about is the cold. Weather patterns could shift violently. You told me the worldwide temperature has dropped two degrees in the last two days. It won't take much more to pull Arctic air across North America, and if this activity is sustainable? The last time that happened, ice sheets and glaciers surged, creating a new glacial period, and we had a 75,000-year mini-ice age."

"Most of this is speculation," the technical sergeant argued. "The data on the electrical storms is fascinating but hardly proof of a potential ice age. That's a huge leap!"

"Millions have already perished in the earthquakes and tsunamis," Min interjected quietly. "Can we really discount anything? If cold is coming, we must prepare as many people as possible."

Another master sergeant stood and shook his head. "We have limited resources. We can't prepare for multiple catastrophes. We need to prove one theory or another. The president is waiting for more information."

Murmurs of agreement filtered through the group. People sat back down and started in again.

Min caught Ben's eye, motioning him back to the monitor displaying the weather over the Caribbean. Someone had changed the view, and Ben realized they were looking at Canada now. Only what a picture it presented. Most of the country was colored blue. Snow shades of dark blue variegated to lighter blue bands as they passed over the border into the states. Ice shades of bright pink highlighted a tear-shaped area right through Chicago.

"What is the temperature forecast in Canada for tonight?" Ben asked, his brow furrowed.

"Below freezing. There's enough moisture in the air to squeeze out some snow. It's not just this storm. It's that this is the first storm. Look how widespread it is." Min ran her fingers over Canada. "This air was over the Arctic. Now, it's being pushed toward North America. The air over Canada is warm and moist because it's summer. Pushing cold pools out of Siberia and the Arctic into the warmer and moister air ahead of it can quickly develop into serious weather. If this were January, we'd call this setup a bomb cyclone."

Ben leaned toward Min. "I need to call my family. I am going to step out for a minute." He kept his voice low.

"Okay." Min eyed him, guessing what he was doing.

"I need to tell them what we are seeing and warn them to batten down for cold. I am sure enough about this 'theory'—I want them to prepare."

Min nodded. They needed to start thinking about approaching the president with this information.

Holden, NE: 2 p.m. CST

"So, what do you think."

Jake put the laser communicator back in the drawer and rubbed his chin before answering. He hadn't shaved in a few days, and the bristles were starting to annoy him.

"If my dad says get ready for cold, we need to do that. It never got above seventy-five degrees today, and this is the middle of July."

Dave tugged on the corner of the wood covering the office window. When he could see outside, he examined the milky blue sky. "Still lots of crap in the air from the quake. Maybe that's why it's cool."

"Maybe. But either way, let's start with the house. We fixed the doors; let's get some more plywood from the shop and see if we can board up the last of the windows. I need to look at that propane tank too, and we should start making plans for the animals."

"What about the neighbors?" Randi stopped him short. She folded her arms, and he knew that meant she was serious. "We should warn them too."

"We can't call," Jake pointed out. "We're the only ones with a Star Wars phone. My cell phone is still out of service. Who knows when or if the cell towers will be back up."

"I could go," Augie offered.

Randi shook her head and picked up the keys.

"No, you need to run the data for Ben. What if I take John in the Jeep, and the girls stay here with Kay and Lily? I'll tell the Loungs. They are only a few miles up the road. "I'll ask Mr. Loung to pass the word up to the next house, and maybe they can daisy chain it to Holden."

Jake's face wrinkled. They both knew he didn't want anyone leaving the property.

She sighed at his stubbornness and pulled the clip out of her hair.

"I'll be back in thirty minutes. You know this is the right thing to do." He knew she wasn't going to let this go. He hated when she was right, and he did not want to agree. But it would take time they didn't have to argue, and she knew he was practical to a fault.

"No, I'll go. You stay here and draw up a list of what we need to prepare for if it gets cold. Dave and John can get started on the windows. As Randi says, it'll be thirty minutes, and I'll be back."

She shook her head but didn't argue. He grabbed the Jeep's keys from her and headed out the door. Pulling out of the yard made him think about gas. He wondered if his dad had stored any for the generator. They had turned it off last night and only turned it on today to keep the refrigerator cold.

Then he thought about Holden. There were probably less than three hundred people in this whole area. These ranchers were used to brutal winters and living without city help. Maybe they should start thinking about pulling together. He'd ask Davis Loung.

Yucatan, Mexico: 2 p.m. local, 2 p.m. CST

On the sixth day of his two weeks in Mexico, Rory Carter scribbled new lines in his notebook, anxious to capture the details after he flushed a group of eleven black-throated bobwhites. A fellow birder had suggested he check the beach scrub, considered one of the better habitats for the sleek birds, and he chortled with glee at his success.

The hot sun wrapped him in a mantle of perspiration, but he shrugged it off, wiping his forehead and replacing the bucket hat on his mostly bald head. His white T-shirt proclaimed, in big brown letters, BIRDWATCHING IS MY PASSION. He hiked up the tan cargo pants weighed down with all sorts of bird accessories, not the least of which was several pockets of different types of seeds, nuts, and dried fruits.

It was time to find a Yucatan Gnatcatcher. He moved up the beach, carefully dodging the salt-stained flotsam left by this morning's high tide. With all that business in the Atlantic and the run-up of water in the United States, he wasn't surprised to find high tide had climbed an unusual extra dozen feet up the sand shelf. Yesterday's earthquake shook things up, but the damage was minor, and Rory was prepared to ignore the whole thing.

As a pensioner, he had saved a long time for this vacation. Bird watching was more than just his hobby these days, it was his primary source of pleasure. He just wanted to relish the two weeks, and then when he got back home to Minnesota, he'd deal with everything else. With that goal in mind, he avoided television, radio, and most of his fellow travelers. It was just him, the blue skies, hot sand, and sea spray while he hunted for his little feathered friends.

An old, giant log blocked his path, and as he carefully navigated the gnarly wood, a gigantic black shadow rolled over him, blocking the sun. Startled, he looked up and almost tripped in amazement. A huge flock of blackbirds blotted the sky, so many it was hard to see blue behind the lithe, flapping bodies. A flock of thousands of birds split apart and then fused together, flying up a few hundred feet and then zooming down right over his head. Despite himself, he ducked in trepidation, a low murmur of wingbeats ringing in his ears as the birds passed by. He was not afraid of the birds, but so many moving bodies! He lowered himself backward onto the sand to avoid any of the flyers accidentally running into him and getting hurt.

The colony sure acted weird, though. The shape-shifting flock circled and spun with not a sound from a single beak. Their flight seemed coordinated, the movements a fluid, intricate pattern. Lying flat on his back in the hot sand, Rory sensed a change in the birds' manner. It felt desperate and deranged; even sadness radiated from the group. He wondered what would cause the birds so much sorrow and gulped back his feelings of impending doom.

Seconds later, the blackbirds rose higher still and then turned. Like black darts, they arrowed down, crashing out of the sky and slamming into the empty beach. Rory cowered against the log, shaking, the snaps of breaking bones and wings filling his ears. It seemed to last an eternity, but when the noise finally ceased, he lifted his head and looked around.

He was surrounded by death, shattered bodies blanketing the sand, motionless on the ground except for when the breeze caught a broken wing and fluttered it. Nothing moved in the sky. Every bird lay on the beach. Rory had no way of knowing that the chaotic wandering of the magnetic poles had terrorized the birds, confusing them to the point of insanity, or that this disaster was happening worldwide to many of the migrating species. All he could see were the results here on this beach.

Rory realized he was crying. It felt like the end of the world.

Chapter Fifteen

Moca, Dominican Republic: 12 p.m. local, 2 p.m. CST

Three hours later, the strange, dry thunderstorms still raged. Worse, the storms had grown in that time, impacting all the islands from Cuba to the British Virgin Islands. If you were observing the phenomena from space, it would look like someone had wiped a long black smear speckled with thousands of glittering strokes across the Caribbean—vastly beautiful. Underneath the clouds, it was much more terrifying.

Hours before, Bendo had carried his abuelo down the stairs, leaving him in the mining tunnels cut deep into the side of the mountain. Providence had seen the town grow over the quarry site, and one of the old entrances was underneath Emilio's building.

It wasn't safe to stay in the bathroom. Bendo felt sure the furious winds could tear away the entire building. Never before in his young life had he witnessed an outburst like this.

With the advent of the storm, the weather had turned sharply colder, with tiny shards of ice whipped on its edge. Most of the town's structures were flattened between the screaming gales and the lightning strikes—charges built up in the people, buildings, and air around them. Flickers swept past, and a weird smell choked those huddling in the few shops and homes, damaged but still somewhat standing. Over and over, streamers discharged like fingers of lightning, grasping for a victim. Explosion debris pelted from all sides as the winds rotated in massive corkscrews.

Bendo had survived many hurricanes, but he wondered if he would see the end of this monster. He and others trying to help suffered electrical burns and bad scrapes. Many compadres he had known his whole life had perished from the bolts of electricity. The side of his leg was abraded, raw skin leaking, and bleeding scorch marks crossed his arms. Everyone was terrified. Above them, an intense battle raged, tearing the air and shredding the clouds.

All electronic equipment was dead. High-pitched crackling sounds preceded the malfunction, leaving them no way to call for help.

Maybe there was no one to call. Maybe this tempest covered the world. Bendo had no way of knowing, and there was nothing he could do but wait for the end—if an end would eventually come.

As the cyclone strengthened, trees began to be uprooted, and giant cedars and palms ripped out of the ground and hurled through the air. Everything was moving. Concussive blasts shook the ground. The ringing in his ears confused him. Still no rain, not a drop of moisture. Just dust and debris, tiny missiles sharp enough to flay the flesh from the bones.

In the mouth of one of the tunnels, Bendo peered out between two broken boards, squinting against the storm for what felt like the one-hundredth time. After hours of darkness, he caught sight of something lighter. Something glowing! His spirits lifted. The storm was coming to an end! He called to the few others sheltering with him in the mouth of the tunnel, and weak cheers answered his good news. Now, he started worrying about what they would find. How many of their people had not made it through? His abuelo was sheltered in the rock, as safe as Bendo could make him, but was it enough?

"What is that?" the thin man beside him asked abruptly.

The light was such now that he could see Flavio's wispy, bearded face, all covered in filth and streaked with sweat. They were all sweating, and he looked down at his shaking hands as he realized the temperatures had climbed dramatically in the last several minutes. A sinking feeling split his gut, and ignoring the howling squall, he shoved past the broken wood beams providing minimal refuge.

Despairing, his hair smoking and skin tingling, he stood against the hot gusts at the center of a fire swirl hundreds of feet tall, as wide as the village he had grown up in. What was left of the wooden houses and buildings caught fire with a roar. Flames closed in from all directions and blazed toward him. Devouring sheets of fire played and flickered, rolling over shattered stone walls, the conflagration consuming anything organic in its path.

Bendo fled back into the tunnel, screaming between coughs racking his chest. He was sure he was going to die.

Cheyenne Mountain Complex: 2 p.m. local, 3 p.m. CST

"We are getting reports of tornadoes on fire throughout the West Indies."

The colonel listened intently, studying the monitors indicated by the technical sergeant as the soldier provided updates. "Burning cyclones thousands of feet tall. See this storm over Moca in the Dominican Republic? It is well over five thousand feet. It's enormous! Jamaica, DR, Cuba, all of them are burning. The coastal cities are trying to evacuate, but most seaworthy vessels were destroyed in yesterday's tsunamis. They're asking for help, sir, but we don't have the resources."

"Everyone is asking for help," he rubbed the side of his face. "There's nothing we can do. Give me a weather update on the remaining states."

"Those electrical storms over the islands aren't reaching our new southern coastline. We're monitoring them, but so far, the superstorms are stationary over the Caribbean. With the ocean surges seemingly settled, the areas below Kansas and Missouri are currently stable. But there is significant cold sweeping in from the north. It looks like all of the cold air in Siberia is running over the top of the planet and sliding down into North America. It's July, but average daily highs have already dropped twenty degrees."

"What do the scientists have to say about that?"

"Not much, sir. This is all unprecedented."

The colonel huffed. "I have to update Tanner in one hour. I need intel. If we are going to direct him down the right path, we need to determine that path before we start telling him what it is. Get Master Sergeant Liu and that geologist up here now."

***

Ben tried not to let his nerves show. Min remained impassive as they rode the elevator up. He also tried to look stoic, but knew his efforts were probably inadequate. He was always better at researching data than sharing it. He wished Max were here. Nobody could state the problem more clearly and with more believable passion than the cyber engineer.

They stepped into the side corridor. The short hall led to a single door, which they pushed through. They found themselves standing before Col. Stanely, whose expression exuded a cold aura of frustration.

He jumped right into the conversation. "I need answers. I am getting too much intel. Where should we be spending our limited resources?"

Ben quickly assessed their immediate surroundings. Three other soldiers were seated at workstations, none looking their way. But he assumed they could hear what they had to say. "Sir, could we talk somewhere privately for a few minutes?" he asked.

Stanely eyed him, exasperated. Without a word, he led them to a small office on the side. As soon as the door closed, he turned on them. "I need this fast and accurate. Master Sergeant Lui claims you have information that severely impacts our response efforts." He threw a pointed look at Min, then turned back to Ben. "What are we looking at here?"

"Ben Stone, sir." The geologist held out a hand, ready to report. Stanely shook it once, hard. Ben delivered the crucial points as concisely as he could.

"Here's what we have. The impacts of the catastrophic damage caused by the events in the North Atlantic are being assessed by your people, who have it as much under control as anyone could. But it's what you don't know that's going to be most significant. My model predicts more, even deadlier impacts as the poles continue to shift. These unprecedented disasters are not over yet. Master Sergeant Liu and I believe the worst is still to come."

Stanely absorbed his words without interruption, taking a minute before he answered. "Did you see the earthquake and tsunami damage? What could be worse than what we have experienced in the last twenty-four hours?"

"Unfortunately, sir, quite a few things, but the one we're most worried about is the start of a new ice age."

Stanely regarded him skeptically. "Because of all the debris entering the atmosphere?"

"Partially, sir," Min picked up the conversation. "But the poles are still shifting, and their activity is having significant repercussions on the weather. Ben's model is predicting a cataclysmic change in the next several days. Literally, we are going from the height of summer to the bowels of a brutal winter in days. The U.S. would not have been ready for this event before the calamitous damage of the last few days. Now, with all the destruction to the infrastructure, most civilians aren't going to be able to survive the plummeting temperatures and storms headed our way."

Understanding the general's need for haste, Ben summed it up as quickly as he could. "The west and the south are going to get cold, but nothing like what's coming down the country's middle. We're talking Midwest temperatures well below zero. We need to transport as many people west to California or south to Arizona, New Mexico, and what's left of Texas as fast as possible. For those left behind, we'll have to determine habitats, food, and heat, or millions more will die."

Stanely took a moment before he asked his next question. This whole scenario felt so incredible that it proved hard for him to keep up. "You said disasters—plural? There's more?"

Ben nodded. "But it is a very fluid situation, and many factors have yet to play out. The highest probability, and the scenario we can do something about is the bitter cold crossing Canada and spilling into the United States. We will keep you updated on anything else we find."

"What about Titan International and their cannon?" Distaste spread across his face as he asked the question.

Ben flicked a look at Min, who started back passively.

"I know everything that goes on in my complex, Mr. Stone. Information stops with me, and I decide what to do with it. Master Sergeant Liu is doing her job."

Conceding with a nod, Ben answered, "I haven't had an update. The team working on the problem will contact me as soon as possible."

"Those cannons need to be dealt with." The general snapped his fingers. "I might be able to help. I understand your brother, Major William Stone, 75th Ranger Regiment Retired, is leading the assault in Argentina."

Stunned that he knew about Will's efforts in the south, Ben inhaled quickly.

Stanely waved off his shock. "My people are just as resourceful as you are, Mr. Stone. Before bringing you here, we ransacked your background, family, and even your ideological beliefs. We need to know who we are working with. I also know about your friend, Max Ungle, his reports out of Titan, and his activities over the last few years to get a warning out. I am sorry his efforts didn't bear more fruit. But now we are left holding the proverbial basket."

"I haven't heard from Will or Max since this started." Ben conceded, the words heavy on his tongue.

"Mr. Ungle flew out of Atlanta yesterday morning before the earthquakes hit. He was on a flight to Bahia Blanca in Argentina. I am assuming he was meeting up with your brother. We've also collected reports out of Bahia Blanca about a terrorist attack in the jungle to the south in the early hours of this morning. It seems a strange, anonymous facility in the middle of nowhere, producing weird noises and pulsating vibrations, suddenly exploded—only scraps left this morning. There were no fatalities, but oddly, there were a few gunshot victims. Local police are investigating, but all the workers and the security team seem to have disappeared into the forests."

Ben brightened; his earlier hesitation was gone. "My brother will call as soon as he can. He understands the stakes. And he knew about the other two cannons. He'll make sure they are eliminated. It may already be done."

"Nobody I'd trust more than a ranger, but I'd feel better if we knew exactly what was happening. Master Sergeant Lui, can you please work with communications to help Mr. Stone contact his brother?"

"Yes, sir," Min said, and began to edge Ben toward the door.

"Wait," Ben held up a hand. "What about President Tanner? What are you going to tell him, especially about Titan International . . ."

"I know," Stanely cut him off. "I'm meeting with him in five minutes. I'll bring him up to date on the weather. We'll start the evacuations and the preparations for the cold threat. We'll leave Titan out of the discussions for now. As soon as you make contact with your brother, have Master Sergeant Liu get in touch with me."

Ben felt a flash of hope as he followed Min out the door. For the first time, someone was listening. Maybe things could finally start to go their way.

Joe Grace and Pete Swanson, two of the numerous civil engineering technicians who managed the infrastructure in the complex, headed through the halls. Their destination was the stone shaft that led to the reservoirs. They had just finished a recap meeting with twenty or so others.

At the top of both their thoughts was the fate of their good friend, Martin Price. All three had worked here for over twenty years, starting within a few days of each other. The rest of the crew called them the Three Musketeers since they worked so well together. They had both dialed multiple times, but their pal had not answered them on his smartphone.

"I wish Martin would call back," grumbled Pete.

"I just hope he is all right. What a week to take vacation hours." Joe sighed and looked at his tablet. Their assignment was to inspect the water basins and the area visually. While it was inspected yesterday, after the quake, it looked as if no one had been down there since. Aftershocks from the big eruption rattled the whole area, but the coiled springs steadied the underground buildings as designed.

The boss wanted to be sure those aftershocks weren't impacting the parts of the facility that weren't resting on anti-movement coils and asked for a complete inspection. Both men groaned inwardly, knowing how long that would take, but they didn't argue. The whole crew was shorthanded and working long hours—desperate times and all of that.

"He was going fishing," Joe repeated the information for the third or fourth time as they cut out of the building and headed to the stone entrance. "He likes to get out early. If he was on the river, maybe he's fine and can't get back."

None of the men had family anymore, and they had formed their own little posse over the years. Keeping tabs on each other was par for the course. They both waved at the security guard manning the entrance to the shaft, holding up their badges as they walked past his booth.

"I just can't believe we had an earthquake like that here in Colorado. I mean, I've lived here my whole life and never experienced an earthquake." Pete hitched the backpack tighter to his shoulders.

They could hear machinery running through the rock and recognized the growl of the generators. Joe tapped on the wall, his fingers absorbing the vibrations.

"They must have all the generators running today," he commented. "They sure are louder than the last time we were here."

"More people to support. I've never seen this place so full, even during 911."

Joe agreed, then pointed to the lanterns lining the tunnel ceiling. "Pretty dim compared to usual." He pulled out a flashlight from his pack. "Just to be on the safe side." He clicked it on.

Pete didn't say anything. Down in these caves, it was better to take precautions. You never knew what could happen. They walked quietly for a bit, the rumbling machinery and their footsteps the only noises keeping them company. His thoughts returned to Martin just as they reached the point where their tunnel ended, and the first of the caverns expanded out and up.

The tunnel had sloped at a gentle angle while they walked, leading them to the junction where the longest pool sat horizontally, bordered by a cement pathway in either direction for about three hundred feet. Three bronze bridges crossed the pool, one at each end and one at the midpoint. Three more tunnels continued into the rock on the other side of each bridge, each housing its pool. This was the area the men had been sent to inspect.

"You want to go right or left?"

"I know it will take longer, but let's stick together. We can go left first." Pete rarely had a preference, but the earthquake and Martin's absence had spooked them both. Joe acquiesced, and they headed left.

A few hours later, their inspection of the left tunnel was complete, and the data was entered into the tablet. Because of the rock, the signal wouldn't connect until they were back on top of the buildings, but the data was logged. They sat on the stone bench carved halfway along the reservoir for this purpose and had a quick drink and energy bar.

"Do you smell that?" Joe looked puzzled and held up a hand.

Pete sniffed. "I don't smell anything."

"It's like I got a whiff of sulfur."

Pete stood up, moved around, and drew in deep breaths. "I don't smell it."

"Hmm, well, it's been a weird couple of days. I don't smell it either now."

They cleaned up their wrappings and canteens, pulled on their knapsacks, and started toward the shaft exit. A dozen feet from the bench, they stopped short and looked at each other.

"I smell it now," Pete said, his voice drenched n fear.

Joe took a deep breath to calm his nerves and was instantly sorry. The sulfur burned.

"Okay, it's probably just a small leak. We need to head topside. Cover your face with something. We're going to move fast." Joe pulled out a bandana and covered his mouth and nose. He waited while Pete did the same. Already, his throat was starting to become irritated. He tried to control his breathing, but his fear choked him.

They took off at a run. Joe tried to factor in how long they'd have to hold their breath. His eyes were stinging, and he could see Pete's eyes over his bandana turning red. They reached the bridge, but Pete was gasping now, sucking down the sulfur, hanging on to the railings, and stopping.

Joe stopped also. He wasn't willing to leave his friend. Pulling Pete's arm over his shoulder, they started stumbling up the cement pathway, trying to reach the main tunnel. The gas was so thick by now that Joe wasn't getting any oxygen. His red, streaming eyes struggled to focus, and Pete had become dead weight. He made it a few more steps and then faltered. Sinking down, his last thoughts were of Martin. He hoped at least one of the Three Musketeers would make it back to base tonight.

Holden: 3 p.m. CST

Lily slouched in the chair, keeping an eye on the girls but mostly brooding. She had volunteered to babysit—more to get away from her mother's probing concern than the desire to spend time with her cousins—but Cassie and Pammie were good, so she wasn't complaining.

She couldn't stop thinking about Grady and all of her friends. Her gratitude that her family made it out of Port St. John didn't stop the tears for everyone else she cared about. She pictured Grady sitting on the bed and how cavalier she was on her way out. She wondered if he saw the water coming or if he died right there in her room.

She glanced upward as a cool breeze rolled over her arms. More acclimated to the hot summer temperatures in Florida, she shivered.

Pammie giggled and pushed the blue ball to her sister. The baby squealed and patted the toy, rubbing the smooth sides. The ball was the new favorite, and both girls tried to keep it moving. Jake had recently taught Pammie how to kick, and the little girl jumped up to send it flying.

Behind Cassie on a big beige rock, something long and sinuous stirred as the baby's high shrieks disturbed it. Yesterday's earthquake had driven the prairie rattlesnake out of its lair, and last night, it had been searching for a place to rest. This rock was still warm from the daylight and shaded the same colors as the snake, providing camouflage from predators. Pleased with the combination, it had curled up hours ago when it had still been quiet.

With the noise the small, warm-blooded beings made, the snake decided to move on. It wasn't hungry, having eaten a few days before. Uncurling, its triangular-shaped head tasting the air, it prepared to slide away. Suddenly, the blue ball smacked the rock, rolling hard into its coils. Startled, the snake whipped its tail, the rattles shaking together as a hissing shot from the blunt-nosed face. Coiling tightly into a strike position, it pulled itself upright.

Pammie chased the ball. She didn't notice the snake, her eyes focused on the blue plastic. But Lily recognized both the posturing snake and the maraca-like sound as it vibrated its tail.

She shrieked at Pammie to stop, flinging herself out of the chair, past Cassie, and scooping up Pammie all in one frantic move. With too many moving objects, the snake panicked and struck out.

John heard Lily's terrified screams a hundred yards away by the garden shed. He didn't stop to think. He just grabbed a shovel from the side of the shack and ran. He saw the snake sink its fangs into Lily's leg, then fall back. Screaming himself now, he ran up and swung the shovel hard at the snake. It connected with the reptile's body, catching the coils up and throwing the snake back across the rock and into the pasture. John threw the shovel after the snake, hitting it again.

He whirled and grabbed a limping Lily, still holding Pammie high. Pulling her away, he caught Cassie up from the ground, all big eyes and whimpering cries, keeping all of them moving toward the house. He had no idea if the snake was chasing them, but he didn't wait to find out. Lily was sobbing, her cries loud, and Pammie was screaming like a fire engine.

The adults tumbled out of the house and the barn, everyone panicking.

"It was a prairie rattler on the rock. It tried to attack Pammie, but Lily saved her. But it bit Lily on her leg," John cried out, repeating the words to make sure his parents understood.

Randi grabbed Pammie, trying to calm the little girl down, and John spilled the crying toddler he held into Kay's arms. Cassie clung to her aunt in tears. Jake lifted a fainting Lily up the porch stairs, and Augie yanked open the newly repaired screen as Jake carried her through the door. Grimly, Dave grabbed a hoe and headed back into the yard, John right behind him.

"John," yelled his mother after him.

"I'll keep him behind me," Dave called back to her, motioning the boy back a few paces.

Cautiously, they approached the rock. No movement. They could both see the shovel where it had landed about forty feet away after John's mighty swing. There was no snake anywhere in the area. Still, it might have coiled up under the shovel blade to hide. Dave motioned for John to move back further. Carefully, he pushed the flat iron over with the hoe. A second later, he released a pent-up sigh of relief. There was nothing under the blade. The snake must have slithered off.

"That was some swing," he complimented John. "You must be a heck of a ballplayer."

"I didn't even think," confessed the boy. "I just swung the shovel to get the snake away from Lily."

"Well, you did a great job."

They carefully searched the yard and paddock for several minutes, but the snake was gone.

Hurrying back to the house, they reached the porch just as Jake and Augie came through the door, Jake carrying Lily again. This time, the girl had a tourniquet tied around her calf, and they could see the area of the bite was swelling fast and bleeding freely. She was moaning, her words confused, about pain in her leg and nausea. Blinking rapidly, she grabbed at John when she saw him, catching his arm.

"Thank you," she whispered, her words slurring. "Thank you for saving me."

"I'm sorry I didn't stop it from biting you." John's face was stricken with guilt.

Jake hurried forward, pulling her away from the boy. He loaded her in the Jeep on the backseat. Kay had climbed in and was waiting to cradle her. Augie and Jake jumped in the front, skidding out with a spray of rocks.

"Where are they going?" asked John.

"Holden has a doctor. He should have the antivenom. They need to administer it as soon as possible." His mom struggled with both girls as she replied. John took Cassie, who went to him with a little whimper.

"The snake's gone," Dave told Randi.

She smiled, relieved. "Thank you, Dave. John, that was very brave of you. The snake could have bitten Lily more than once, or struck out at Pammie or Cassie. You're our hero today."

He blushed. Dave ruffled his hair. "I told you that was a great swing."

"I just hope Lily will be okay." He gazed down the road, holding Cassie tight. "I hope they get home soon."

Cheyenne Mountain Complex: 3 p.m. local, 4 p.m. CST

"This would be easier if your brother had one of our laser communicators," Technical Sergeant Mia Montgomery told Ben.

"I've used them, and you're right. I wish I could have sent one with him." Ben flipped over the device she had handed him. It was identical to the one he had in his knapsack.

"Not to worry. I have some other tricks I can try." Her fingers danced over the keyboard while she worked through the compatibility issues.

"Mia is one of our best," Min told Ben proudly while they waited. "If anyone can figure this out, it will be her."

"Thanks, Min!" The communications expert leaned forward. "I won't let you down. Just this, this, and this . . ."

The device in Ben's hands chimed.

"And Bingo!" Mia chortled happily.

Ben lifted the laser communicator to his ear and could both feel and hear the device ringing. It picked up on the other end, but no one spoke.

"Will, can you hear me?" Ben said loudly.

"Ben, it's Max!" Ben sat up straight, excited to hear the cyber engineer's voice.

"Max! I expected Will to answer. Are you both okay?"

"Fine, we're both fine. What phone are you calling on? This call isn't encrypting."

"I know." Will hesitated. "Max, I finally got us some help. I'm in Cheyenne Mountain Complex with the Air Force."

"The Air Force? Huh, I never tried the Air Force." Max sounded tired. "Did you hear about Beijing? We didn't stop Titan. So many more people died. All that effort, and we didn't make an ounce of difference."

"I heard. I'm sorry, Max, for them and us. This whole thing is such a cluster. But there are still millions of people left alive, and we can make a difference for them. We can't give up now. We heard there was an explosion in the jungle. Was that you and Will? Did you destroy the cannon?"

"Yeah, the facility is flat, and the cannon is destroyed. I saw that cannon in action. They are brutal, violent tools. Blake and Murph sank the other two ships carrying the cannons that attacked Iceland and the North Atlantic. But, Ben, there's another Mantle Cannon in the Pacific.

A fourth cannon. Will left hours ago on a jet. He has a plan to sink the ship that's hauling it."

"What? How is he doing that? Wait, I can get us some help from the Air Force. Does he have your phone?"

"No, my phone was in my backpack, and everything but my laptop was destroyed in the explosion. Will left me his. We thought it was broken. I've been trying to get it to work, then your call came through. Listen, I don't know if you can reach him or the submarine they've commandeered, but it's called the *U.S.S. Topeka* and close to where Titan's third ship is. Will is meeting Murph and Blake on the sub. They're transporting on a jet from Sydney. He said they should all be aboard by midnight, central time. I've got the coordinates. Let me give them to you."

Will wrote as fast as the numbers came through the phone. Min leaned over, copying the GPS coordinates, then pulled out her phone, dialing quickly.

"These coordinates . . ." he frowned as he compared them to the map Mia had pulled up on her display. "The antipode is somewhere in the Middle East. That's the next target. Okay, let me see if we can help at all. What about you? Are you headed back here?"

"Soon."

Ben shook his head, frustrated: vague answers like usual.

"But Ben, one more thing. Will has to stop the cannon before it is initiated. MAC was right. Those mutated pulses are slowing the core. The next run won't just take out the Middle East. If they stop the core, it could be the end of the human race." Ben heard the weak undertones in Max's voice and started to worry the hacker was giving up.

"I know. We're already seeing the effects. I figured that's what happened. Listen, Max, you need to get back to the States and to our place in Nebraska if possible. Things are turning bad here. The U.S. is heading into a mega winter. I'm not talking about September. In the next week, we are going to really feel the results of the slowing core. The military is starting evacuations to the south and west. We are getting the word out, but setting up enough shelter and food is a Herculean task. And to make things harder, the poles are still shifting. We don't have any idea when it will stop, but this activity is aggravating the climate all over the world. MAC is predicting some pretty strong consequences. South America may seem calm now, but I don't think it will last. I need you. Get back here fast so we can weather the storm together."

"Keep this phone with you," Max instructed. "I'll stay in touch."

"Got it, you too. Get home, Max." He hung up and sat for a minute, drained.

"Here," Mia handed him a cold cup of coffee. "Sorry, it's all I have."

He thanked her and took a quick gulp. It was awful, but the caffeine gave him a much-needed kick. He looked up as the door swung open, and Colonel Stanely hustled through.

"Master Sergeant Liu updated me. I've got my people checking those coordinates now. You should know there are weather issues in that part of the Pacific, and they are worsening—a non-frontal, low-pressure system developed over that area. The sea surface temperatures are elevated, even for this time of year, and there is little vertical wind shear. The weather boys predict that a tropical cyclone will develop in the next three to six hours. I don't know how or if that will affect one of these cannons, but it will be a hell of a mess for your brother to fly into. On a positive note, we confirmed the *U.S.S. Topeka* is deployed in that area, so your friend's information was credible."

Ben stared at him. "Sir, we have tried to get someone in authority to wake up and listen to us for years. Our success rate was zero. Not that I'm not grateful, but why, with almost no proof, are you willing to believe us?"

"I wouldn't," the colonel snapped. "But I don't have any other explanation for what's happened in the last two days. I can't reach most of our allies; the Pentagon is underwater, along with just about everyone I report to, and the president wants answers he's willing to accept. I want to ensure we don't lose any more Americans. Your theory makes the most sense, and . . ." he hesitated. "This does not leave this room. Is that understood?"

He glared at Mia and Min, who nodded rapidly and then returned to Ben. "This is not the first I've heard of a potential threat from Titan International. I am sorry to say I gave little value to what was shared with me, so I'd like a chance to redeem my mistakes."

Flabbergasted, Ben threw up his arms. He wanted to swear, throw things, and throttle Stanely simultaneously. He wondered how many others they had tried to persuade were still alive and thinking the same thing. But he stopped himself from snapping at the colonel. The only way forward was to work together; he needed Stanely and the military more than Stanely needed him. The colonel was correct. The weather forecast added a new layer of complexity to the situation. He wondered if there was anything they could do to help.

Chapter Sixteen

Southwest Argentina: 7:30 p.m. local, 4:30 p.m. CST

Ana Cruz pulled a full bucket out of the old well. She loved the aquifer and knew its story. Over the last hundred years, the underground aquifer had been the wellspring for the Guarani population in this area, and women just like Ana stopped every day to bring up a bucket of clean, cold water. That was one of the advantages of living so far out in the country. She smiled to herself and leaned against the well ledge. This was a good home.

Worries about Marco seeped into her thoughts, and firmly, she pushed the anxiety away. When she married Marco many years ago, she knew what he did for a living. She promised herself that she would not worry ahead. The bad times may come, but she intended to be happy every minute until that day happened. Still, she had hoped this kind of activity was behind them when Marco lost his leg.

Not one to keep secrets, Marco had explained the stakes to her this morning. She understood why he had to go, but now that he had left, she struggled to control the bitterness. The greed of Titan International threatened everyone. Madmen driven by desire for power and money. She stared into the bucket, formulating wishes in her head. Marco was a good man, who didn't hesitate to put himself in harm's way when needed. But it was hard to let him go.

"Senora." The hiss startled her out of her thoughts. Glancing around in the bright sunshine, she caught sight of a round, brown face peeking between the juvenile soapbark trees and wild scrubs.

It was Mateo, one of the children in the area, a favorite of hers and Marco's. She knew all the kids well; their mothers regularly brought them to her for vaccinations and first aid. But this particular young boy liked to shadow Marco as he worked around their yard and cajole alfajores out of her, crumbly shortbread-like biscuits sandwiched with jam that she baked most mornings.

"Hi Mateo," she answered cheerily, only to frown when he shushed her urgently. He motioned her to join him. Leaving the water pail on the ledge, she crossed the path, slipping into the scrub with the ten-year-old. He was clearly bursting with something to tell her.

"You must not go home. He is coming," he told her earnestly as soon as she was close enough to hear his urgent whisper.

"Who's coming?" she asked, willing to play along.

"In the field, I heard the men speaking where they were working on the crops." He stopped to peer between the bushes anxiously.

"What did you hear?" Only half believing now that Mateo was playing a game, her smile slipped, and her brow wrinkled. His serious countenance was starting to spook her.

"Senora, do you know who Lobo Gris is?" he asked her.

He gazed straight into her eyes, his dark stare containing more than a little fear. At this moment, he seemed more adult than a child.

She frowned again. Lobo Gris meant grey wolf. "No. Are we playing a game, Mateo?"

"No game." Despite the day's heat, he shivered and moved closer to her. She leaned in and slipped her left arm around his thin shoulders.

"He is the baddest of the bad men, senora. He kills people for money. The men, they say he is very good at killing people. He always gets his mark." He repeated the words he had heard, mimicking the men who spoke them.

A chill ran up her back, and she pushed her black hair back with a nervous hand. She knew Mateo could feel her arm tremble. "Well, if he comes here, we will just stay out of his way," she attempted to comfort the boy.

"No." His small face was solemn. "He is coming to *your* house, senora. He is coming to find someone in your house."

Will's face flashed into her mind, but he and Marco had been gone for hours. That only left Max. Could this Lobo Gris be chasing Will's girl? After all, the young lady did have a gunshot wound. Puzzled, she didn't know, but knew she couldn't take the chance. Marco cared about Will, and Will cared for Max. That was good enough for her. She'd get Max and get them both out of there, at least for the time being.

"You can't go back there," Mateo said as if reading her mind. "I don't want you to be co-lat-ir-al damage." He sounded out the unfamiliar word. Tears filled his eyes.

"I can't abandon my friend, Mateo. Do you know how much time I have before this Lobo Gris gets here?"

"No time." He shook his head as fast as a bird shaking off water.

She bit her lip, trying to think of what to do. She wasn't leaving Max behind.

"Hide," said Mateo, seeing her distress. "You can hide in the forest where we play. I will go into your house through the back door and bring your friend so you can hide together."

She hated to involve the boy, but her options were limited. She knew how easily the children slipped in and around the forest. Maybe Mateo was right. Indecision was eating their minutes, so she gave in, nodding sharply. "Let's hurry. But we go to my house together. I'll stay in the forest while you slip in and get Max."

A ten-minute walk through the trees delivered them behind her house. It looked as peaceful as she had left it, and for a minute, she found it difficult to believe there was any threat. But she was married to an ex-ranger and knew better than to take things at face value. Besides, Mateo could be full of fun, but she had never known him to make up wild stories. Forcing her to crouch in the bushes, the little boy took off. She didn't see him move around the pond, but a minute later, she saw his small shadow slip into the back door.

Worried that Max wouldn't cooperate with Mateo, she chewed on her nails nervously. Just as she decided to follow, the back door opened, and two forms, crouched low and moving tentatively, sped through the garden. The second form moved stiffly but kept going. She recognized one of Marco's bags hanging from the slim shape and the baggy clothes as her own. When they reached her, Max almost collapsed.

"It's a good thing you gave me that powder stuff for the pain," Max said, gasping where she lay. "I don't know if I could have done that run without it."

"Silverweed. It's a good analgesic. I can't believe you came. You don't even know Mateo." Ana shook her head in disbelief. "I thought you'd balk for sure. I was coming in to convince you."

"Huh," Max said, sitting up with Ana's help. "I've been on the run for years. As soon as I saw the look on his face, I knew we were out of there. I appreciate the warning, Mateo."

The boy grinned, shifting his feet anxiously. Too much talk.

"We need to go now," he urged the women up and back into the trees.

***

Sixty minutes later, a man walked out of the tree line on the other side of the Cruz house. He stopped under the canopy of a large beech tree, slowly absorbing each detail of the area. His close-set eyes missed nothing, even as dusk set. Every leaf, every insect, even the breeze was identified and categorized.

He was of average height and plain features, neither angular nor rounded, and typical in every regard. Brown skin, too pale to be bronze, and thin strands of tan, bowl-cut hair made him a figure to forget after one glance. Even his clothes were unremarkable: khakis, a short-sleeved mocha shirt, and dusty boots.

It wasn't until you looked closer and met the gaze of this man that you quickly realized you were in the presence of barely restrained violence. Death reflected back. Few men met that gaze without shrinking away. Lobo Gris was a loner with one purpose. To look into his eyes was to see your future, measured in moments as he took your life.

The only thing in this world that gave him pleasure was killing. He had been this way as a young boy and only grew more dangerous as he aged. These days, he was paid for what he would do for pleasure. It was an irony that was not lost on him.

He studied the thatched house. No movement. The whole area was the same. The natives who made this low country home seemed all to have vanished. The timber and grass houses he had passed were empty, and the fields with their full crops had no one tending them. Just the animals remained, and they ignored him. His mouth twisted in what passed for a smile. His reputation had preceded him.

He stepped forward, his confident control over his surroundings still in place, but he was irritated that the chase would not conclude there. The dog had slipped away. It had only taken him twelve hours to find the person Victor Newsom hunted. It would not take long to find him again. But in the meantime, Lobo Gris would send a message. He liked to warn his victims almost as much as he liked to dispatch them. Sharpen their fear for his pleasure. He crossed the threshold, whispering the name of the person he hunted.

"Max Ungle, Max Ungle, Max Ungle . . ."

***

Mateo was more help than Ana could have ever imagined. He led them across the hard plain, thick with clumps of inflexible grass that left no sign of their passing. Earthquake activity had broken the ground with fissures and holes, but they were all thankful for the mess as it disguised their passage. They stayed low and moved between big rubber trees and vast boulders, with the youngster scouting ahead while Ana half carried a weak Max.

When Ana asked how he knew so much about the surrounding area, Mateo told them about his family. "My father is a tracker. He made sure I was familiar with the ways of the forest and the pampas. He taught me how to find anything and, better still, how not to be found." He winked, but Ana felt a lurch of fear and guilt, knowing he was too young to risk his safety for them.

It was full dark when they finally reached the Rio Negro. Mateo left them for a few minutes to return dragging a worn dugout canoe littered with dead leaves and twigs from where he hid it. The boy was settling them both in the bottom when the night sky behind them burst with an explosion. All three jerked around and gaped at the sight.

"Your house is that way," Mateo told Ana, his eyes wide.

She struggled to slow her breathing, fear etching itself across her face. Max moaned and laid her head on the side of the canoe.

"It's me they want. You guys should drop me off and hide. They'll forget about you while they're chasing me."

Ana hefted the wooden paddle she found on the hollowed-out bottom of the skiff. "They won't have to do much chasing. You're too weak to get far. But Mateo, you go back to your family. We'll follow the current downstream until I can find us a place to hide."

"No, senora. I have a better plan. My cousins are downstream. We'll go there and get help."

"Mateo, I don't want to bring this trouble to your cousins," Ana protested.

Mateo laughed and touched her arm. "Do not worry, senora. My cousins are much badder men than Los Gris. They are smugglers! We will get them to smuggle you and your friend away!"

He hopped in the dugout behind Max and pushed off before Ana could stop him. Digging deep with the other paddle, he caught the current and sent them downstream.

Smugglers! This just kept getting worse and worse. But what else could they do? With Marco gone, she didn't have a lot of options. Ana kept an eye on the empty shore, satisfied they still had a lead. She thought about her little house, regretting its loss, but more than that, she worried about the people of her hamlet and the trouble she had brought on them.

As if reading her mind, Mateo reassured her. "Don't worry, senora. No one would confront Lobo Gris. My family knows what to do when they are in danger."

She hoped he was right and no one would get hurt. A house could be replaced, but not the friends and acquaintances they had made in the last few years. She dug hard in the water, helping to speed the canoe along. The physical labor helped dissipate the intensity of her anger toward Titan and the threat they posed to everyone. She pictured Marco's face and said a prayer.

Smugglers. Oh boy. She said another prayer for herself and Max. With clenched fists, she paddled, praying they were doing the right thing.

St. Louis, MO: 8 p.m. CST

Art's loafers slipped on the makeshift raft's uneven, wet boards. His grip tightened on the pole, and he hefted it again. He tried to keep his body movements in time with the river's roll. Almost three-quarters of the way across the muddy river. He didn't want anything to stop them now. Jack manhandled the outboard motor repeatedly, forcing the propeller back into the water and the raft forward. The sweat poured off both men. Tepid, wet air blew over them. It was not hot, but they were both exhausted with the effort of shoving the heavy barge a few feet at a time.

Multiple times, chunks of wreckage had banged hard into the raft, causing it to yaw wildly one way or the other. Art used the pole to angle around the garbage or deflect the pieces around them whenever he could. A couple of times, with a few good blows, he broke the chunks into smaller pieces, and they floated harmlessly away.

The raft was pretty solid, even if it was made from scavenged boards and planks. It was still hard to steer, however. The jerry-rigged craft was unwieldy, causing them to slew in the water. Art braced himself again, trying to maintain his balance.

Six vehicles floated over on their barge, including Pastor Don's minivan. The kids huddled in the middle, and Ed and the adults lined up along the sides, wielding makeshift poles like Art. He was grateful Jack was navigating the raft. It took a lot of muscle to keep moving east against the current and the weight of the barge. There was no telling how far they had drifted, but Jack was attempting to hit anywhere along the shore with the barge and ground them on the Missouri side. The Gateway Arch no longer loomed to their right, so they must have traveled some distance by now.

Everyone wished they could have started earlier. The sun was going down by the time they were ready to try a crossing. They discussed holding the launch until morning and better light, but in the end, with little food and water available and no security on the road, the decision was made to try now. Multiple gunshots echoed from the city throughout the afternoon, leaving no doubt about the threat of potential dangers, and which side of the Mississippi River Art wanted to be on.

Jack hunched over the engine, trying to guide it with his weight. The Mercury 400 was a powerful machine. It was too much for the raft, but there weren't any better alternatives. Jack tamed the beast with brute strength. Art worried every foot of the way. Again, the raft floundered in the water, slipping partially under the surface before forcing itself and the barge forward a few more feet.

It was almost completely dark before the barge thumped into the shore. Tired cheers rose up in front of them. Art was glad to see a few of their people scrambling over the flat sides and onto the shore. Working together, they pulled the anchor ropes around the first broken bridge truss, keeping the barge from floating away in the current. His strength drained, Art struggled to tie the raft to the barge. First Jack and then he climbed wearily onto the flat bottom boat. Ed held out a helping hand to both.

"Look at the sky!" he exclaimed as they were pulled aboard. Pale green and blue veils of light pulsated gently above them. Tiny dots of white stars pricked the glow. The activity shifted, fading away, and then deepened again.

"It's beautiful." Ed sighed with pleasure.

"It sure is," Art stretched, aching in every muscle. "Let's get the trucks and minivan off the barge, and then we can admire it."

Forty-five minutes later, the barge was empty. Rolling the last truck off the barge sapped the last of everyone's energy, so when Ed suddenly stiffened, it took Art a minute to notice. A small group of dark figures slipped along the sand, approaching furtively from the west, moving shadows masking their numbers.

"Stop right there," Jack demanded, his voice low and rough on purpose. A mean growl accented the threat.

"Get the women and children in the vehicles," Art whispered to Ed. He nodded and scrambled away.

The strangers stopped immediately, and a few even backed up.

"We don't want any trouble," the lead figure stated calmly, raising his hands palms forward. "We just want to know if we can use your barge. We want to cross the river back to the Illinois side. Look, to prove our good intentions, there is a gas station up the road. No one was there, but we rigged the pumps and filled up our vehicles. If you stop there, you can do the same."

Jack hesitated and looked at Art.

"I'm low on fuel," Art admitted.

"Me too." He raised his voice again, keeping it rough. "Sure. Keep back. When we are out of here, you can have it."

The group stayed back in the shadows without saying anything else. Art's group quickly jumped into their vehicles, and in a few minutes, they left the Mississippi River behind. The leader gave them a casual wave as Art pulled away. Grateful to have avoided a fight, he called back, "We left the keys to the outboard on the raft."

The men quickly moved toward the barge, and Art pressed harder on the gas pedal. The confrontation on the river bank seemed weird, but a few minutes later, the filling station and promise of gas turned out to be true.

Art let the others fill up first. They pulled out in a hurry to get home, one at a time, shaking hands and expressing gratitude as they left. Being on the Missouri side of the river was great, and Art appreciated the teamwork. Yet after some time, he grew weary of the chatter and moved to lean against the minivan, waiting patiently to fill his tank. Ed joined him after a few minutes, still staring at the glowing green sky. Jack came over to shake his hand.

"Look at this," he said, holding out a keychain with a small glass compass attached. The centered, elongated needle wavered back one way and then the other, unable to settle in a direction. "You think it has something to do with that?" He gestured at the waves of color in the sky with his chin.

"Aurora borealis," Ed stated. "The northern lights, or aurora borealis, are beautiful dancing waves of light. . ."

"Thanks, Ed," Art stopped him hastily. "We know what the aurora borealis is; we were just surprised to see it so far south. I don't know what's happening. My brother might know, but I still can't get the cell phones to call out or even text."

Jack nodded. "Probably the towers."

It was quiet for a minute.

"I appreciate the partnership today," Jack said to Art sincerely. "Ditto."

"Listen, we live in Danville, about seventy-five miles west from here. Ed told me you were headed to Nebraska. You won't get there tonight, but we're on your way. Why don't you stay with us, provided our house is still standing and the roads are passable? We can get you a meal, and you can start tomorrow fresh. It's my way of saying thank you."

Ed's stomach chose that minute to grumble loudly. Art smiled. He looked over at Marta, who was standing with Angie and Bobby. She nodded at his unasked question; her tired eyes grateful for the suggestion.

"I appreciate the offer. Let's head that way and see how it works out. Seventy-five miles is a long way, and maybe we'll need to partner again."

"Deal!" Jack shook his hand hard. "I'll wait until you are ready to pull out."

Art looked up while the gas pumped. Despite the beauty of the aurora, he felt a flicker of dread crawling up his spine. The strange behavior of the compass added to his worry. He did not know why, but he felt threatened by the unusual haze in the sky. They needed to get to Nebraska.

Chicago: 8 p.m. CST

Ironically, their own apartment survived the quake with only broken tableware and a few cracks. Everything else stood firm. How could the expensive condo they had worked so hard on for the last six months be a pile of crumbled stone? It defied his sense of justice.

Del splashed cold water on his face and looked in the bathroom mirror. Dripping irregular features stared back at him. He didn't look like someone who was enjoying the irony.

Both of their other builds had also taken damage, but the bulk of their investment was the West Briar Place renovation. When the opportunity came up last year, they didn't have the collateral to borrow from a bank. Their previous ten jobs were solid and delivered great referrals, but that wouldn't get them a 300,000-dollar loan. So, they agreed they could manage a short-term loan from a non-traditional loan agency. Call it what it is, he told himself harshly—a loan shark.

Josh came in as he was toweling off. "I made some sandwiches. We should use up the cold stuff as fast as possible. I don't know when the electricity will come back on."

"Okay, I'm not really hungry anyway." Del pulled on a clean blue T-shirt.

"In any other circumstances, we would pack right now and head to my father's place in Nebraska."

Del shook his head. "Even in this chaos, Sam will come after us if we leave."

"I know."

They shared a despondent glance.

"I don't know what we can do. All we have is the other two places." Josh spread his hands. "I'd say we can fix and finish both of them in a few weeks, if we can get supplies, and then offer them to Sam. But he wants cash."

"Maybe we can sell them fast. People are going to need housing. Maybe we can sell this place too and live out of our trucks." Del looked hopeful.

"When I got back, I talked to the neighbor's downstairs. It sounds like the whole country got hit with this earthquake. I should have listened to my father. I don't know when the currency systems will be back up and running. If we can't pay Sam cash today, he wants us to work it off by doing something dangerous, or even illegal. We could be at his beck and call for weeks—months. We don't have any other options."

"If we had another place to borrow cash, we would have done that last year." Del followed Josh into the tiny kitchen. They each grabbed a plate of food and a can of beer.

The little food and beer they had stored here would not last long. I better eat what we have right now, he thought glumly.

They sat down at the table, automatically avoiding the crooked right side. Even their wonky table survived the quake. Why couldn't the condos on West Briar Place still be standing? Bitterly, he took a bite, his eyes wandering to the window.

"Look at that," He remarked, the bite of the sandwich stuck in his throat.

They both stared out the window. Dusk had fallen, and with no streetlights or illumination in the apartment, it seemed darker than early evening typically was at this time. A soft green glow lit up the upper portion of the northern sky. As they watched, the green deepened, and undulating waves of purple and red lights danced through the emerald. Silvery ribbons shimmered and exploded with intense coronas as rainbow arcs filled the atmosphere.

"Is that the northern lights? How can we see them here?" Del asked, his face lit up with astonishment.

"I don't know." Josh did not look astonished; he looked worried. "But I don't think this is a good thing. I wish I could call my dad."

They sat and watched the show.

Southern Pacific Ocean: 10 p.m. local, 10 p.m. CST

Rain lashed the Sikorsky canopy, and gusts of wind tossed the helicopter. According to the pilot, the storm had blown up out of nowhere. Thanks to all the crazy business in the Atlantic, forecasters called it just one more weather anomaly.

Newsom was scared, though he'd never admit it. Cynthia sat belted into her seat, hands clasped, and eyes closed. He wondered if she was praying.

Hart stared stoically ahead, watching the two pilots struggle with the controls. Newsom doubted that his boss was negotiating with a higher being. He sniggered to himself. More likely negotiating with the devil himself.

"Your ship is ten minutes out, sir," The captain called back to him. "This storm isn't getting better, but we will have to land. Make sure everyone is belted in because it will be a rough landing." Not waiting for an answer, he reached up and turned a knob to the radio. The static squawked deafeningly, drowning out the sound of the deluge for a minute.

When it cleared, he called out. "Come in, *Titan Three*. This is the L2AE Coast Guard, about five minutes off your vessel. I have Dror Hart on board, and he requests permission to land over."

Static squealed again and then cleared. "L2AE, understood. We are preparing for you now. You should see our lights any minute."

Everyone peered out the windows except Cynthia, who kept her eyes closed and hands clenched tight. It was so dark that Newsom couldn't even make out the waves. They were completely wrapped in darkness, smothered in a blanket of night. A few minutes later, he caught sight of a glow. It brightened fast as they swept toward the three-hundred-foot cargo ship. Their pilot switched on the outside beacons and moved to hover over the deck.

Titan One and *Titan Two* were old liners purchased from cruise companies ready to sell their outdated vessels. The refit had been fast and easy since the vessels were seaworthy, and most of the cabins weren't needed. They tore the middle out of the ships and built the cannons into the remains. It had been different with *Titan Three*.

Newsom had purchased the cargo ship from the Australians sight unseen, trying to save money. It wasn't advertised as seaworthy, so he had scooped it up for a bargain. He used his own people to install the cannon because of security considerations, but he hired a team of marine mechanics out of Sidney to get the ship ready to sail. He hadn't worried about aesthetics, but even in the rain, he was shocked at how derelict the vessel looked under the bright beam of the flood lights.

Rust coated most of the surfaces. In some places, it had eaten clean through the metal, leaving gaping holes in the railings and cabin walls. Slime and rot discolored the wood surfaces. Decking boards were coming loose or were outright missing, exposing beams. Piles of paraphernalia blocked doors and littered decks, old nettings, gear, riggings, and unidentifiable damaged barrels scattered and rolling in the storm. The superstructure was partially caved in, the windows all smashed out, and the deckhouse rocked with the motion of the ocean. Newsom wondered how they had convinced anyone to sail on such a dilapidated wreck. The ruin must be in better shape than it looked, he decided.

The sailors on deck rushed to clear the landing pad of debris. The wind dropped off, and the rain eased for a few minutes, giving the pilots the chance they needed to start the descent.

The landing was every bit as terrifying as Newsom expected. They dropped fast. With a thud like the deep bass of a giant drum, the helicopter's wheels met the deck hard enough to jar their teeth loose. The aircraft skidded sideways, jerked to a stop, and slid back. The pilots were swearing, fighting the controls. He heard men yelling, and through the streaked windows, he saw them run forward and start lashing the helicopter to the deck before the angry sea could slide the bird into the ocean. Dror was on his feet, shoving open the door before they finished.

In the few seconds it took to cross the deck, they were soaked. Captain Bodhi was smart and subservient enough to have dry clothes waiting. He also prepared hot food and drinks in the galley, the only semi-clean room on this ship, though the fare was pedestrian and tasted off. He heard Cynthia murmuring thanks to the tall, skinny cook who served them, but he didn't bother. It was the least they could do.

"I can't get a signal for my laptop. Probably the storm. I need to get to your communications room," he told the man.

"Up one level and forward," the hash chef told him. "Jackson! Show Mr. Newsom to the Communication Room," he called out to a roughneck seated by the door. The crewman didn't argue, but scowled the whole way through the ship.

Six hours had passed since he last had a signal. He was anxious to check on the transfer pending from Tanner. Hart flashed him a look as he left. Hart was anxious, too, though he'd never admit it.

It wasn't easy making his way through the halls. The ship groaned as the ocean roiled beneath the hull. The heavily burdened boat wallowed as it moved against the waves. Newsom recalled the previous owners' disclosure of the ship's lack of seaworthiness with a pang of misgiving. He hoped the team he hired to repair this ship knew what they were doing.

Finally, they reached the communications room. A lone sailor staffed it this late, but he was more than willing to help Newsom connect to the internet. It took several minutes, but he eagerly accessed the banking information when the laptop connected.

His breath caught in his throat: a one followed by the correct number of zeros populated the balance field. Tanner had come through and paid for the Beijing job.

As he stared at the amount, everything fell away: the giant storm, the wave-tossed ship, Hart, even that little weasel whistleblower. Solid joy flashed through his body like a nuclear blast. This was the best moment of his life.

Chapter Seventeen

Cheyenne Mountain Complex: 12 a.m. local, 1 a.m. CST

In the fifty-seven years that the Cheyenne Mountain Complex had been operating, not once had a full complex evacuation been ordered. Barney Post, an 832nd Civil Engineer Squadron supervisor firefighter, was well aware of that fact, and he brooded over it tonight as the alarm ripped through the facility. The mountain's unique environment rendered even the most common threats challenging. He constantly prepared for super complications in ventilation, smoke, and occupancy.

Even so, he didn't expect a flood of sulfur dioxide gas to rise from the back of the complex. He was gratified to note that the goal was the same: to get people out on the safest routes to the outside. He was ready to go with his men when the sirens went off, getting the job done.

Insidious vapors crept through the caves and the building ventilation, fingers of death grasping at their victims, scorching their airways and burning them into unrecognizable mounds of red meat. It happened so fast that even those who recognized the sharp odor could not get a warning out.

The toxic gas permeated most of the bottom level before security recognized a threat. The first that anyone was aware of trouble came just before 11 p.m. when maintenance managers discovered that two of the civil engineering technicians sent to inspect the reservoirs had never returned. Calling the guard booth at the mouth of the shaft did not yield an answer. Still, no one was too worried. Communications had been spotty since the earthquake.

Security was contacted, and a team of airmen and engineers headed down the elevator. Airman Brian Laslie wasn't concerned. In an extensive facility like this, it was easy to misplace people. He figured the engineers screwed up who they assigned where again. This wasn't the first time he had taken a team out, only to discover it was more miscommunication and less security issue.

He glanced at the three men accompanying him while the elevator dropped to the lowest level. From the looks on their faces, he figured they were thinking the same thing. But nobody complained, and when the chime dinged their floor, they got ready to exit. Brian was already through the door when the overpowering smell of rotten egg smacked him in the face.

"Oh God, what is that?" he complained, throwing his arm over his nose.

His partner grabbed him and pulled him back. "Look!"

Two mounds in white lab coats sprawled on the floor about ten feet down the hall. Neither was moving. Brian had started to exit the elevator again to check when one of the civil engineers yelled, "No!" Jerking Brian back, he jammed the up button hard. The doors slid shut before Brian could stop them.

"What's with you? Why'd you shut the door?" he asked, rubbing his irritated eyes. "We have to check that out."

"You're not going out there," declared the civil engineer. "Did you smell that? That's sulfur. Are your eyes hurting? Your nose? Throat? That's the effects of sulfur poisoning." He rubbed his face and his eyes. "For it to affect us that quickly, it must be over 500 parts per million. You could die in a few minutes breathing that shit in."

Brian blanched. He realized that his throat and eyes hurt, and his skin was prickling like a sunburn. He pictured the two at the end of the hall and shuddered. As the elevator door slid open, he pulled out his radio. Twenty minutes later, the first-ever evacuation order for Cheyenne Mountain Complex was issued. The alarms whooped, and lights along the floor flashed, identifying the fastest routes to the main tunnel, where buses waited to evacuate the population out to the assembly points in the State Park. In minutes, the halls were jammed.

Between the two missing civil engineers, guards, and the scientists working evening shifts in the labs, over three dozen people were assumed to be lost. Post had airmen counting heads in the rush to evacuate, but he knew it would be a tough ask. Getting people out was the priority.

With no information on how or where the sulfur was being pumped into the lower level, and with the size of the area to search, Col.

Stanely didn't waste time trying to stop it. He couldn't fight the gas, especially as it corroded everything it touched. It would have to be plugged at the source. They had protective gear in storage, but until the gas was analyzed, no one could be sure it would hold up. From what they'd seen in the security videos, the gas appeared to have super acidic qualities. It was hard to tell, because even the first-floor cameras were malfunctioning. Then, there was the possibility of this being an attack.

With everything that had happened in the last twenty-four hours, he wanted to assume this was another symptom of what the scientists were calling the "Broken Earth Event" because as bad as another geological occurrence would be, an attack by a foreign military would be worse. But this was the military. He was wired to expect a first strike, especially when America was at its weakest. The better response was to retreat until he could gain some intel, gather resources, and mount an offensive.

That meant he needed to evacuate the president and Mrs. Tanner, and then get his team out of the mountain, through a mile-long tunnel, and to the State Park. He'd set up over there and get digital eyes inside the complex. They'd figure out the next steps then.

Trying to be in three places at once, Fireman Barney Post ducked into the command center to update him. Communications across the hand-held devices tended to overlap, and he wasn't sure how much Col. Stanely heard. "Forty-three casualties on the first level. That includes the two civil engineers. We don't know for sure they are down there, but odds are that's what happened."

"Damn," Stanely growled, slamming the desk with his fist. The other five airmen at their stations kept their eyes on their screens. "Has the President been evacuated yet?"

Post barely restrained himself from rolling his eyes. "It was a struggle. He didn't want to get out of bed, but I have men moving the president, his party, and his security through the main tunnel right now. He should be at the landing zone in thirty minutes."

"His helicopter is being prepped. I already contacted Area 51. They are expecting him. What about everyone else?"

"We're evacuating. All circulation has been turned off, so at least we aren't filtering the gas into the buildings anymore. But it continues to rise, which I am told means it must still flow into the mountain somewhere. These walls are not airtight. Until we find the ingress, we need to vacate the premises. That stuff is toxic; the civil engineers say it can kill in minutes."

"They have no idea where it's come from? If we're under attack?"

Post shrugged, then stood a little straighter, remembering who he was talking to. "They know as much as you do, sir. Right now, they are trying to figure out what components the gas is made of besides sulfur, but the labs were all on the first level. They've captured samples, but they'll have to be processed at the labs off-site. We need to get you and your team out of here also."

"Let me know when you have everyone else out. We'll be on the last bus."

"Yes, sir," As Post hurried from the command center, he raised his hand-held to his ear and listened to the reports. Gas was impacting the second level, not yet in the amounts that wiped out the first level, but people were complaining of foul odors and coughing. They needed to work faster. He ran down the corridor.

Ben jerked awake when the alarms started broadcasting. Before he could shake off the sleep, someone was pounding on the door of his tiny billet. He sat up fast, hit the light switch, and swung his legs over the side. Before he could stand, the door flew open, and Min was standing in his space. Blushing, he was glad he opted to sleep in his jeans.

"We have to abandon the complex," she urged. She was dressed in khakis, a loose shirt, and a jean jacket, with a knapsack across her shoulders and boots on her feet. A Cheyenne Mountain Complex baseball cap covered her dark hair.

Trying to wake up, he blinked hard. Reaching for his shirt and boots, he asked, "Why, what's going on?"

"Some toxic gas, maybe sulfur or some sulfur compound, has penetrated the mountain. The leak must be low, but there must be an incredible amount of it. It's rising, filling the mountain like an underground pool. We think the ingress must be located by the reservoirs. The lab we used all day was flooded, and some technicians were overcome. They're dead." Her tone was stark.

"What!"

Min didn't wait, simply grabbing his equipment and shoving it into his bag. She handed him his jacket and gave him a cap matching hers. He tugged it on.

"Col. Stanely issued orders to abandon the complex. We'll go to the buildings around the mountain and a meeting zone over by the State Park for the families."

She pulled him out of the billet, and they hurried through the barracks to the corridor.

He was thinking fast. "Min, we need specialized equipment to track the pole shifts. Are they going to have it outside of the mountain?"

"No. You're right. I'll speak to the colonel about evacuating you to Area 51."

"No," he stopped walking, forcing her to also stop. People rushed past them, heading for the rally points.

"I am not heading further west with the cold coming. I'd never get back to my family. At my ranch, I have a quantum computer and artificial intelligence already working on the pole shifts and the potential ice age. I can't risk being out of communication with them. I need to go back to Nebraska."

She bit her lip. "We won't stop you, Ben. You're not a prisoner. But how would you get there?"

"I'll walk if necessary. Maybe my brother can drive back and meet me part of the way. We'll work something out. I think the laser communicator is still working, and I'll use it until it doesn't. This is the right move. I'll stay in touch with your people as well."

They started down the corridor again. The first step was to get out of the mountain. They had almost reached the bus rally point when Min spoke again.

"I have a car."

Amazed by what he thought she was offering, Ben asked, "You'd let me borrow your car?"

"No," she twisted her lips wryly. "But I'll drive you there."

He didn't know what to say. They looked at each other.

"Can you leave?" he asked finally.

"I'll have to get permission from Col. Stanely, but I'm not a prisoner, either. It makes sense. I'm closest to your research. I know all of the procedures and intelligence here, and I don't have any family, so I wouldn't be leaving anyone behind. I'm the best choice as a liaison. Unless you don't want me to come?" She said the last part so softly that he almost missed the words in the clamor from the evacuations.

He was surprised at how much he wanted her to come. An excitement he had not felt in a very long time woke up and fluttered in his chest. The world was reeling under multiple blows and mass confusion. They may all be dead in a year or less, but he couldn't think of anyone he would rather ride out the storm with.

"I think that is the best idea I have heard in a very long time." He told her solemnly, but his eyes sparkled with enthusiasm.

She smiled, recognizing his excitement. "Let's go get my permission granted."

***

The last bus rolled out two hours later. Colonel Stanely ordered the blast doors closed behind them. He commandeered a two-story office building a quarter mile from the complex, and his people started setting up immediately. Glad to have the president off his hands, he was relieved when he heard the helicopter had landed safely at Area 51.

The next set of problems was more perilous. Medical first. Multiple people had been affected by the gas and needed care. A makeshift hospital was set up in the old gymnasium. Too many critical operations people had been incapacitated, leaving them shorthanded. The worst cases were flown to Area 51 for emergency treatment. The doctors were hopeful they could pull the rest through the debilitating effects right here in Cheyenne, even though Colorado Springs Hospital was inundated with earthquake victims and had no room.

The rest needed shelter and food while trying to retake the complex. With the bitter cold headed their way, their timeline would be twice as life-threatening. He didn't fool himself; he understood the complexities. Just then, a strong aftershock rocked the parking lot, as if the planet itself wanted to underscore their desperation.

"Mother Nature always gets the last word, sir." Stanely turned to see Min standing behind him, balancing herself with one hand resting on the bus. He noted the full backpack on her shoulders. Around them, soldiers milled in the parking lot.

"Report, Master Sergeant," he ordered.

"Sir, I'm requesting permission to accompany Ben Stone back to his ranch in Nebraska. He claims to have access to a quantum computer and artificial intelligence that may help us better forecast the weather anomalies we will experience. I might be able to give you more time to prepare and pinpoint the locations most at risk."

"You can't do that here?"

"I could work with him long distance, but here we are short on equipment, food, and shelter. I believe I would be better able to serve by supporting Ben in Nebraska in this instance. Also, we don't have the equipment or the programs here to track the pole shifts. We need to understand what's happening on the ground and up in the magnetosphere."

"We need every bit of knowledge we can get. These are unprecedented times." He stared back through the dark skies at the black mountain. "How are you going to get there?"

"My car survived in the parking lot. We are going to try and drive it."

"I want you back here, Master Sergeant before the cold makes that impossible. Do you understand?"

"Yes, sir. That's my plan."

He dismissed her, then called her back. "Tell Mr. Stone I will work with those I trust to help his brother. You both need to stay in touch. Be careful, Min. Everything has changed."

"Yes, sir. I understand." She walked away quickly, anxious to get started.

Ben gripped a flashlight in his teeth and spread a map over the hood. He was using his finger to trace their route when she came around the corner. The parking lot lights were out, but the early morning moon was bright. She chose to take the illumination as a good sign.

Unlocking the car and sliding into the driver's seat, she waited until he joined her. She pushed the start button when he sat down, and the car rumbled to life. Driving carefully around the other vehicles that had jumbled in the earthquake, she thought it was a good thing she liked to park some distance from other cars. Her quirk had saved the Toyota 4Runner from more than door dings this time.

She pondered the future as they picked their way off the hill. With so much uncertainty, she'd never had less of an idea where she was headed, but the stakes had never seemed higher. What would happen next? Min was ready to find out.

Southern Pacific: 12 a.m. local, 12 a.m. CST

Murph and Blake made it to the *U.S.S. Topeka* before the storm wound up. It was overcast, and the water was choppy, but they parachuted safely within pick-up distance of the sub. It was different when Will and Marco reached the point of contact hours later. By then, the storm had whipped itself into a frenzy, and night had fallen.

"You guys sure you want to do this? The weather is not cooperating, and you will have one hell of a landing." The note of concern in the pilot's voice rang through the earpieces in their helmets.

"Sure." Will had stopped looking out the windows; between the rain and the dark, there was nothing to see.

Marco's laugh overshadowed Will's clipped answer. "Just another swim in the Pacific," he told the pilot and the co-pilot. "You guys spend too much time in the air."

Marco's guy had come through, delivering the specialized equipment just before they took off from the airfield. Both ex-rangers were fitted in heavily insulated and armored suits, lightweight enough not to drag them beneath the waves but strong enough to protect them from the elements.

Will knew the cold would be their biggest threat. They needed to ward off hypothermia until they could be picked up, which in these waves might take minutes or hours—hopefully, the former. The suits were equipped with fast, secure, robust comms, strobe light emitters, and GPS to guide the Navy to their landing spot as quickly as possible.

Marco sat beside the other delivery, keeping it close to his thigh. A sizable waterproof chest designed to float and equipped with its light emitters and GPS, the box was packed tightly with more equipment and weapons.

"Ok, we're a go," the co-pilot called, his tone apprehensive. The back hatch dropped open. Bitter-wet wind and icy drops of moisture tore through the cabin. Will felt the plane dive and then slow, almost to a stall. He knew this stunt was as dangerous as hell in this storm, but he was grateful for the help. Every foot closer to the water reduced the impact of their landing.

He grabbed the side walls of the cargo bay, squatted to make as small a package as possible, and fell forward. As soon as he was away from the plane, he pulled the orange cord hanging off of his chest. Shiney, waterproof wings popped out of his backpack, and a short parachute popped over his head. The squall grabbed at him, almost collapsing the chute, but the wings, designed to help him glide, allowed him to follow the drafts of wind, soaring down like a bird. The parachute slowed his descent, ensuring he wouldn't smash into the surface of the ocean, traveling at terminal velocity.

The plane was gone. He couldn't even hear the engines anymore. A strobe of lightning lit the sky, and closer than he expected, he saw Marco, his parachute deployed and wings unfurled, riding the airstream to the water. From this height, he could see that the chest had hit the water already, and the strobe lights were winking between the waves. Angling himself in that direction, he landed with a splash, only to be immediately doused with a freezing wave. Using his strong arms to pull him through the water, he swam toward Marco, hoping the sailors on the sub would hurry.

***

The ship rocked in place and pulled hard on the anchors deployed earlier. The captain was, more or less, following orders, keeping them in the same spot. Ignoring the motion, Victor Newsome stared at his phone, but he wasn't really looking at it. All he could see was the bank deposit screen and the very large number displayed earlier.

He had informed Dror Hart of the deposit, just like the CEO had ordered. President Tanner had come through. He could tell the big

German was deeply satisfied. Even Cynthia was smiling, though he knew she was seasick from the storm. Her makeup had long worn off. The green sheen highlighting her cheeks and the way she kept swallowing gave her away.

Hart either didn't notice or didn't care. He kept her busy transcribing his dictation, plans for more cannons, improvements, and new customers to increase business. Tanner wondered if Hart understood the damage they had caused so far. Not that stuff about the core—Newsom still didn't believe Brecken's micromanaging carried any weight.

But it was obvious that the Mantle Cannon over-performed and caused incredible damage to whatever it was aimed at. You couldn't destroy every decent, civilized part of the planet, because then where would anyone want to live? Where would he live?

Look at Beijing. The original specs for the cannon predicted that one or two volcanoes would vent, and ten to twenty miles would be affected. Not two or three or even eight hundred miles, with new, unexpected volcanoes and fissures erupting. That super crater would be inhabitable for a century or two.

And Iceland? Well, Iceland no longer existed, save for one or two pieces of basalt poking above the waves. He hadn't heard any predictions of that. Brecken had claimed a few volcanoes would throw out some magma or lava or whatever, mess up the surrounding countryside a little bit, and then go quiet again. Instead, the whole freaking island cracked, broke, and tumbled into the Atlantic Ocean. The point was that Iceland was toast.

They were going to have to start using the cannon more judiciously. At some point, the weapon would have to be retired or maybe used as a threat against other countries.

Hey, that could work. Titan International could charge other countries *not* to fire the cannon at them. Some people called that extortion, but the right word in this case was *protection*. They could collect big, and a few more examples would certainly convince any reluctant stragglers to pay. Then he could set up shop, say in San Francisco or Monaco or Dubai, and start living the life he was meant to live.

Oh, wait, not Dubai. See, this was just what he meant. Taking out the Middle East would impact Dubai and eliminate pretty much any city in the United Arab Emirates. He shook his head. He was going to have to start thinking about this strategically.

His thoughts returned to the bank deposit screen and all of those zeros—time to interrupt the boss.

"Dror, the storm's getting worse. If we're going to fire the cannon tonight, we should probably get on it. The captain is having a hard time holding this location. The pulses work best if we keep hitting the same spot."

"I haven't been able to get Tanner on the phone." Hart gave Cynthia a sour look.

"It's not the connection," she said defensively. "He's just not answering. I called the Cheyenne Mountain Complex, too, and no one is answering there either."

"Maybe it's the storm," Newsom suggested.

"Whatever," Hart waved his hand dismissively. "So, the question is, do we chance it and hope Tanner coughs up the payment?"

"I say yes. We're here, the opportunity is wide open, and who knows if or when we will get a better shot at the Middle East?" Newsom knew he was pressing hard. Hart didn't generally like to be pushed, but there was a lot at stake tonight. His thoughts wandered back to the bank deposit and all those zeros.

"You really are a piece of work, Victor," Hart barked a brief laugh, and his eyes seemed too wide for a moment. "Let's run the cannon tonight. We'll send Tanner an invoice. I'm ready to reshape the world."

***

Will met Commander Spike Porter in the Control Room of the *U.S.S. Topeka*. His suit had drip-dried. Another perk of the specialized fabric weave was that it kept water and bullets out.

"Captain, appreciate the assist," he told the slender man, holding a gloved hand to shake.

"Our pleasure." The CO's grip was firm. "Most of my people had family on the East Coast. Admiral Maddocks filled me in, and I talked to everyone ship-wide. Just so you know: we are not here, and this mission is not happening. But, working in those parameters, we will stop those bastards."

"Have you picked them up on radar yet? And will they be able to pick us up radar?"

"Yes, to your first question. *Titan Three* is about four kilometers off our bow. We're headed in that direction at eight knots, so we'll be close in about thirty minutes. To answer your second question: not likely. This sub is covered with sound-absorbing tiles called anechoic coatings. They look like perforated rubber tiles, and they help us avoid sonar detection from a distance. Now, if we get close, chances are our signal could be picked up, but we have some defense tricks to help with that, too. Also, *Titan Three* dropped anchor in the middle of the ocean, and they are fighting the storm. They might be too busy to notice us."

"They need to stay in the same location to fire the Mantle Cannon. Have you picked up any pulsing activity yet?"

"Not yet. We're monitoring," he pointed to the helmsman at acoustics, a small man with an aquiline nose. A giant headset covered his head, and he stared at his sonar screen with hawk-like intensity. "He'll let us know the minute he hears something."

"Sir, when we took out the last three cannons, we did so without taking any enemy lives because these were Americans. Most of these tech types don't even know the outcome of what they are doing. But this time, with the storm and the critical nature of stopping them before the cannon runs, I am having trouble forming a strategy that I can anticipate will work."

The captain was nodding before he finished, a fierce look on his face. "We've already debriefed your team. Lt. Blakely and Lt. Murphson explained your previous ops. As commendable as your concern for the lives of those aiming the cannon is, it could be that millions would not have died if you had struck out with no regard for those people."

He held up a hand as Will started to protest. "I lost people on the East Coast too. I'm not second-guessing you, but we'll never know if the timing could have changed. It doesn't matter now. What matters is stopping this before the planet takes a final kick in the nuts. Let's look at our options."

"I'm sorry, sir. We tried to do what was right. If I knew forty-eight hours ago what I know now, my men and I would have reacted with far more lethal force." Will's face reflected the sorrow he felt.

"I know." Porter's voice was low and intense. "It's the military's curse. Either we react with too much force or not enough. Somebody always pays. Look at this."

They moved to the strategic planning table; a four-by-six flat digital display embedded in an iron frame. The screen was backlit blue, the ocean floor superimposed, and the depth marked in a grid. According to the map's legend, the red blot indicated the *Titan Three*, the only vessel in over one hundred miles. A black oval was moving toward it. Will assumed this marker was the *U.S.S. Topeka*.

"The *Titan Three* is a cargo ship, about three hundred feet long. I can put two torpedoes in it, and she'll be on the bottom in minutes. But your men tell me you think you should board her and confirm the target before we shoot. Isn't it enough of a confirmation if the pulse is activated?"

"I prefer to stop the cannon before activation, Captain." He touched the red mark and then clenched a fist. "But we need to stop the men who started this madness. Dror Hart and Victor Newsom should pay for what they have done. Either way, we must know their whereabouts even if we tie them to the rail and watch them go down with the ship. They may have stashed backups of this weapon elsewhere; I wouldn't put anything past them. I want them in my hands while we find out. Then we can let the rest of this play out, whether it be a watery grave or law courts deciding their fate."

The CO nodded grimly. "I wouldn't like their chances of making port if they board this sub, but we'll play this op your way for now, Ranger."

He called over the executive officer. "XO, we're going to board the *Titan Three*. Get two of the Zodiacs ready and assign two of our men with each boat."

"Aye, sir. Two Zodiacs ready to launch with two men each." The XO turned to the COB. "Chief, I need four of your best drivers sent aft.

Lieutenant, we'll need to surface to launch the boats, but keep it short. I don't expect that ship has any armaments, but let's not test our luck."

"Aye, sir, preparing to surface on the COBs orders," the lieutenant called out.

The chief of the boat stood, arms behind his back at attention. "Aye, sir. Four of the best drivers on their way." He leaned over the comms lieutenant, speaking to him in soft tones.

Porter turned back to Will and gave him a cold look. "That gives you a team of eight to search a damn big boat, Major Stone."

"Understood, sir. When we find our targets, I'll radio you. I plan to load them back in the tenders and get back here before torpedoes are launched. But, Captain Porter, don't wait on us if that cannon activates. Bring that ship down with all force necessary. The life of every person left on this planet may depend upon it."

Porter nodded sharply. The XO gestured to Will to follow. Now, it was a game of timing.

***

Newsom paced around the cannon. He stopped and craned his neck up, trying to see the top of the machine, and then resumed his pacing. He could not stop thinking about that deposit. What he needed to do was make some decisions. The New York office was gone, drowned, and most of their people with it. He accessed their system tonight with the help of that communications guy and changed all of the server passwords for the whole company. Even if one of the IT resources had survived and made it to a working computer, it didn't matter because, right now, Newsom was the only person with active passwords to get into Titan International servers. That included all the financial records and banking accounts as well.

So, what was he going to do with that? Sure, the United States was a mess right now. However, the legal system would be back up and running in a few weeks or months. When Hart made it back to land, he would demand access to everything. His stomach twisted at the thought.

Newsom growled and paced faster. They were set to activate the cannon in an hour. The techs preparing for the run were careful not to look at him. Heads down, they worked away at their stations. No one made eye contact with him.

He knew he seemed insane, but when he arrived, he stopped at each desk, forcing the person to look up as he carefully examined their face. He may have shot that whistleblower last night, but maybe not. No matter, that little shit wasn't going to sneak into this lab. He was staying right here until after the cannon run.

Anyway, this ship was derelict, rundown, and smelled of rotting fish; it wasn't like there was anywhere better to wait. He eyed the door, his eyes tight with strain—fifty-five minutes to go.

***

The inflatables launched without trouble, but steering them through the turbulent ocean was another story. Will was thankful for his insulated suit and lightweight armor, keeping the bullet-like drops of ice and spray off his skin. Marco had provided identical armored suits for Blake and Murph, squatting low in the craft behind them. The crate also produced four of the Fabrique Nationale FN SCARs, a Special Op Forces combat assault rifle they were all comfortable with. With one of these automatic weapons in his hands, he felt the familiar urge to leap into action.

Captain Porter sent four seasoned sailors to man the Zodiacs. Their armor was not as badass as the suits Will's team wore, but it was better than the usual gear the Army provided. The sailors surfed through the ferocious breakers. The rubber boats were tossed mercilessly, but the drivers held them steady enough to reach their target. Beside him, Marco planted himself stoically, rifle in hand, waiting for the action to begin.

He wasn't worried about anyone on the vessel hearing their approach. The growl from the supercharged engines was no match for the thunder and crashing whitecaps. Big breakers slammed into the cargo ship, with booms that echoed over the water. Even the lightning crisscrossing the night sky didn't concern him. The rigid-hulled boat, the armor they wore, the weapons, and the water were all a deep, soulless black. He doubted they could be seen even if someone were staring directly at them. More suddenly than he expected, a towering gray wall rose from the waves.

His team wasted no time scaling the metal ladders bolted into the sides. Everyone knew they were on a clock this time. Hart could switch on that cannon any minute. Porter's team stayed back just long enough to lash the Zodiacs to the ladders, hoping for a chance at a quick getaway. Then, rifles leading, they joined Will and the team midship.

Dropping onto the deck, they stopped short, appalled by their surroundings. The ship was FUBAR.

Will thought this had to be the most decrepit vessel he had ever seen. Sheets of rain swept the deck, but they didn't help at all. Everything—every surface, deck panel, and railing was rusted or corroded. Crap was dumped everywhere: nets, ropes, boxes, old equipment, and broken pieces of the ship. Nothing was tied down; unidentifiable junk slid with the rain, piling up against the crooked railing. Every now and then, something sailed over the side, lost to the maelstrom below. Working on this cargo liner had to be a nightmare. He'd be doing Titan International a favor sinking this transport. Shaking his head, he tried to focus on the mission.

Motioning to Blake and Murph, he sent them and the two sailors they came over with to the aft. They'd cover more ground if they split up. Everyone knew what they were looking for. Any sign of a Mantle Cannon or Hart and Newsom. Radio if you found either. He had warned everyone about the pulsing.

If the vibrations start, abandon the mission and get off the ship immediately. He did not doubt that Captain Porter would come through with the torpedoes if the cannon activated. With a signal to Marco and the other two seamen, they started forward.

It was hard to walk. The sailors with their sea legs didn't struggle as much, but Will had to plant his feet firmly with each step. Thunder roared over his head. He accepted the cover for what it was worth: at least no one would hear them coming.

Within the first five minutes, the unit located an access door. There was no need to worry about picking the lock. It wasn't even latched. It was just swinging back and forth in the wind, banging each time the ship rolled. Will shook his head. This ship and its crew were a travesty.

Being out of the storm was a relief, but the cessation of wind and rain ramped up his senses. The ship groaned with every breaker. He turned on the bright searchlight attached to his rifle, then, pointing in the direction he wanted to go, they moved down the steps. Marco was on his heels.

In his earpiece, he heard Blake whisper, "Major, we are in the bowels of the ship. We haven't made contact yet. I'm not sure there are that many people on board. We haven't seen anyone."

"Roger, Blake. There is nothing here either. Stay frosty."

They moved undetected through the corridors—the air stank of mildew and oil. Will was disgusted to see orange slime growing on the walls. Something crackled under their feet, and Will hoped the deck floor wouldn't give out and drop them into the ship's guts. Most of the doors along the hall were open.

Glancing in exposed more rot and ruin. Mold grew on carpets, and crazy patterns and colors of fungus lit up in the beam from his rifle. He was no expert, but Will couldn't help but wonder why this ship hadn't been ordered scuttled. This place would give derelicts a lousy name.

He realized they were approaching a bridge of sorts. A glance at the symbols on the wall revealed they were at the wheelhouse. He quickly looked around the door and counted three men standing at stations. They were arguing among themselves about the storm and the control of the ship—or lack of control due to the heavy breakers.

If Will heard them right, they had pulled up the anchors and were attempting to keep the ship afloat by driving straight into the big waves. Not the best strategy. He wasn't Navy, but even he knew to approach oncoming waves at a forty-five-degree angle. He recognized the Australian accents and got a quick peek at their rough garb—jeans, shapeless shirts.

He deduced they were mercs picked up for this specific voyage. He doubted they cared about the cannon. They were focused on keeping the ship afloat and not dying in the storm. He gestured for his three to keep low and keep moving. Hart and Newsom would be with the cannon, and that was where he needed to be.

"Major, we found Hart and his assistant. They're in a cabin on the second level. She looks sick and is lying down. He's making notes of some kind," advised Blake. He drew in a breath. "Hart's getting up and heading toward the doorway. If he steps through . . ." Blake cut out.

Will held up a fist. The other stopped short.

Seconds ticked by while Will waited impatiently.

"Major, we have two prisoners. Do you want us to move them or lock them in here?"

"I'm not sure any of the locks on this rust bucket work. See what you can do to contain them. We're going after Newsom and the cannon."

"Hart says Newsom won't activate the cannon without him present."

"Yeah, and he might even believe that. I don't. Did he tell you where the cannon is located?"

"Yes, a cargo area for hauling liquid-type containers. It's three levels high. There's only one access door from the inside. You can reach it on the third level, which is just about midships. It's a maintenance door, but it's big enough to walk through. Otherwise, the only way in is to roll back the roof hatch. He says it's big, like a double garage door size, and the cannon is right underneath it. They lowered a pre-built cannon through that hole, which is how they got this cannon onsite so fast."

"He's pretty talkative for someone you just captured."

"Yeah, well, right now, he is threatening us with his lawyer. He's telling the girl to call stateside, but apparently, they've had trouble getting calls out with the storm."

"Contain them and take away their communications. I don't want them warning Newsom. The cannon has to be stopped first. Then, head back to the topside and find that roof hatch. We might need a second entrance."

"Yes, sir." Blake cut out, and Will moved his team down the hall to a junction, where they took the stairs single file.

Two levels down, Marco cocked his head, then pointed right. As they moved deeper into the ship, the stench intensified. Rotting sea life overlaid by burned rubber and sour oil. With no ventilation, thick, stagnant air filled the corridor. Filthy walls wept with moisture. Will grimaced and tried to breathe in shallow breaths.

They found the access door to the liquid cargo hold a few minutes later. Some artist years before had helpfully drawn a continuous sea wave across the door. The marker was still visible. Battered and scratched, most of the paint was scuffed off in its years of use. However, the latch still caught when closed. No windows, so he couldn't get a look inside. He needed a distraction before his team broke through. He hadn't forgotten the guns from last night. Newsom was willing to go lethal if necessary. Time for the roof hatch, he thought.

"Blake, come in," He motioned for Marco and one of the sailors to move to the other side of the door. They flanked it, weapons up, bracing their feet as the ship rolled again.

"Go, Major," Will could hear the storm behind his shout.

"We're at the access door. We need a distraction. This ship stinks. Do you think you could give them a little ventilation?"

"Yes, sir." He heard Blake grunting and Murph calling out instructions to the other two. "Get ready, Major. We're about to let a little fresh air in."

***

Newsom stood, arms crossed, with a blank expression. He had backed up to the cannon, using it to balance against the hammering wave motion, facing the door. When Hart came through, he wanted the CEO to see how irritated he was at having to wait. He was supposed to be here five minutes ago.

He was getting very tired of Dror Hart.

Something creaked loudly high above in the shadows of the ceiling. Newsom ignored it. The whole ship screeched and groaned with every wave. He'd be glad to get off of this dump, that was for sure. Ten minutes ago, he had called the pilots and ordered them back to the helicopter. As soon as the cannon completed its run, he wanted to fly out back to the United States.

Of course, the pilots objected. The weather was a mess. But they caved in a lot faster than he would have expected. He figured they wanted off this piece of crap, too. He knew Cynthia wouldn't argue, and he wouldn't let Dror stop them.

Suddenly, the entire top of the room was torn open with a long shriek of metal. To his shock, screaming wind shot through the room, with heavy torrents and sprays of cold seawater washed over the edges, pouring down on top of them. For a terrifying moment, Newsom feared the ship was finally sinking. He splashed forward a few steps, trying to understand what was happening, when the access door flew open, and multiple soldiers in black armor filled the space. Gaping, he stepped back and grabbed the strut next to him, intending to duck behind it.

At that very moment, *Titan Three* drove into a massive rogue wave, taller than the ship was high. Thousands of gallons of water poured through the hatch, knocking everyone off their feet and flinging them across the room. With salt burning their eyes and noses, and choking on the spray, the four men took minutes to regain their footing and retrain their weapons on their targets.

The room was a swimming pool, the water chest-high. While some poured out of the open access door, even more cascaded from above. Abandon ship alarms started howling in the corridor, and they could see red lights strobing off the water in the hall.

"Where is he?" Will shouted. "Where's Newsom?"

"He went out the door," a bedraggled man in a white coat panted, pointing to the door they had just entered. "He must have held on to something when the water flowed in from the top."

"Shit!" shouted Will. He waded toward the door.

"Wait! What about us?" screamed the man.

"Don't you hear those alarms?" Marco, the last one out the door, turned back. "Abandon ship! Get to the lifeboats!"

He splashed after the others up the hall.

***

Dror Hart was on his feet when the abandon ship alarms started wailing. He knew what the sirens meant. The men who captured them hadn't tied them up, thank God. Locking the door behind them, they warned Dror and Cynthia to stay put or else. Dror wasn't afraid of the soldiers, but he had a healthy fear of this ship sinking. He knew Newsom could be a cheap bastard; hell, that was one of the reasons he hired him. But this time, the little skinflint had miscalculated. This ship was a deathtrap, cannon or no cannon.

Hart strode over to the door, fingering the frame. The original owners used cheap materials, and like everything else on this ship, the frame was in the final stages of decay. He stepped back, braced himself, and shouldered the door as forcefully as he could. It splintered on the first try, and the door swung open.

"Where should we go?" Cynthia asked behind him. "Not down to the cannon, surely?"

He could barely hear her over the warning bells. She had her laptop bag swung over her shoulder, and despite still looking green, her face was set in a determined expression.

"No, hear that? Those are evacuation warnings to abandon ship. We're headed to the helicopter." He stepped out the door, looking both ways to ensure the soldiers didn't leave a guard.

"Good," she looked relieved but added, "What about Mr. Newsom?"

Hart grunted and started walking as fast as the ship's motion would allow. He squinted ahead, trying to gauge if the corridor seemed slanted.

"He knows where the helicopter is," he threw back over his shoulder. "We'll meet him there."

She didn't argue. He was glad she kept up because he wasn't in the mood to coax her. Maybe she knew that, because she didn't say anything else. They found the staircase they had come down hours earlier and started up.

***

Newsom was furious. He didn't know where the soldiers had come from, but he clearly understood that their appearance meant he wouldn't be firing the cannon at the Middle East tonight. Who knew when he could pull this all back together again? Every time he put one of these together, it was a lot of money and resources. And these guys showing up meant they had lost a second payment from Tanner. This was bullshit.

He pounded the railing as he pulled himself up. He didn't know why the abandon ship warnings were activated, but he doubted the boat was sinking. Still, he couldn't stay here with those black ops guys. Who knew their motivations?

So, he'd get to the helicopter and get out of here. Good thing he'd sent the pilots up to get ready earlier. He could take off as soon as he was seated. He spared a thought for Dror Hart and Cynthia, but not for long. Maybe the mercenaries would take care of them. That idea helped calm him. Maybe the mercenaries would take care of everyone on the ship. That would leave them with the Mantle Cannon, which was sitting in four feet of seawater. It might be ruined.

Or, if not, hell, maybe he could work something out later when he found out who had the nerve to raid his ship. Maybe they would sell him the cannon back. They could keep the boat. Newsom was finally convinced of its worthlessness.

He pushed through the outside door into the raging storm. The gales of wind and the frigid temperatures slapped him motionless for a minute, his breath blown from his body. This storm was a lot worse than earlier. He staggered over to the outdoor staircase leading to the helicopter landing pad. He had to pull himself up, arm over arm, hugging the railings when the wind grew too fierce, or another wave broke over the ship. Gasping, soaked through, and shivering, he finally gained the top step and almost cried with relief.

The helo's lights were all lit, bright beams splitting the black night. He could see the blades turning in the wind, and his heart jumped at the sound of the engine rumbling over the roar of the wind. The craft was unlashed and slid slightly to each side as the vessel rocked or the wind buffeted the glass bubble. He squinted back over the length of the cargo ship as lightning briefly punched back the darkness. Huge waves surged up and over the ship. The brine streamed down the giant square hole embedded in the deck, now open. He wondered if the soldiers were responsible. The ship lurched and sloped further, leaving no doubt it was going down—time to go.

He slipped and slid across the platform, noting the growing vertical slant under his feet. Not much time left. He reached the helicopter, jerked open the door, and fell in.

"Let's go," he yelled at the pilots, who whipped around to face him. They exchanged uneasy glances.

"What about Mr. Hart and his assistant, sir?" asked the co-pilot nervously. The ship lurched underneath them again.

"They didn't make it. Do you feel that?! Get us out of here." Newsom knew he was screaming, but he didn't care. He pulled himself up and stared out the window.

The pilots didn't say anything else. The aircraft revved up, the blades turning faster. The pilot flipped a switch and pulled up on the yoke, and they lifted off.

Barely a few feet off the helideck and rising through the sheets of rain, Newsom caught sight of a person pulling themselves up the same staircase he had just ascended. Two people, as a blond head popped up beside the big man.

He shot a fast look at the pilots struggling with the controls, trying to keep the wind shear from bringing them down. They hadn't seen Hart and Cynthia gain the helipad. With a surge of fuel, the helicopter took off, leaving the sinking ship behind.

Newsom dropped back into his chair, shaking from the cold, and realized what he had just done. He had just taken the most significant risk of his life. If it worked out, the company and the mega payment from Tanner, not to mention all of the data to build and wield the cannons, were his. He'd be king of the world.

***

Hart knew they were in trouble. The helicopter was gone, and the ship was going down fast. Newsom had outwitted him, and now he would pay for that mistake with his life. He screamed into the night, wishing he could go back in time and kill that little prick instead of making him an employment offer.

He should have known the beady-eyed weasel would double-cross him. Hell, that was why he hired him. He knew there was nothing Newsom wouldn't do for money and power.

The ship settled deeper into the water as the bulkheads filled. Deep shudders tore at the vessel as the cold sea water hit the blazing hot boilers. The bottom of the ship ripped out in the explosion and started sinking faster. Heavy waves could finally reach the top deck, crashing over the landing pad and back into the sea. A few seconds later, the platform was empty.

***

Will was beyond relieved to rendezvous with his team on the deck. In this hellhole, anything could have happened. Risking their lives, Blake and Murph returned for their prisoners, but Hart and the blond had broken out and disappeared.

"Shit! I can't believe they got out," Murph raged, but Blake, more practical, shook his head, wiping the rain out of his eyes.

"It was inevitable. This ship is a shithole," he told his friend.

Will agreed. They couldn't have dragged the two civilians behind them, and they wouldn't have come willingly. The main objective of this op was to prevent the cannon from activating. Apprehending Hart and Newsom was always a secondary goal. Stopping the cannon and not losing one of his men felt like a win.

The ship lurched, and when it settled at a forty-five-degree angle, the deck was too close to the ocean surface for his liking.

He saw a helicopter lift up, a bright firefly in the gloom, and knew at least Newsom had gotten away. But the ship under their feet was sinking, the cannon had not been activated, and no other parts of the world were currently in catastrophic upheaval. There'd be another day to bring Newsom down. He wouldn't rest until he wrapped his hands around that scrawny chicken neck.

Marco updated him on the rest of the lab team heading for the lifeboats in the rear, and he radioed Porter to send out rescue boats. Maybe they could save some.

His sailors were able to reach the Zodiacs, free the inflatables, and pull Will and his friends off the sinking deck. He thought he heard someone screaming as he threw his leg over the hard rubber side, but the waves tore their boat from the hull before he could go back and look.

Dropping onto the seat, he started to plan his next move.

Epilogue

It had been three days since the end of his world. Alvar Haarde stood next to his plane and gazed at the fragments that remained of Iceland. Scarcely one hundred square kilometers of land remained, and a handful of Icelanders huddled on this rock. Aircraft from the Faroe Islands flew multiple rescue missions, and now they were down to the last hardy souls who did not want to go.

Alvar had the fuel but not the will to leave his home. He had been to the Faroe archipelago. It was beautiful. He knew he could make a new home there. But it was hard to fly away from what had been the center of his universe. He burned to understand why this end had come. He vowed not to give up until he had answers to the questions spinning in his head. He just needed to figure out where to start.

***

The *Hungry Gullet* limped ashore someplace in Maine, or Vermont—Captain Pete wasn't really sure. More things were broken than intact on the trawler's structure. They fought a hell of a battle climbing that last tsunami, and Ridley broke his arm in the struggle. Pete wasn't entirely sure how they crossed the crest without being tossed off. He could still feel gravity pulling them off the watery face of the ocean. It must have been half a mile high at that point.

They spent a day in deep water to avoid any more monster waves, but yesterday, he headed in, looking for medical help for Ridley. The boy was going to be okay physically, but they were both mentally battered. All he had left were this boat and his friendship with the teen. He didn't know where they would wind up or how it would all work out, but they'd stick together and see it through. They'd figure out a plan.

***

Rob Smith reached his parents' house late Thursday. The elder Smiths lived in Columbus, Ohio, and were thrilled to have their only son walk through the door. But his travels weren't over. The Smiths and everyone in Columbus received evacuation orders. More catastrophic weather anomalies were headed their way, and the military moved the population out in scores.

With a knapsack containing the sum total of his worldly belongings and his parents at his side, Rob boarded one of the buses to Texas. He understood this was just a landing zone, and they'd have to move on from the Lone Star state. With luck, he could volunteer his skills to help organize wherever they found themselves. For once, he wasn't worried about deadlines and business meetings. He was just glad to be alive and with his family. He didn't spare much of his thoughts for his employers. With any luck, Dror Hart and Victor Newsom were dead.

***

Freney Peterson sat warm and dry on Joe Jackson's floral sofa in Cullman, AL. Tigh Hayes sat next to her, sipping iced tea. Word about evacuations south had come through in just the last few hours but they didn't worry. At this point, they sort of felt blessed and figured whatever happened was in the hands of a higher being anyway. The rescue boys who pulled them from her old Mazda called them "the miracle twins."

Joe, his old Army buddy, was happy his text did some good. Truth be told, when he sent it, he wondered if it was just a fart in the wind. But having Tigh sitting on his sofa with his friend Freney was a great outcome. They were going to play poker tonight. He couldn't wait.

***

Weng Xi, arms tangled in the burned branch of a cherry tree, floated on the Dongbiamen River for hours. Beijing, his family, his bike, and everything he knew had been lost to the terrible heat and appetite of the volcanoes. How he was still alive, he had no idea. Without even the strength to swim, he floated along with the other detritus of the tide, face and arms burned, eyes swollen closed, waiting for the end.

The peasant woman who pulled him out of the water wouldn't let him despair. She screamed at him to live, dressed his wounds, and prodded him out of his lethargy. He resisted her efforts, just wanting to die, but she would have none of it. She understood he owed it to his family to survive: he had a duty to bear their memory. Xi knew he could never forget that horrific inferno. The scars he wore would always be a reminder.

***

The village of Moca, in the Dominican Republic, had literally been seared off the face of the earth. Emilio's apartment building and every other structure, all the massive trees, the beautiful forest—all obliterated. It looked like the face of the moon. Ash rode the breeze, and everywhere Emilo looked, he saw another reason to make him cry.

More than half the town had made it into the tunnels, and the rest were presumed dead. No bodies and nothing organic remained from the fiery tornadoes. It was barren in every direction. Emilio wasn't sure how they could regroup and start over. Bendo and the few other men scouted out, trying to find information, water—anything that could help. Emilio feared there was nothing left in the Dominican Republic to find. He wondered if that were true for the whole planet.

***

Rory Carter sat in the hotel bar nursing his Diet Coke. To his despair, the birds that had committed suicide on the beach were not the only flock affected. There had been multiple reports of the same strange behavior from all over the Yucatan Peninsula. News from Minnesota was just as bad. The earthquake had caused enough damage that he wouldn't be flying home anytime soon, and rumors of bitter winter conditions and mandatory evacuations of his city were even worse. Maybe he could never go home? He hung his head, saddened and powerless to do anything.

"Señor Carter?"

He looked up to meet the gaze of a small Spanish man, deeply tanned under a thick thatch of dark hair.

"Yes, that's me," he answered, wondering what could go wrong next.

"I am Tomas Beltran, the director of Punta Lastre Nature Reserve here in Yucatan. My brother owns this hotel and told me about your expertise with birds. Have you ever thought about taking a job here in the Yucatan? Conditions in the United States seem . . . complex, at the moment. Perhaps I could interest you in a sabbatical here in the Yucatan, working to preserve our birds?"

A jolt of joy replaced some of his hopelessness. A smile twitched at the corners of his mouth. "Tell me more, please."

****

Thank you for reading Broken Earth: Devastation. I hope you enjoyed this story.

Please visit my website bewaretheend.com and sign up for my mailing list for updates and new release information.

Your support is invaluable to me. I welcome and respond to your feedback. Please feel free to email me at bb.bewaretheend@gmail.com.

www.ingramcontent.com/pod-product-compliance
Lightning Source LLC
Chambersburg PA
CBHW051944220626
47052CB00004B/792